Tangled Up In You

Whisper Lake #6

BARBARA FREETHY

BARBARA FREETHY BOOKS

Fog City Publishing

PRAISE FOR BARBARA FREETHY

"ALWAYS WITH ME is a heartwarming second chance romance, with a captivating mystery, that keeps you reading and wondering what happens next." Doni - Goodreads

"A beautiful second chance love story with a bit of drama and mystery. I loved it!" Peggy - Goodreads on ALWAYS WITH ME

"Tragedy haunts her, regrets shadow him and passion lures them into a mystery as dangerous as their feelings for each other. Freethy captivates with a sensuous game of tainted hearts and tempting romance. My Wildest Dream is a hotbed of intriguing storytelling. Brodie and Chelsea are sure to get under your skin." Isha C – Goodreads

"My Wildest Dream has just the right mix of romance and suspense to keep the reader interested from the first chapter to the final page. I loved everything about this book. Visiting Whisper Lake is like coming home and reuniting with old friends. You won't be disappointed. Norma – Bookbub

"I have just finished CAN'T FIGHT THE MOONLIGHT and WOW such an emotional book. The characters of Justin and Lizzie were so well written, with so much depth. There were scenes in this book that gave me a lump in my throat. Absolutely loved this book...and can't wait for the next one!" Booklovers Anonymous

"I love the Callaways! Heartwarming romance, intriguing suspense and sexy alpha heroes. What more could you want?"
— *NYT Bestselling Author Bella Andre*

PRAISE FOR BARBARA FREETHY

"I adore the Callaways, a family we'd all love to have. Each new book is a deft combination of emotion, suspense and family dynamics." — *Bestselling Author Barbara O'Neal*

"Freethy is at the top of her form. Fans of Nora Roberts will find a similar tone here, framed in Freethy's own spare, elegant style." — *Contra Costa Times on Summer Secrets*

"Freethy hits the ground running as she kicks off another winning romantic suspense series…Freethy is at her prime with a superb combo of engaging characters and gripping plot." — *Publishers' Weekly on Silent Run*

"A fabulous, page-turning combination of romance and intrigue. Fans of Nora Roberts and Elizabeth Lowell will love this book." — *NYT Bestselling Author Kristin Hannah on Golden Lies*

"PERILOUS TRUST is a non-stop thriller that seamlessly melds jaw-dropping suspense with sizzling romance. Readers will be breathless in anticipation as this fast-paced and enthralling love story evolves and goes in unforeseeable directions." — *USA Today HEA Blog*

"Barbara Freethy is a master storyteller with a gift for spinning tales about ordinary people in extraordinary situations and drawing readers into their lives." — *Romance Reviews Today*

"Freethy has a gift for creating complex, appealing characters and emotionally involving, often suspenseful, sometimes magical stories." — *Library Journal on Suddenly One Summer*

TANGLED UP IN YOU - BOOK BLURB

Molly Trent is an adventurous, free spirit whose turbulent childhood has driven her to a new mission in life—to make people feel better. Unfortunately, a series of burglaries at her wellness shop puts her in the path of a cynical and suspicious detective, who thinks she does more harm than good. She's used to criticism, but she sees something in the tightly-controlled, grumpy police detective that she wants to unleash, if only she could get him to trust her.

Trust doesn't come easily to Detective Adam Cole. He has been a loner for as long as he can remember. He's very good at protecting people. He's great at being a friend, but relationships that go beyond that—not so much. After a heartbreaking tragedy in his early twenties, he put up walls that are never coming down. Despite what Molly Trent might think, he does not need help or herbs to be happy.

Unfortunately, what he needs is her. The chemistry between them almost makes him wonder if she hasn't cast some sort of spell over him. But he fights their attraction hard, because he doesn't do forever, and he can't imagine that an optimistic romantic like Molly would settle for anything less. But when they get tangled up in life and love, anything can happen...

TANGLED UP IN YOU

CHAPTER ONE

"Everything is great." Molly Trent gripped the phone tightly in her hand as her gaze swept the cluttered mess of boxes crowding the back room of the health and wellness store she'd recently inherited. "It's perfect."

"You're lying. You're doing that thing you do," Layla Warren said.

"What thing?"

"Pretending everything is okay when it's not. Looking for the rainbow in the middle of the storm."

"Okay, it's not perfect. But I'm good at starting over. It's what I do. I was getting itchy feet anyway. Change is good for me. I'll make this work." Despite her words, she felt a bit overwhelmed by the task in front of her. "I just wish Phoebe was here, and that I was working with her, the way I used to. I should have realized that her unexpected call a few months ago might have had a more significant reason behind it. Clearly, she had health issues."

"She obviously didn't want you to know, or she would have told you."

"Maybe, but I should have visited her after that call. I just figured there would be time for us to reconnect."

Unfortunately, that time had ended eight days ago when

Phoebe had had a heart attack in the middle of her store. She was dead before they got her to the hospital. The next day, Molly had heard from Phoebe's lawyer, who'd told her that Phoebe had left the building to her, which included the wellness store, the yoga studio, and the apartment upstairs. She'd been completely blown away by the inheritance. She'd only been part of Phoebe's life for a couple of years, a long time ago. But Phoebe had never married or had children, and, apparently, she'd decided that Molly was the only one who could take over her business.

"Did you tell your mom you were leaving San Francisco?" Layla asked.

"Yes. She was disappointed to hear I was returning to Whisper Lake. She doesn't believe in revisiting the past. She's a big believer in moving forward and never looking back."

"How do you feel about being in Whisper Lake again?"

"Too soon to know. I just got here last night. But this store was a refuge for me when I was sixteen. Phoebe's passion for natural healing was the reason behind my studies and my career, as unimpressive as that has been so far," she said dryly.

She'd been dabbling in various parts of the health and wellness industry for the past six years, never sure where she fit in, and most of her jobs had been easy to leave. In fact, she'd been about to quit her most recent job at a skin care center when she'd gotten the call from Phoebe's lawyer.

"I want to carry on Phoebe's legacy and make the store even better if I can," she continued. "Phoebe was proud of the way she could help people, whether it was with natural healing sleep aids, stress-reducing lotions, aromatherapy candles, herbs, yoga, meditation, or a combination of all the above. I wish the store hadn't come with Phoebe's death, but I have to admit I'm excited about the challenge."

"I'm glad," Layla said. "I just hope this doesn't mean you won't come back to San Francisco."

"We'll see. You know I don't like to plan. How are you doing with your beautiful babies? I'm surprised you even have time for this call."

"Both sets of parents have come to help with the twins. They are having a blast, and I'm taking a break."

"Good for you. I should get going. Kiss your babies for me."

"I will. Don't work too hard, Molly."

She'd no sooner ended the call when a jolting crash reverberated through the building. She rushed into the showroom, seeing one of the heavy displays on its side, the front door wide open. She ran through the door, wondering who had knocked over the rack and fled.

As she hit the sidewalk, she barreled straight into a man—a man on crutches.

The force of her body sent them both to the ground in a tangled mess of arms, legs, and crutches.

"Oh, my God, I'm so sorry," she said. "I didn't see you."

"Clearly. Do you want to let me up?"

She suddenly realized she was lying on top of an incredibly attractive man. He had dark-brown, wavy hair, a strong jaw, and dazzling blue eyes, the same deep blue as the lake. He wore a cream-colored knit shirt and faded jeans.

She cleared her throat, realizing she was staring at him for far too long. Then she flushed, becoming aware that he was staring back at her. Time seemed to stand still for a few long seconds. Then she pulled her arm out from under a crutch and forced herself to get to her feet.

"I am sorry." She extended her hand to help him up.

"You said that." An annoyed grimace ran across his face as he ignored her hand and got up, putting his weight on his right foot, his left foot encased in a walking boot.

She grabbed his crutches and handed them to him. "I hope I didn't injure you."

"I'm fine. You should watch where you're going."

"I know, but I think someone stole something from my store.

There was a crash, and the door was open. I ran outside to see who it was and knocked you over."

He frowned at her words. "You're saying there was a shoplifter?"

"Maybe. I'm not sure. One display was knocked over. Did you see anyone run out of the store?"

"No. I just came around the corner and collided with you." His gaze narrowed. "Did you say this was your store? You're the new owner?"

"Yes. I inherited the store from Phoebe Haller. I'm Molly—Molly Trent. You are?"

"Adam Cole. Detective Cole," he added.

"Oh. You're a police officer?"

"Temporarily on leave." He tipped his head toward his injured foot. "Do you know what was stolen?"

"Honestly, I have no idea. The store is packed, and I'm not even a tenth of the way through the inventory. I just arrived last night." She paused. "Maybe the person didn't steal anything. They might have just knocked over the display and ran so they wouldn't be charged for the broken items."

"Seems possible," he murmured, but his frown made her nervous.

"What are you thinking?" she challenged.

"There was an attempted break-in here a couple of days ago. The alarm went off, but no one was caught."

"Really?" she asked in dismay. "I didn't know that. Although Phoebe's lawyer gave me a new set of keys and said the locks had been reinstalled. I guess that was the reason."

"The store doesn't have a working security camera. You should replace that as soon as possible."

"I will." She paused. "Is your foot broken?"

"Hairline fracture and a twisted ankle. Apparently, I just need time to heal."

She had a feeling this wasn't a man who appreciated

patience. "Massage can help stimulate healing circulation. I also have some lotions that can offer a similar effect."

"Spoken like someone who manages a wellness store. I'm not a big believer in mystical lotions. I prefer evidence-based facts."

It wasn't the first time she'd heard that kind of skepticism. "Natural healing has plenty of evidence-based facts behind it. I'd be happy to share them with you."

Before he could reply, a woman came out of the shop next door, a high-end clothing boutique. Jackie Hunt was dressed in a sleek, red sheath dress, wearing her usual Botox-tight expression of unhappiness. Jackie was somewhere in her early fifties, and she'd already stopped by with pointed questions about whether she'd be selling CBD products and suggesting that she might want to sell the store to one of the other merchants on the street who was looking to expand.

"What is going on out here?" Jackie asked. "Is there a problem, Detective Cole?"

"There's no problem," Adam said. "Everything is fine."

"I don't think it is fine," Jackie said, with a sharp shake of her head. "Phoebe sold marijuana products, and that's why someone probably broke in last week. I'm worried about what kind of clientele this store will draw if this woman continues in the same vein."

"You don't need to worry," Molly said. "CBD products are legal, and they are used for medicinal purposes only."

Jackie crossed her arms, giving her a haughty look of irritation. "Of course you'd say that."

"It's the truth."

"Why don't you show me that lotion you were talking about?" Adam said, tipping his head toward the door.

For a moment, she stared at him in confusion. He'd just said he had no interest in her lotions. Then she realized he was offering her an escape. "Oh. All right." She opened the door and walked into the store, Adam following close behind. As the door shut behind him, she said, "You don't really want to see any lotion, do you?"

"No. But you didn't need to hear anything further from Mrs. Hunt."

"I really didn't." His actions surprised her. He'd made it clear he didn't believe in what she was selling, but he was nice enough to give her an escape from Jackie Hunt.

"Is this what fell over?" Adam asked, eyeing the shelving display that was now laying on top of a table that had contained vitamin bottles and ointments, most of which were now scattered on the floor.

"That's it. I'm not completely sure what was on it, except what we can see. There's a lot to organize."

"There certainly is." His gaze swept the room, noting the crowded shelves and the dozen boxes in the middle of the store. "You have your work cut out for you." He idly picked up a piece of glass from a nearby counter. "Do you really believe this piece of glass can work some sort of miracle?"

"Crystals are minerals that can interact with the body's energy field, creating balance and alignment. They can reduce stress and enhance focus. There's archaeological evidence that amber was used for protection as far back as ten thousand years ago," she replied.

"Sounds like a very long con," he said cynically. "People will buy anything, I guess."

"Well, I don't con people out of money and neither did Phoebe. Just because you don't understand something doesn't make it false. When I get this store back in shape and running again, it will be great for the entire community. I owe Phoebe to keep her legacy alive."

He gave her a speculative look. "You owe Phoebe? Who was she to you? I know she didn't have any relatives."

"She was like a grandmother to me. She gave me a place to work and a purpose in life when I was a teenager. She had my back. Now I have hers."

Adam nodded, then suddenly started. He checked his watch. "Damn! I'm late. I have to go."

"If you change your mind about some natural healing options, they're on the house."

"If you can find them," he said dryly. He moved to the door, then paused. "Keep the lock on this door if you're not yet open for business."

"I didn't think anyone had to lock their doors in Whisper Lake."

"The town is much bigger than it used to be. Lock the door."

CHAPTER TWO

ADAM HURRIED down the street as fast as he could on an injured foot and two crutches. Despite brushing off the fall he'd just taken, he felt a new ache in his calf and knee on his good leg. He'd probably instinctively tried to guard against re-injuring his foot. Hopefully, those aches would go away quickly and without the need for any healing crystals or lotions.

He smiled to himself, thinking it was the first time in over a week that he'd felt like smiling, but Molly Trent was something else. He'd never imagined he'd get knocked over by a beautiful woman on his way to breakfast. He'd never seen eyes with that particular shade of green on a woman. They were like cat's eyes. Her long, curly light-brown hair had felt like silk against his face. She'd also smelled of lavender—not overpowering, just tantalizing. And her body had curves in all the right places.

He shook that thought out of his head. Molly Trent might be pretty, but she was not on the same wavelength as him. He didn't believe in most of what was sold in that store. Not that there weren't believers in town. Phoebe had done a good business until she'd gotten too sick to keep up with the store. Then it had gone downhill fast.

Before that, though, she'd been thought of as part witch, part mystic, part miracle worker. With her wild red hair, raucous laugh, dramatic eyeliner, and apparently an ability to call up the spirits during her monthly séances, she'd been a legend around town.

He wondered if Molly would carry on Phoebe's traditions. He also wondered about the relationship she'd had with Phoebe. There was a story there, and he was curious as to what it was. Ordinarily, he wouldn't have time to be curious. But it had been eight days since he'd been injured in the line of duty, and he was already bored out of his mind. At least on Monday, he'd go back to desk duty. He needed to use his brain again.

He picked up his pace, hating to be late for anything, especially when he was trying to set a good example for the person he was meeting. He arrived a few minutes later at the Blue Sky Café. It was ten thirty on a Friday morning, in between the breakfast and lunch rush, so there were plenty of tables and only a few people inside the restaurant. Unfortunately, his sister Chelsea was one of them. Blonde, beautiful, and four months pregnant, Chelsea was sitting at the counter, chatting with another pretty woman, Chloe Morgan, the owner of the café.

He really should have picked another restaurant.

"Adam," Chelsea said with a happy smile. "How are you? We were just talking about you."

"Why is that?" He stopped by the counter as his gaze swept the interior of the café. He frowned when he didn't see who he was looking for.

"We're worried about you not having anything to do," Chelsea said.

"And not answering our texts or calls," Chloe put in, giving him a pointed look.

"Sorry. I was doing what the doctor ordered—resting."

"More like brooding," Chelsea said knowingly.

He ignored that comment. "How are you feeling?" he asked, noting the full bowl of oatmeal in front of her.

She sighed. "Hanging in there. Trying to get some food into my stomach without it coming back up."

"The morning sickness sure is hanging on."

"Only it's not in the morning, it's all hours of the day." She gave him a tired smile. "But it feels good to get out of the house."

"Do you want something to eat, Adam?" Chloe asked.

"Not yet. I'm meeting someone."

"Who are you meeting?" Chelsea asked curiously.

"No one you know."

"Well, that sounds interesting. I thought we knew all the same people." His sister gave him a speculative look.

"I thought so, too," Chloe put in, an interested gleam in her gaze. "Is it a date?"

"I don't have dates in the morning."

"It could be a coffee date," Chelsea said.

"It's not." He checked his watch again. "Did someone come and leave?"

"Do you want to be more specific about the someone?" Chloe asked.

"Yeah, what's with the mystery?" Chelsea asked.

He sighed at the determined look in both of their eyes. "There's no mystery. It's a nineteen-year-old guy. And there he is," he said, as Drew Kilborn came into the café.

Drew was about five nine with long brown hair and brown eyes. He wore ripped jeans and a T-shirt with an indie band's logo on it. He sauntered into the restaurant with a look of careless boredom and a complete disregard for the fact that he was thirty minutes late. Not that Adam hadn't been late, too, but Drew didn't know that.

"You're late." It was the wrong way to start the conversation, but he couldn't take it back.

"I was looking around town. Isn't that what you suggested I do?" Drew challenged.

"Let's get a table."

"Aren't you going to introduce us?" Chelsea asked.

He wished he could say no, but he couldn't. "Drew, this is my sister Chelsea. My friend Chloe. This is Drew Kilborn."

Chelsea's gaze widened. "Wait a second. Kilborn? You're Gina's little brother?"

"Yeah," Drew said shortly. "I need coffee."

"I'll bring some over," Chloe said. "Sit anywhere you like."

Adam ignored the look in Chelsea's eyes that told him he would have a lot of questions to answer later. He waved Drew over to a booth along the wall. Chloe dropped off two mugs and some menus.

Drew drank his coffee in a couple of long gulps. Chloe had barely finished refilling the coffee at the table next to them when Drew banged his empty cup on the table. She came back and refilled it.

"I guess you were thirsty," she said.

"And hungry," Drew said. "I'll take the Denver omelet, with a side of bacon, and an order of pancakes."

"You got it." She turned to him with a smile. "How about you?"

"Egg white spinach omelet."

"In other words, the usual," she said dryly.

He knew he was predictable, but he couldn't eat like a nineteen-year-old anymore.

As Chloe left, he turned to Drew. "Where did you go this morning?"

"I walked around."

"Did you check out any of the Help Wanted signs?"

"I didn't see any."

"Really? Because I saw at least three on my way over here."

"I might not even stay."

"Well, you don't have a lot of options. Your college kicked you out. So did your dad."

"I have friends," Drew muttered. "I don't know why you want me to stay with you. It's not like you're anything to me anymore."

Drew was right. They hadn't been anything to each other in a very long time. "I just want to help, Drew. I know you've had some rough years."

"Whatever."

Drew's uncaring attitude was at least partly a cover for the pain he'd been through, and Adam wanted to help. He just didn't know how to reach the kid who had once idolized him and then hated him and now probably didn't give him a second thought. But he had to keep trying. Drew's father had asked him for help, and he owed the Kilborn family more than he could ever repay.

"If this is going to work, you need a job," he told Drew. "You'll enjoy being here more if you make friends and get to know the town. A friend of mine runs a sports adventure company down by the harbor. I'm going to hook you up with Jake. He has some fall hikes coming up, and I know he can use extra guides."

"You want me to lead someone through the mountains?" Drew asked doubtfully. "I can't imagine why you think I could do that."

"You wouldn't be the lead guide, but you'd meet other kids your age."

"I'm not supposed to meet other kids. I'm not supposed to have fun. I'm supposed to sit in this hole of a town until Christmas, until I've repented enough for my unacceptable behavior, and I can go back to UC Santa Barbara for winter quarter."

That was basically the plan, although he would have put it in more positive terms. "The next couple of months can be fun, Drew. You might enjoy being here if you're willing to have an open mind."

"Why are you doing this? Why do you suddenly care?"

"Your dad asked for help."

"And he turned to you because you're the son he didn't have. You're the son he always wanted," Drew said bitterly.

He shook his head. "You've got that wrong."

"I don't. He thinks you can straighten me out because you

straightened yourself out. But I don't need your help. I only agreed to come here so I could get the hell out of my father's house. I'm going to do whatever I want to do until you kick me out and then I'll go somewhere else."

"If I kick you out, your dad won't pay for your return to college."

"Then I'll drop out. It's not like it's getting me anywhere."

He sighed, seeing the stubborn light in Drew's gaze. He had a huge chip on his shoulder and the unyielding cockiness of a teenager who was daring him to try to take control. "You can stay with me until Christmas as long as you get a job. You don't have to be happy, but you do have to work. I'll give you a week to make some progress. If that doesn't happen, you're out."

"I don't think you'll kick me out. You owe my dad. If you get rid of me, you'll owe him even more."

He wished he could say Drew was wrong, but he couldn't. Instead, he said, "Those are my terms."

Drew stared back at him with an assessing gaze. In the end, he just shrugged. "Maybe I'll check out some jobs."

"Good." Their conversation ended as a server brought their food from the kitchen.

He'd meant what he said about giving him a week to get a job but kicking Drew out would be tough. He hoped it wouldn't come to that, for both of their sakes.

When they finished eating, Drew took off on the pretense of checking out some jobs.

As he left, Chelsea slid into the booth across from him.

"What is going on?" she asked curiously. "Why is Gina's brother here?"

"He's going to live with me until Christmas."

Her brows shot up in surprise. "Seriously? How did that happen?"

"Drew got into trouble at school. He's suspended for the quarter. His father wants him away from his party friends. He asked me if I'd take him in for a few months, try to get him on the right path."

"I didn't realize you still had a relationship with Gina's parents and brother."

"We reconnected after Gina's mother passed away a few months ago," he said. "I went to the funeral."

She gave him a surprised look. "Seriously? I had no idea. Why didn't you tell me?"

"Because it wasn't any of your business."

"I just thought…well, I thought they didn't like you."

"They didn't, but when Teresa was dying, she asked Steven to contact me. She wanted to breach the distance between us. She said she felt like Gina would have wanted us to apologize to each other and she didn't think that would happen if she didn't force the issue. I talked to her on the phone a week before she passed away and then I went to the funeral. Since then, Steven and I have kept in touch. He's concerned about Drew. I think losing his sister and now his mother has messed him up."

"So, you offered to take him in. When did he arrive?"

"Last night."

"How's it going so far?"

"About as bad as you'd expect," he admitted. "Drew doesn't want to be here. He doesn't know if he should like me or hate me. We'll see how it goes."

She gave him a thoughtful look. "You still blame yourself for Gina's death, don't you?"

"This isn't about Gina; it's about Drew. I'd appreciate it if you and Lizzie could get on board." He knew that Chelsea would share the news with their younger sister as soon as she left the table, if she hadn't already.

"We'll always support you, Adam. I just hate to see you getting dragged back into the past."

"I'm not in the past. I'm in the present. And on that note, I have to go." He put some cash on the table and got to his feet.

"Why do you have to leave in such a hurry?" she asked dryly, as she slid out of the booth. "Do you have a busy day of sitting ahead of you?"

He gave her an annoyed frown. "As a matter of fact, I have a case to look into."

"I thought you weren't working yet."

"This is a minor case, nothing the department would have time for, but I might as well do something instead of nothing."

"What's the case?"

"Possible shoplifting at the wellness store—A Better You."

"Really? I didn't know the shop was open again."

"It's in the process of reopening. A woman named Molly Trent is taking over for Phoebe. I was walking by when she ran out of the store, looking for whoever knocked over a display case."

"Well, it doesn't sound like a crime that will get you into too much trouble. I hate worrying about you."

"You never have to worry about me. I can take care of myself." He gave her a hug, then hobbled out the door, knowing that the crime he was about to solve wasn't going to get him into trouble, but the woman he was trying to help just might.

CHAPTER THREE

MOLLY ALMOST KNOCKED Adam Cole down again when he came out the door of the Blue Sky Café, but this time, Molly managed to stop herself from barreling into him. But as she stepped back, she couldn't escape the sizzle of attraction that surged between them.

"That was close," she said breathlessly.

"Are you always in a hurry?" he asked.

"I have a lot to do."

"Well, slow down a little. Whisper Lake doesn't move at the fastest pace."

"Phoebe used to say that to me, too. She told me I was too impatient to get to the next thing. I needed to enjoy where I was standing." The memory made her sad. "I had a hard time following her advice."

"You said you knew Phoebe when you were a teenager… You lived here when you were a kid?"

"From age fifteen to seventeen. It was a long time ago, but it feels like yesterday." She paused. "Did you grow up here?"

"No. I grew up in Denver. I moved here four years ago, so we wouldn't have met."

"I didn't think we had." She would have remembered

meeting this man. She licked her lips, feeling oddly nervous. "Can I buy you a coffee or something as an apology for knocking you down before?"

"I just ate. But thanks."

"Okay. If you change your mind on any natural healing products, let me know."

"I won't change my mind."

"Once it's set, it's set?"

He frowned. "I wouldn't go that far." He cleared his throat. "I was thinking about what happened at your store earlier. I'm going to look into it. Without evidence of anything missing or stolen, you won't get much attention from the department, but I'm on leave at the moment, so I have a little time."

"That's very generous of you."

"It's not just generosity; it's also curiosity. It bothers me that there was an attempted break-in exactly one week ago, and possibly one today. I don't like patterns."

His words made her a little nervous. "Do you really think it's a pattern?"

"It could be a sign that someone is targeting the shop, knowing that it's in transition. Items could be taken with no one knowing."

"That's true. I have no idea what's even there to be taken. Do you know anything about Phoebe's death? Her lawyer said she had a heart attack while she was at work, and she died instantly. But he didn't give me any other details."

He shook his head. "I'm sorry. I don't know the details. That was the day I broke my foot. I believe the store manager found her and called for help, but it was too late. Did you talk to the manager?"

"No. The lawyer said that Nina moved to Miami the day after Phoebe died. I thought it was a little strange that she left so quickly. If you can find out anything about the previous break-in, I'd appreciate it."

"I'll let you know. In the meantime, lock your door."

"I will. I only unlocked it earlier, because I took a package down the street to Amelia Stone, one of Phoebe's long-time customers. She'd ordered something before Phoebe died, and it had just come in. When I got back, I forgot to lock the door behind me. When I lived here before, this was a sleepy town, especially in the off-season. It feels much bigger and busier now."

"It has become a top resort destination, which should be good for your business."

"I hope so. Phoebe left the store in a mess. But I know it can be good again, despite what some of my retail neighbors might think. Mrs. Hunt acts like I'll be selling drugs and casting spells on my customers."

"Phoebe did little to negate the rumors of her being a witch. I think she enjoyed them," Adam said.

"You're right. She didn't care what anyone thought. And she used to say that there was magic inside each of us. Some people just never recognized it, never used it."

"Do you believe that you have magic inside of you?"

"Are you asking me if I'm a witch?"

"Just wondering how much you're like Phoebe."

"I'm not a witch, but I believe we have powers inside of us we rarely tap into. It's more awareness of your gifts and using them instead of running away."

He rolled his eyes. "Whatever that means."

"It means we all have more potential than we realize. We often define ourselves too narrowly. We fall into stereotypes and use negative language about our own flaws, like saying you're not good at math, or you can't dance, or there's no way you could write a book."

"Hey, some people just don't have certain talents."

"I prefer to think that they just haven't explored those talents. Obstacles can be opportunities."

"That sounds like something I'd read on a poster."

"Well, it was one of Phoebe's favorite sayings, so it might be on a poster. Did you know Phoebe very well, Adam?"

"Not well, but we had a few conversations over the years. She was an interesting woman, someone who thought outside the box. She was also very charitable and an eager volunteer in the community."

"Phoebe loved kids," she said. "She used to give scholarships to the summer camp so that all the kids could go. And she had a free yoga class on Saturday afternoons for any child who wanted to bend and stretch. She was my first yoga teacher. She thought it would slow me down. It did for at least an hour. She was a really special person." She drew in a breath. "And I don't know why I'm telling you all this. I guess I'm still trying to process her death."

"That makes sense. If you went to high school here, you probably have some friends in town."

"I hope so. I heard Chloe Morgan owns this café. She was really nice to me when I lived here."

"If you were friends with Chloe, then you probably knew some of her friends, too."

"She used to hang out with Gianna Campbell, Hannah Stark, and Keira Blake. Do you know if they're around?"

"Definitely around. All except Keira. She's with her fiancé in Florida. He's a pitcher for the Miami Marlins."

"Wow. That's exciting."

As their gazes clung together, she felt another shiver of attraction. She told herself to get over it. She hadn't come to Whisper Lake to find a man. She'd come to start over—again.

That thought reminded her of her mother, who was always starting over. She'd been raised by a nomad, someone who was always in search of a better life. And while she sometimes longed for roots, there was also a part of her that wasn't sure she could ever truly settle down and stay somewhere.

"I'll let you go," Adam said.

She realized she was staring at him again. "I don't want to

keep you, either. I'll try to be more careful entering and exiting doors."

"If I hadn't been on crutches, you wouldn't have taken me down. It's just hard to balance on these damn things."

"I bet. How did you hurt yourself?"

"I stumbled," he said vaguely.

"I've done that a few times."

As the door to the café opened and an older couple came out, Adam moved to the side to make room for them.

"Detective Cole, how are you?" the woman asked.

"I'm fine, Mrs. Barker."

"What you did to save Amy Polofsky last week was amazing," the woman continued. "Amy might have died if it hadn't been for you."

"You're a true hero, Adam," the man put in. "We are lucky to have you on the force, watching over everyone. I hope you're feeling better."

"I'm fine," he muttered.

Adam looked more than a little uncomfortable with their praise. Clearly, he'd downplayed his stumble.

"Take care of yourself," the man said as he ushered his wife to the sidewalk.

"Stumble, huh?" She gave him a challenging look.

"I was just doing my job."

"Sounds like you went above the call of duty."

"There is no above the call. When you're on duty, you do what needs to be done."

"Like save someone's life? How did you break your foot?"

"I got between a speeding car and a little girl. Unfortunately, the driver of that car got away, which still pisses me off."

"But you saved the girl's life."

"I was in the right place at the right time."

He was not a man comfortable with praise.

"I'll look into the details of the break-in," he added. "I'll get back to you."

"Thanks."

She watched him walk down the path, feeling more intrigued than she had in a long time. She'd just met a man who didn't like to talk or brag about himself, even though he had plenty to boast about. That was a rarity.

As she turned toward the restaurant, the café door opened again. She grabbed it, holding it open for another woman, who was chatting on her cell phone. Then she moved inside.

She recognized Chloe immediately. It might have been a long time since high school, but Chloe, with her brown hair and hazel-colored eyes, looked just like the girl she'd gone to school with.

As she approached the counter, Chloe's eyes widened with surprise and the same recognition. "Molly? Is it really you?"

"It's me."

Chloe came around the counter and gave her a hug, followed by a warm, friendly smile. "This is wonderful. I heard a rumor that Phoebe might have left you her shop, but I wasn't sure."

"Yes. I am the new owner of A Better You."

"That's amazing. It's sad about Phoebe, but your coming back to Whisper Lake is definitely the silver lining." Chloe stepped back. "And you're looking as beautiful as ever."

"I was going to say the same for you. I don't think you've aged a bit."

"Oh, please, I've definitely aged. I have a baby now. Actually, Leo is three, so he's a toddler, not a baby."

"That's wonderful. And Kevin?"

"We're not together."

She frowned as shadows filled Chloe's gaze. "I'm sorry to hear that. Phoebe used to write me and fill me in, but it has been a few years since I got one of those newsy letters."

"It's all good now. Kevin is in the military, still deployed more often than he's not, but it's his life, and he loves it. My son, Leo, Whisper Lake, and this restaurant are what I love."

Despite her words, Molly got the feeling there was more pain behind their separation than Chloe was letting on. Chloe and Kevin had been together since high school.

"Do you want something to eat?" Chloe asked as she moved behind the counter.

She slid onto a stool. "I would love to start with coffee."

"You've got it." Chloe filled a mug with coffee and then set it in front of her. "So, where are you living?"

"In the apartment over the store."

"What have you been doing all these years?" Chloe asked curiously.

"A lot of different things. Most recently, I was working for a skin-care company in San Francisco. But it wasn't a job I was going to do forever. When I heard about my inheritance, I thought it was a sign that it was time to make a change. So here I am. Impulsive as ever."

"Well, I'm glad you're still impulsive. When you left us in high school, I was really sad, Molly. You were so much fun. I missed you."

"I missed you, too. You were very nice to me. You brought me into your circle of friends the first day I started school here, and I was always grateful for that."

"I just didn't understand why your mom couldn't wait and let you graduate."

"She could never wait. When it was time to leave, she had to go."

"Are you still close with your mom?"

"I stopped following her around the country two years ago, but we talk often, and she still pops up every few months, usually bringing chaos in her wake."

"She did bring the drama," Chloe admitted. "But she was so beautiful, so free. There was something special about her. Whenever she talked to us about our dreams, our goals, it felt like we could do anything. Anyway, I can't wait for everyone to see you again," Chloe said.

"I heard that Hannah and Gianna are here, but that Keira is in Florida with a baseball player?"

"That's right. Keira doesn't even like sports, but she somehow fell in love with a pro athlete. But Dante is a great guy, so I'm happy for her. Hannah is working as a nurse at the medical center. She was gone for a while and then came back. She married Jake McKenna."

"Wait! Her high-school boyfriend? The one who cheated on her and broke her heart? When I left, he was her sworn enemy."

"That vow lasted ten years," Chloe said. "But when Jake came home a couple of years ago, they finally worked their way past the hatred and back to love. He runs an adventure sports company down by the harbor. Gianna Campbell is also here. She's a graphic designer and does web design. She's married to an architect, Zach Barrington."

"A lot of changes," she murmured.

As a group entered the restaurant, Chloe handed her a menu. "Take a look at this. I'll come back to take your order once I get everyone seated."

"I'm going to need to take it to go."

"No problem. I can wrap anything up for you. And it's on the house."

"You don't have to do that."

"Consider it a welcome home present. Oh, and if you're free tomorrow night, you're coming to a barbecue with me."

"I am free, but—"

"No buts. Everyone will be there that you used to know, and they'll want to see you."

"Then I won't say no."

Chloe smiled. "I'm glad you're back, Molly."

"I don't know if I'm back forever," she said quickly, not sure why she felt the need to say that, but she did. "I need to see what I can do with the store before I decide anything."

"Understood, but I think you're going to want to stay in

Whisper Lake. The town is much more sophisticated and bigger than it was when you were here. You're going to love it. There's a lot to do and even some interesting men to meet, if you're single."

"I am single, but I'm not looking for a man. I have the chance to own a business, call my own shots. That's what's exciting to me these days."

"There's nothing that says you can't have it all."

That might not be written anywhere, she thought as Chloe left. But she'd learned two important lessons from the wandering years of her life: no one could have it all, and nothing lasted forever.

After a quick takeout lunch in the apartment upstairs, Molly returned to the store, ready to dig into the work ahead of her. She tackled the showroom first, which, while daunting, was not as cluttered or as messy as the back room. If she could get this room ready for retail, she'd be that much closer to making some money.

She'd worked in several retail stores over the years, many of which had sold similar products, but she'd never been in charge, never had to order, or take inventory, or worry about hiring and cash flow. She felt a little daunted as she thought of everything she didn't know, including whatever accounting system Phoebe might have on the one computer on the counter—if there even was an accounting system.

Back in the day, Phoebe liked to keep track of everything by hand and with a simple cash register. The cash register was still on the counter, too, but she hadn't been able to figure out a way to open it yet. Not that she'd had much time. She was only twenty-four hours into this new adventure. She needed to cut herself a break.

She just needed to start—somewhere.

Maybe with the boxes. Many of the boxes had one name on

them: Caroline Montgomery. The attorney had told her that Phoebe had recently inherited items from the estate of Caroline Montgomery, Phoebe's long-time friend. Caroline had passed away only three days before Phoebe, so Phoebe had apparently never looked at what had been left to her.

Phoebe had talked about her friend a lot. Caroline had grown up in Whisper Lake with Phoebe but had moved to LA when she was sixteen and had eventually become an award-winning movie star. She had been married at least three times and as she'd gotten older, she'd become a world traveler, often sending Phoebe items from her travels: an incense burner from India, a crystal from Nicaragua. Molly remembered how excited Phoebe would get when a package would show up from Caroline.

But those packages had usually come one at a time. There were now a dozen large boxes in the showroom and another ten in the back room. She was curious what was inside all the boxes, but she really needed to concentrate on the practical first. She needed products to sell and concentrating on the boxes that had come from various manufacturers was a priority.

Before she could move, a knock came at the door, and she looked up in surprise. There was a tall, lanky boy standing outside.

She walked over to the door and opened it. "Hi there. I'm sorry, but we're not open."

"I saw the sign. Do you still need help?"

As he tipped his head toward the Help Wanted sign, she realized it must have been put there by the previous manager. "Oh, I didn't even realize that was up."

"So there's no job?"

"Well..." She hesitated. There was a mountain of work to be done, and she could definitely use some help. She also remembered standing at this door a long time ago, asking the same question, hoping someone would give her a chance to make some money, to be independent. "I'm getting the store up and running again. Right now, I just need someone to help me clean up, re-shelve items, take inventory, and do that kind of thing. Maybe two hours a day to start, and then it could work into more once I reopen. I can start at minimum wage. What do you think?"

"Two hours a day works for me," he replied with a careless shrug.

"Okay. Do you want to start tomorrow? Can you come in at ten and work until twelve?"

"Sounds good."

"What's your name?"

"Drew Kilborn."

"I'm Molly Trent."

"See you tomorrow," he said, then shuffled down the sidewalk.

As soon as he was gone, she realized she should have asked him for more information than just his name, but there was so much to do and having another pair of hands could only be a good thing.

For the next hour, she cleaned off shelves, checked expiration dates on products, threw some away, and put others into piles to organize by category.

Besides vitamins, herbs, lotions, and bath products, the store also sold yoga gear, meditation assets, health and wellness books, sleep aids, aromatherapy products, and other mystical miscellaneous items designed to create a harmonizing environment. There was also a new display featuring the latest in medicinal CBD products, the area that apparently incensed the shop owner next door, even though the products were all completely legal to sell.

She took a couple of trash bags out to the dumpster. As she came back into the room, she moved to the area behind the door and climbed up on the stepladder to clear off the top shelf.

She was halfway up the ladder when the front door opened.

Startled, she realized she hadn't locked it after Drew left.

She also realized it was Adam Cole coming through the door.

In her haste to get down, she missed the step and let out a squeal as she fell off the ladder.

But she didn't hit the ground.

She was caught by a pair of strong male arms.

"Are you trying to kill me?" Adam asked in bemusement as his crutches fell to the ground.

Locked against his hard chest, his arms still around her, the last thing she wanted to do was kill him. Her heart was pounding, sending blood racing through her body, tingling every nerve. She was filled with a reckless desire. Impulsively, she acted on that feeling. She put her hands on his face and then went up on tiptoe to take the kiss she wanted.

CHAPTER FOUR

ADAM'S SURPRISE turned to passion as he took her spontaneous kiss to another level. And when they finally broke apart, his blue eyes were burning with a fire that sent another wave of heat through her.

"Damn," he muttered.

They stared at each other for a couple of seconds and then she took a step back, her breath still coming fast. "So that happened."

She felt like there were other things she needed to say, but she couldn't find any words. Adam wasn't helping. He was just staring at her, his gaze unreadable.

"What are you thinking?" she finally asked.

"That you're going to be trouble."

"I'm sorry. I shouldn't have kissed you."

"I'm not complaining."

She pushed her hair behind her ears, feeling a little awkward after her impulsive kiss. "Thanks for catching me. When the door opened, I was startled, and I lost my footing."

"I thought you were going to lock the door."

"It was locked and then someone came in, and I forgot to lock it again. I'm glad I didn't knock you over this time. I'm really not trying to kill you."

He gave her a dry smile. "All evidence to the contrary." His gaze swept the room. "You've made some progress."

"A little." She drew in a breath and let it out, wondering why he'd come back, and then she remembered... "What about you? Did you find out something about the break-in? Is that why you're here again?"

"Yes. I reviewed the police report. The alarm was tripped at nine-fourteen p.m. last Friday night, one week ago."

"And Phoebe died last Thursday."

"One day prior to the break-in," he confirmed. "A key was used to enter the store. The alarm company responded at nine-twenty p.m. No one was in the shop when they arrived. The company contacted Phoebe's attorney, George Marconi, who arranged for the locks to be changed that night. No one could determine if anything had been taken."

"You're saying that someone came in with a key?"

"Yes. Who would have a key to the shop?"

"I don't know. I would assume the manager, but the attorney told me she left Friday morning, the day after Phoebe died. I don't know if anyone else worked here. The attorney also said that Phoebe didn't discuss the business with him, except to say she wanted to leave the building to me, which includes the shop, the yoga studio, and the apartment upstairs, where she was living."

"What kind of condition is the apartment in?"

"It's cluttered. It feels very much like Phoebe just stepped out for an hour. I couldn't sleep on the bed last night. It felt too strange."

He gave her a sympathetic look. "It's never easy when someone dies."

"I miss her more than I imagined. I always thought I'd see her again, but now I know I won't." Her voice trailed away. "Phoebe didn't have any close relatives, but it's still surprising that she left everything to me when I hadn't seen her since I was a teenager."

"You obviously made an impact on her."

"I loved her. But distance came between us. Should I be worried that someone is going to come back?"

"Well, the locks are new, so no one will enter with a key besides you. And there haven't been any reported incidents since last Friday."

"Until today when someone knocked over the display." A chill ran through her. "I hope no one comes back."

"That you're here now should be a deterrent. But I would stay alert and keep the door locked until you're ready to be open. Where's your phone?"

"It's on the counter."

"Why don't you get it? I'll give you my number. You can call me if you have any more problems."

"Okay, thanks. This is nice of you," she said, as she got her phone and put his number in.

"To be honest, I don't have a lot else to do, and I hate that."

She smiled at the frustrated note in his voice. "How long will you be off work?"

"I'm back to desk duty on Monday. No on-site investigations until I can move without crutches. But I'll be more productive than I am now." As his gaze moved toward the boxes next to her, he said, "So, are these boxes from the film actress who recently died?"

"Yes. Phoebe and Caroline were friends since childhood."

"I met Caroline a few months ago, shortly after she moved back."

"Caroline was living here?" she asked in surprise.

"In a remote house on the west shore of the lake. She had a security issue that I spoke to her about."

"What kind of issue?"

"A trespasser, a broken window, but once her security system was in place, she had no further issues."

"What did Caroline look like? Was she as beautiful as she looked in the movies?"

"She looked like she used to be pretty, but she was very sick and extremely tired. She only said a few words to me."

"What did she say?" Molly asked with interest.

"That I was as handsome as her second husband, but she hoped I wasn't an asshole."

She smiled. "What did you say?"

"That I usually tried not to be an asshole. She didn't look like she believed me. I never saw her again after that."

"It's sad that they died only days apart. Phoebe never even had time to open these boxes. I know Caroline used to send Phoebe treasures from her travels. I suspect that's what I'll find inside. I was going to leave these boxes for last since I need to get the saleable items out first, but now I'm getting more curious."

"What's your story, Molly?" Adam asked. "How were you able to suddenly drop everything in your life to come here and take over for Phoebe?"

"I was getting ready to leave a job when I got the news. It seemed like a sign that I should change my life."

"Anything can be a sign if you put meaning on it."

"That's one way to look at it. Or it could have been the universe telling me to make a move," she said stubbornly. "Sometimes we need an external force to help us make a decision we've been avoiding."

"What decision were you avoiding?"

"Whether I should stay in a job I didn't like all that much or if I should take a risk."

"And now you're taking the risk."

"I've always wanted to work for myself, to make the rules, set the prices, do what I felt was right, and now I have it. I just need to make it work, and I will, because I have to." She decided to turn the tables. "Why did you come to Whisper Lake? It seems like a man of action would want to work in a bigger city."

"I've worked in bigger cities, but after my sisters moved here, I came to visit, and I liked what I saw."

"You have sisters in town?"

"Two. Lizzie owns the Firefly Inn and Chelsea is a singer. They're both married now. In fact, Chelsea is married to a fellow police officer, Brodie McGuire; they're expecting a baby."

"It's nice that you have family here. What about your parents?"

"They're in Denver. I have a brother there as well. Another one is traveling the world."

"Five kids. That's a big family."

"I suppose. What about you?"

"It has been my mom and me for my entire life, with some assorted men moving in and out of our lives. I always wished for a sibling or a dad. A few men seemed like they might be stepfather material, but it never happened."

"Where is your mother now?"

"New York." She didn't want to talk about her complicated relationship with her mother, especially not with a man who seemed to have grown up in an idyllic family. "Anyway, thanks again for coming by and for saving me from what might have been a nasty fall. You really are the hero type, aren't you?"

He shrugged. "Right place, right time."

"For me, anyway. Maybe not so much for you."

"Well, I have to admit, I am wondering how we'll run into each other the next time."

Her pulse leapt at his words. "There might not be a next time. You clearly have no interest in health and wellness products."

"Oh, I think there will be a next time."

"Why?"

"Whisper Lake isn't that big, and you and I...I don't think we're done, Molly."

She looked into his eyes, thinking she didn't want to be done. On the other hand, he was a complication she didn't need.

"Maybe we should be done. I have a lot to do, and I'm not really interested in getting involved with anyone."

"You should have thought about that before you kissed me." He moved toward the door. "Lock this behind me."

"I will," she promised, thinking the person she really needed to keep on the other side of that door was him.

After leaving the wellness store, Adam got into his car and let out a breath. He rarely felt unsettled. In fact, he was known for being cool under pressure, an expert at compartmentalizing, at keeping his emotions away from his decisions, from his actions. But one beautiful brunette had knocked him off-balance, both literally and figuratively.

He hadn't expected her to fall into his arms.

And the kiss…

Well, that had been surprising, too. It had also been good, really good, better-than-he'd-had- in-a-long-time kind of good.

Which was why he should stay away from Molly.

She was a whirlwind of energy—impulsive and reckless. He'd seen firsthand the downside of spontaneity. It could be exciting, and hot as hell, but it could also lead to danger, to pain, to the hurt he never wanted to feel again. Molly was a threat to the calm and the predictability he'd worked so hard to build into his life. He needed to keep his distance.

A few minutes later, he pulled into the parking lot for Micky's Bar and Grill. It was happy hour, and the bar was crowded, but Brodie had a table in front of a wall of television screens, one of which was playing a baseball game between Miami and Houston.

Brodie had brown hair and eyes, and wore jeans and a button-down shirt. He had a pitcher of beer in front of him along with two glasses, one of which was half full.

"Is Dante pitching?" he asked as he sat down at the table.

"He has a no-hitter going. Miami is up by two in the seventh inning. Maybe they'll let him go the distance."

"That's great." He watched as Dante DeAngelis went into his pitching motion, landing the perfect slider for a strike-out. "His shoulder is back to normal."

"He's having a great month," Brodie agreed. "I caught a glimpse of Keira in the stands, and she was screaming her head off. She looked happy."

"They're making it work." He filled the empty glass with beer. "How did your day go?" Brodie had just finished a shift for the police department where they both worked.

"Uneventful, which is a good thing."

"It is," he said with a knowing smile.

Brodie liked action. He had been an Olympic skier and a very active person his entire life.

"And your day? The same?" Brodie asked.

"Actually, not as uneventful as every other day this past week." He took a long sip of beer.

"Does that have something to do with the brother of your former girlfriend showing up in town?"

"I see you spoke to Chelsea," he said dryly.

"Only briefly, but she expressed concern. What's this kid's story?"

"He's nineteen and lost. His sister died when he was a little kid. His mom passed away a few months ago after a long illness. Drew got into some trouble at school. He was partying too much and got put on probation. His father asked if I could help straighten him out, so he's staying with me until Christmas. My only requirement is that he gets a job. If he doesn't, I'm sending him back."

"And this kid is the brother of your former girlfriend, the one who died tragically?"

"Yes," he said shortly. "Gina passed away when she was twenty-one, only a few years older than Drew is now. He's had a lot of loss in his young life, and his father is exhausted after taking care of his wife during her last days. He has nothing left in the tank for Drew."

"It's good you're helping, but you remember nineteen, right?" Brodie gave him a pointed look.

"Yep. Stubborn, know-it-all, no-one-is-going-to-tell-me-what-to-do attitude," he replied. "This idea might result in an epic fail. But I'm going to give it a shot. By the way, do you have any hikes going on this weekend?" In his time off, Brodie ran adventure hikes for Jake's Adventure Sports company. "I'd love to get Drew out in nature. The mountains are great for changing perspective."

"They can definitely do that. I'm leading a hike on Sunday morning, eight miles round trip, medium level. I've got a group of six going. Two are guys in their early twenties, and one has a sister who's eighteen, so he might enjoy it."

"It sounds perfect. I'll talk to him about it."

"Just don't force him, Adam. I only want willing participants. If he's complaining the whole time, he'll ruin the trip for everyone."

"Got it. I'll throw in the eighteen-year-old girl as incentive."

"Always worked for me," Brodie said with a grin.

"There's something else I wanted to ask you. You responded to the 911 call for Phoebe Haller last week, didn't you?"

"Yes. Why?"

"What did the scene look like?"

"Chaos. I've never seen so much junk in my life. I knew Phoebe was eccentric, but I didn't expect her store to be filled with so much stuff. She died right in the middle of all of it. When I got there, she was on her back, with her hand on her heart, her lifeless eyes wide open. Her manager, Nina Williamson, was hysterically crying. She found Phoebe when she came back from lunch. She was so shaken she didn't think she could ever be in the store again. When I checked back with her the next day, she was already on a flight to Florida."

As Brodie finished talking, Adam felt a little uneasy. "I wonder why she left so fast."

"Her neighbor said she'd been planning to retire to Florida, but she didn't think she'd made specific plans to go until Phoebe died. I guess she was spooked. She told the neighbor she'd be back later to get the rest of her things." Brodie paused, his gaze narrowing. "Why are you asking me about that call?"

"The manager's hasty departure from the state seems suspect. There was also a break-in at the store a day after Phoebe died. And today, someone might have stolen something from the store or just wanted to do some damage by pulling down a rack filled with products."

"And you know this how? I thought you were off work."

"I was walking by the store when the new owner came running outside and barreled right into me. She'd been in the back room when she heard a crash."

"What was taken?"

"She has no idea. She just arrived, and, like you said, the store is a mess. Apparently, the late Caroline Montgomery sent half her estate to Phoebe. Which makes me wonder…" He could see the awareness enter Brodie's gaze.

"Whether there's something at the store that's worth stealing," Brodie finished.

"Yes. Or the break-in might have been a crime of opportunity. Everyone in town knew Phoebe was dead, and the store was temporarily unattended. Phoebe's lawyer had the locks changed, and there wasn't another incident until possibly today when the door was open."

"Are you sure you're not just looking for a crime to solve?"

He sipped his beer, then gave him a dry smile. "That's entirely possible."

Brodie grinned back at him. "At least you're owning it. Who's the new owner? Is she another Phoebe?"

"Not even close. She's young, probably late twenties. And she's…" His voice trailed away as he searched for the right words to describe Molly. "She's very interesting."

"As in hot, beautiful, sexy, interesting?"

"Yes," he admitted, seeing the speculative gleam in Brodie's eyes. "But she is not my type. She's into crystals and magical thinking."

"So what? You don't have to marry her. When's the last time you had some uncommitted fun?"

"I have fun," he grumbled.

"That's not what Chelsea and Lizzie say."

"My sisters don't know everything, and neither do you."

"I don't doubt that."

Their gazes moved back to the screen as Dante took his no-hitter into the final inning.

"Three outs and Dante will have a no-hitter," Brodie said. "To think, a couple of months ago, Dante wasn't even sure he'd pitch again. Now look at him. Just goes to show you never know what might be around the next corner—good or bad."

"You never know." He sipped his beer, his gaze on the screen, but his thoughts on Molly. He didn't know if her arrival would be good or bad, but he was curious to find out.

CHAPTER FIVE

SATURDAY MORNING, Molly went down to the shop a little before ten. She'd planned to get in earlier, but after rolling around on a hard couch for too many hours, she'd finally fallen asleep close to dawn. She really needed to get over her fear of taking over Phoebe's bedroom. She couldn't sleep on the couch indefinitely.

Tonight, she would change the sheets and force herself to sleep on the bed. Phoebe would want her to make herself comfortable. She would want her to look at the apartment as home. In fact, she'd probably want her to look at the store as home, too.

Phoebe had left her a life to step into, the same life Phoebe had lived.

But as Molly gazed around the cluttered showroom, she wondered if she could take Phoebe's life and make it her own.

It was a complicated gift she'd received. The store could be a new beginning or a mistaken detour. She could spend a lot of time and fail. She could spend a lot of time and be a success. *But then what?*

She was afraid of roots, terrified of commitment. Roots could get ripped up; commitment could disappear; heartbreaking disappointment could follow. She'd seen it happen to her mother, and in turn, it had happened to her. Caring too much could bring pain. She'd started to believe her mother had the right idea: move on before anyone gets hurt.

But she was tired of moving on, starting over. This could be the last stop. This could be the place she was meant to be. But it felt like too big a risk to believe that.

She blew out a breath. She was thinking too far ahead. Plans were for other people, not for her. She lived in the moment. And when change came, she embraced it. She hurried through life, never letting herself linger too long anywhere. Even now, her pulse was racing along with her thoughts. She needed to slow down. She should probably go into the yoga studio and work out, but she didn't have time for that. She had too much to do.

She suddenly heard Phoebe's voice in her head, telling her to stop thinking so much. She didn't need to solve every problem right now. Phoebe had urged her to find the joy in discovery. That's what she needed to focus on now.

She just wished she could have one more conversation with Phoebe, that Phoebe could tell her what to do next, what was most important. Because, along with the store, Phoebe had also left her ashes to her, with a note that the lawyer had read to her over the phone. She needed to read it again, because she'd been so overwhelmed, she'd barely heard it, but she knew that Phoebe wanted her to decide where she should spend eternity. She had no idea why Phoebe would trust her to do that. Nor did she have any clue where that should be, but she could push that off for a few days at least. The attorney had possession of the ashes now and had simply asked her to stop by one day next week to collect them. She'd deal with that problem then.

A sharp knock drew her attention to the door, and she saw the face of the lanky teenager she'd hired the day before. She let him in, relieved to have company. She needed a distraction from her own thoughts.

"Hello, Drew. I'm happy to see you," she said.

He didn't respond to her smile. "What do you want me to do?"

He might not be cheerful, but he seemed willing to work. She'd take that. "I'd like you to start in the back room." She paused as she locked the front door. "I want to keep this door locked when we're not here in the showroom. There was a break-in last week. Until we're ready to really be open, I'd appreciate if you'd keep the bolt on."

He shrugged. She had a feeling that would be his response to everything.

She led him into the back. "You can start opening boxes. I cleared some space on the table. If you can organize products that look like they go together and/or are by the same manufacturer or distributor, that would be very helpful. You can then break down and recycle the boxes in the bins that are just outside the back door."

"Got it."

He pulled headphones out of his pocket and put them in his ears.

"One second," she said.

He took out the headphones. "What?"

"Can you tell me a little about yourself before we start? We didn't get acquainted yesterday."

"What do you want to know?"

"How old are you? Do you live around here? Are you in school?"

"Nineteen. I'm in town until Christmas. Then I'm going back to school."

He definitely wasn't chatty. That was one difference between her teenage self and him. She'd peppered Phoebe with questions and had been happy to have any conversation she could get from someone who was actually interested in her opinions.

"You said you're in town until Christmas," she pressed. "Are you visiting with your family?"

"No, I'm staying with a friend of my father's. Well, he didn't used to be a friend, but I guess he is now."

Finally, a little detail. There was a story behind that answer. But Drew had already put his headphones back on, and she needed him to work more than she needed to know about his life.

As he started in the back room, she moved out to the front. She had a plan of attack for today. She would begin in one corner of the store and stay there until it was clean and organized. Then she'd move on. She couldn't keep getting distracted by different tasks. They all had to be done at some point.

The next two hours passed in a blur, but she finally filled one shelving display with sleep aids: meditation tapes, eye masks, aromatherapy candles, and more. It was a start. But there was still a lot to do.

Just after noon, Chloe knocked on the door.

She let her in with a smile. "Hello. What are you doing here?"

"Bringing my friend some lunch." Chloe handed her a large paper bag. "Sandwiches, salads, and cookies. Whatever you don't eat for lunch, you can have another time."

She was touched by the kind gesture. "This is so sweet of you, Chloe. Thank you."

"It was no problem, and I thought you might be too busy to eat."

"You're right. I also hired a teenager to work for me part-time. I'm sure he'd love some food, too."

"That's great. You're already hiring people."

"Just a couple of hours a day until I can figure out what I have to sell and reopen."

Chloe glanced around the showroom. "I guess I haven't been here in a while. I don't remember so much stuff."

"Apparently, Phoebe inherited some things from her friend, Caroline Montgomery."

"Really?" A curious gleam entered her eyes. "Anything interesting? I heard Caroline was quite a collector."

"I haven't gotten to her boxes yet. Did you meet Caroline?"

"No. After she moved here, she never left her house. I'll be curious to know what she left Phoebe. From what I heard, Caroline traveled all over the world and received some incredible gifts from her three husbands."

"It's hard to imagine being married three times."

"I hear you," Chloe said with a laugh. "I'm not even sure I want to do it a second time. Not that I didn't love being married, but people can change. One day you're in love, and the next day you're not. I don't know if I want to go through that kind of pain again."

"I'm sorry things didn't work out with Kevin. You fell in love when you were so young."

"Which was part of the problem. We were young. And because Kevin was in the military, he did most of his growing up far away from me, in a world I couldn't understand. He was injured right before Leo was born. In fact, he missed his birth. I was in labor, and I didn't even know if my husband was going to live long enough to see his son. I thought he'd quit after that. And I think he tried. Not as hard as I would have liked, but he took a stab at being home. He was just really unhappy. His heart was with his team. I finally had to accept that."

"I can't even imagine how difficult that must have been, especially with a baby."

"It was a tough couple of years, but Leo and I are good now. We have each other, and Kevin is probably more supportive because he's free of the marriage that wasn't working for him anymore. He sends me money. He calls at least twice a month to check in, and he comes to visit when he can. It's not what I wanted for my son, but hopefully one day Leo will understand that his father is fighting for the world he wants his child to grow up in."

"That is admirable."

"Kevin is a good guy. Anyway, I didn't mean to bore you with all that."

"I'm not bored. And in case you have forgotten, I am a fantastic babysitter, so just say the word."

"I'll let you get settled in first. But I do remember that you were a good babysitter. All the kids loved the way you did voices in your stories. I also remember you saying that you used to tell yourself stories when you were a kid, because it distracted you from being scared when your mom left you alone at night."

She frowned. "I told you that?"

"It was one of the few things you said about growing up with just your mom. I might need some tips on what not to do as I raise Leo on my own."

"You will never be like my mother, Chloe. She was too young when she had me. Sometimes I took care of her more than she took care of me. When she got stressed, I was the one to comfort her, to tell her it would be all right. Then she'd feel better and go out, and I'd tell myself a story before I went to bed."

"That sounds lonely." Chloe gave her a compassionate smile. "When you were living here, your mom was with the fire chief, Neil Loeffler. You thought she was going to marry him."

"I did. Neil was great. I hoped he was going to be my stepfather, but like every other man my mom dated, he wasn't interested in marrying her, only sleeping with her. Their breakup was the reason she pulled me out of high school early and moved me to New Orleans. Anyway, that's all in the past. I'm looking forward."

"You may have to do a little more reminiscing tonight. You're still up for a barbecue, right? Gianna and Hannah will be there, and they want to see you."

"I'd love to come."

"Great. I'll pick you up at five. You'll get a chance to meet Leo. He'll be my date."

"I can't wait."

After Chloe left, she locked the door and then took the bag of food into the back room, where Drew was breaking down a cardboard box.

"I know your two hours is up, but my friend dropped off some lunch," she told him. "I have plenty to share. Are you hungry?"

"I could eat," he muttered.

They sat down at a small table in what Phoebe had called the lounge, which was really just a kitchenette with a refrigerator, microwave, coffeemaker, and a table with two chairs. As she pulled out the food options, she said, "You've made a good start in here. I appreciate the hard work. Pick whatever you'd like to eat."

He selected a turkey and cheese sandwich, which left her with the chicken Caesar salad.

They ate in silence for a few moments, then Drew said, "What kind of software do you use for inventory?"

"Uh, I'm not really sure. I haven't looked into all that yet."

"Does the store have a website?"

"No. Phoebe never got around to making that happen."

Drew looked shocked at that fact. "You must have a website. You have a lot of shit to sell. I don't think there are enough people in this town to buy everything. You need to sell online, too."

He had a point. "I agree, but that will have to be down the road. I just got here last night. My friend, the previous owner, passed away and left me her business, but she was sick recently and everything fell apart. I'm going to clean it up and make it shine again."

He didn't say anything as he swallowed and then took a slug of soda.

"Where do your parents live, Drew?" she asked.

"My mom is dead. My dad lives in Denver."

"Oh, I'm sorry about your mom."

Her comment was met with another shrug. "What does your dad do?" she asked.

"He's a lawyer."

"Are you close to him?"

"No."

"You don't want to talk about him, do you?"

"No."

She nodded in understanding. "I get it. I used to hate when people asked me about my parents, mostly because I didn't have a dad, and my mom was not someone I was proud of."

Her words were met with silence as Drew finished his sandwich.

"Phoebe let me work here when I was an unhappy teenager," she continued. "I loved having a place where I could make my own money and not have to listen to my mother's next great idea that was sure to fail."

"My dad has shitty ideas, too."

"Like what?"

"Like me getting straightened out by some guy I haven't seen since I was eight years old."

"Is that the family friend you're staying with?"

"Yeah. He used to be a partier like I am now. But then he got his act together and became a cop. My father thinks I can learn something from him."

Her body tensed at his words. "He's a police officer? What's his name?"

"Adam Cole."

Her heart flipped over. *This kid was living with Adam?*

"Adam only agreed to my father's stupid plan, because he owes my dad" Drew continued. "It's not about me at all." Drew gulped down the rest of his sandwich and got to his feet. "I gotta go. Do you want me to work tomorrow?"

"It's Sunday, but if you want to help, I won't say no."

"I have to go on some stupid hike in the morning, but I can come around three."

"That's great. I'll be here all day."

The back door banged shut behind him, and she got up to lock it, her mind racing with what Drew had just told her.

Adam was supposed to straighten Drew out, because he used

to be a partier, and now he was a cop. But what really puzzled her was what Drew had meant when he said that Adam owed his father. *What was that about?*

She'd spent most of the day forbidding herself to give the sexy cop one more minute of her time, but now she couldn't think of anyone else.

CHAPTER SIX

ADAM ARRIVED at Brodie and Chelsea's home a little after five on Saturday night. He'd hoped to get Drew to join him for his sister's barbecue, but Drew had refused, saying he wasn't hungry. He'd told him if that changed there were frozen pizzas in the freezer and a salad in the fridge. Drew had given him a grunt, gone into the guest room and closed the door. He was beginning to wonder if having Drew stay with him was a big mistake. He hadn't realized the level of antipathy that Drew held for him. At one point, the kid had idolized him, but, of course, a lot had changed since then.

Still, it was early. Maybe Drew would loosen up after he was in the mountains for a while. He'd agreed to go on the hike tomorrow with Brodie's group, so that was a start. Meeting some younger people might make him realize he could have some fun here.

But Adam did remember being nineteen and wanting his own life. Maybe he needed to tell Drew that, let him know he understood, that he just wanted to be a friend, not a jailer or a pseudo-father figure. That conversation would have to wait until tomorrow.

As he got out of his car, he ran into Hannah and Jake on the sidewalk. Hannah's fiery red hair was swept up in a ponytail, and she wore white linen pants and a tank top falling off her fair, freckled shoulders. Jake was in his usual jeans and a T-shirt. They both looked incredibly happy since tying the knot a few months ago.

"How's your foot?" Jake asked him.

"It's getting better."

"Are you resting it?" Hannah gave him a suspicious look that had probably been honed by her years as a nurse. "Or are you trying to impatiently move that part of the healing process forward?"

"I've been resting it."

"Make sure you do. In the long run, the healing will go faster and better."

"That's what I've been told. Patience is not one of my strengths."

Hannah frowned. "You have to take the time off, Adam. The world will not end if you're not in action for a few weeks."

Hannah was never one to sugarcoat her suggestions, but he liked that she was direct. Yes, Nurse Hannah," he teased.

She made a face at him, then led the way to the front door. They didn't bother to knock, just walked into the house, which was beautiful, large, and new. Brodie and Chelsea had taken the previous home down to the studs to rebuild and had turned the adjacent barn into a recording studio for Chelsea's very successful music career.

Brodie came through the patio door, wearing a bright-red apron that was labeled Grill Master.

Adam grinned. "Nice apron."

"Chelsea thought it was funny, and I'm wearing it so she has something to smile about."

"What's wrong?" he asked quickly.

"She's just spending a lot of time in the bathroom. The baby doesn't seem to care for anything that she eats."

"Poor thing," Hannah said. "I'll go check on her."

"She's upstairs."

As Hannah left, Brodie gave them a worried and helpless look. "I hate to see Chelsea suffering like this. I thought she'd be better by now. There's nothing I can do that makes anything better."

"I'm sure she'll appreciate you wearing the apron," he said. "Hopefully, she's almost out of this morning sickness phase."

"We both keep thinking that, but it goes on and on. Anyway, come on back. There are cold beers, wine, and Zach just made very strong margaritas."

"I'm in," Jake said, heading first through the French doors leading out to the patio.

As Adam followed the guys outside, his gaze swept the crowd. The usual suspects were all there: his sister Lizzie and her husband Justin, Zach and Gianna, Hannah and Jake, Chloe, Leo, and…

He stiffened in surprise, his stomach flipping over as a beautiful brunette with stunning green eyes smiled at Leo and tickled him in the stomach, drawing a giddy little laugh from Chloe's little boy.

Chloe must have invited Molly. They had been friends when they were young. He should have anticipated that she'd be here, that Chloe would want Molly to reunite with her old friends.

He shouldn't care. But his lips tingled as he remembered their hot and very unexpected kiss.

Her gaze suddenly swung to his. Her lips parted, her eyes wary.

Had she known this barbecue was at his sister's house? Was that why she'd come—so she could see him?

"Hello? Earth to Adam."

He turned to see his younger sister Lizzie's bright, inquisitive gaze. "Sorry. Did you say something?"

"I just said hello. Who are you staring at? Oh, wait, it has to be Chloe's friend, Molly." She gave him a knowing smile. "She's very pretty. And friendly too. She told me she's taking over Phoebe's health and wellness store."

He cleared his throat and deliberately focused on Lizzie. "Right. How are things going with you and the inn and with Justin?"

"Good, great, and amazing," she said with a radiant smile.

"I'm glad to hear that." Lizzie had always been a positive person, but since she'd married Justin, she was even happier.

"I just wish things were going better for you, Adam. How's the foot?"

"It's fine. No one needs to worry about me."

"You always say that. But it's difficult not to worry about you. Your job can be dangerous. You almost died saving that little girl."

"But I didn't. I just got banged up."

"Did you ever catch the driver of the car that almost killed both of you?"

"No. The car was found abandoned on the north shore. It had been stolen from an elderly man, who had no clue it was even gone until it was returned to him."

"So nothing will happen to the driver?"

"Not until we get another lead."

"That's disappointing."

"Yeah," he said shortly. "But I haven't given up."

"You never do." Lizzie's smile widened as she glanced past him. "Hi, Molly. Have you met my brother Adam?"

"I have." Molly gave him a tentative look. "Hello, Adam."

"You've met?" Lizzie asked in surprise.

"Yesterday," Molly replied. "I literally knocked your brother over. I hope your foot isn't any worse today."

As he gazed into her eyes, he found himself suddenly short of breath. He'd spent most of the day convincing himself Molly had not been that pretty, that sexy, that kissable, but he'd been lying to himself. She was all that and more. And he really wanted to kiss her again.

"It's okay," he said, realizing he needed to say something. "How's the store?"

"I've made some progress. I probably should have kept working, but Chloe invited me to meet up with some of my old friends. I didn't realize it was at your sister's house until I got here. I haven't met Chelsea yet."

"She's having a bout of morning sickness, but hopefully she'll be out soon. Hannah is with her."

"I'll check on them," Lizzie said.

As Lizzie moved into the house, Molly gave him another questioning glance. "Is it weird for you that I'm here? I don't want you to think I'm stalking you."

"It's not weird. And I don't think that. You're more than welcome. It's good that you reconnected with Chloe."

"She is just the same as she always was. Chloe was one of the first girls I met when I moved to Whisper Lake. She lived across the street from where my mom and I were staying, and she took me under her wing the first day I went to high school. I was very grateful. Then she introduced me to all her friends, who were just as nice to me."

"She has always been very inclusive."

A sudden squeal of surprise and delight interrupted their conversation. He turned around to see Hannah run out of the house. She moved straight toward Molly.

"Molly?" Hannah said. "Molly Trent?"

"It's me. Hi, Hannah," Molly said, as Hannah threw her arms around her and gave her a hug.

"I can't believe you're here. This is wonderful," Hannah said, as they broke apart. "I mean, sad about Phoebe, but great that she left the store to you. Were you shocked? Or did you know it was going to happen?"

"I had no clue. I spoke to her a couple of months ago, and she didn't mention it. It's still difficult to believe that she's gone and that I'm in charge of A Better You."

"I remember how close you two were. I'm sorry."

"Thanks."

"You look good, Molly," Hannah added.

"So do you. I heard you're married."

As Hannah showed Molly her ring, Adam muttered something about getting a drink and then headed to the built-in bar where Justin and Zach were hanging out. He grabbed a beer out of the cooler, popped the top, and took a much-needed drink. He couldn't remember when he'd felt this unsettled by a woman.

Justin and Zach were engaged in a friendly but heated discussion about baseball, including Dante's recent no-hitter. He joined in to distract himself, but while he threw in a comment now and then, he couldn't stop his gaze from moving to Molly. First, Gianna joined her, then Hannah. Then his sisters came out of the house, and his uneasiness increased. He really didn't need his sisters to become friends with Molly, but that was going to happen. They were tight with Chloe, Hannah, and Gianna. Whether he liked it or not, Molly was going to end up in the middle of his friend circle.

But the last thing he wanted was for Molly to be his friend.

As they finished a lively meal with great food and many laughs, Molly realized how much she'd missed these women. But it also felt like she'd never left, like the time between had passed in the blink of an eye. Chloe, Hannah, and Gianna were very much the same. Hannah still had her dry, sarcastic wit, while Chloe was warm and kind, and Gianna brought a creative energy to every conversation.

She loved hearing about their lives and their loves and meeting their new friends, Lizzie and Chelsea, and their spouses.

Lizzie was a talker. It was easy to see her as the manager of an inn. She seemed like someone who loved being the hostess. Even at Chelsea's house, she had taken charge of the schedule, from appetizers to drinks to their main course. But she wasn't pushy, just eager to make everyone happy.

Chelsea was quieter. She didn't know if that was because she was still feeling sick or if that was more her nature. It was difficult to imagine her commanding a stage, but over dinner she'd heard a lot of stories about Chelsea's fantastic music career.

Adam said little during the meal. But his gaze had found hers several times. She wished she could read him better. She wasn't sure if he was happy she was at the barbecue or annoyed she'd become part of his circle.

It was definitely a tight circle. The women were close and so were the guys. Everyone was matched up except for Chloe, Adam, and her. If she wanted to be with her old friends, she was going to have to find a way to coexist with Adam. She really wished she hadn't impulsively kissed him.

She had a bad habit of acting on impulse, but she probably should have thought that idea through, especially since she was starting over in a new town, or at least a town she hadn't lived in for a long time. But it was too late for regrets, and they were a waste of time anyway. She would find a way to make peace with Adam and hopefully get the perpetual scowl off his face at some point.

As Leo let out an unhappy squeal, Chloe grimaced. "I think this little guy is done with this party," she said.

"He lasted a long time," Gianna said.

"He did. I need to take him home and get him to bed." Chloe's gaze turned to her. "I don't want to drag you away, Molly. Maybe Adam could give you a ride home." Before she could say she didn't need a ride, Chloe had turned to Adam. "Can you do that, Adam?" Chloe asked.

He hesitated. "Sure. No problem."

She inwardly sighed. He clearly did not want to get stuck with her, but he was too nice of a guy to say no. And she didn't want to make a big deal out of a ride that would only last a few minutes, so she simply said, "Thanks."

"Are you sure you don't want to stay for cake, Chloe?" Lizzie asked.

"The last thing either Leo or I need at this point is sugar," Chloe said with a laugh. "I'll see you all soon."

"Well, I want some cake," Hannah said. "Who else is in?"

There was a chorus of assent. Molly got up to help, but Lizzie waved her back into her seat. "Hannah and I have got this."

As Hannah and Lizzie left, Chelsea came around the table and down next to her.

"It's really nice to get to know you, Molly," she said.

"You, too. You have a beautiful home."

"Thank you. Would you like to see my recording studio?"

"I would love to."

"Let's take a walk."

She got up and followed Chelsea down a well-lit path to a big barn-like building.

Upon entering, Chelsea switched on the lights. "This is where it all happens these days."

"It's very cool. I've never been in a studio before. This looks so sophisticated."

"I wanted it to be state-of-the-art so I could work from Whisper Lake." Chelsea swept her hand toward what appeared to be a massive control panel with more knobs and buttons than Molly could count, as well as three digital screens. "My sound engineers work there. I stand behind the glass and sing. Sometimes, I'm joined by musicians as well. When we're not working, we're lounging over there." She pointed to a seating area of comfortable couches and chairs, and a small kitchen.

"How often do you record?" she asked.

"It depends. I just finished an album last month, so I'm taking some time off, which worked out well since I've been feeling rather sick with this pregnancy."

"Sorry to hear that."

"Thanks. I actually spoke to Phoebe the day before she died.

She said she had an herbal tea that might help my morning sickness. She was going to put it aside for me, but then, well, the worst thing in the world happened, and she passed away. I was just wondering if you might know what she was talking about, or if you might have found something with my name on it."

"There's a lot of stuff that I haven't gone through yet. But I'm fairly sure she was talking about a ginger-lemon tea. I can look in the store tomorrow to see what Phoebe has. If she doesn't have it, I can order it or give you some suggestions if you want to do it yourself."

"I've looked online, but it's so confusing, and I'm a little afraid to do something too radical. I don't want to hurt the baby. Brodie is also very concerned about me taking any unregulated herbs."

"These teas are very mild. Besides tea, there's a mint-based lotion that also seems to help."

"A lotion?" Chelsea asked doubtfully.

"Yes," she said with a smile. "It's relaxing and smells really good."

"Well, that doesn't sound dangerous."

"It's not. Why don't you come by the store tomorrow afternoon? Let me see what I can find that might help you."

"Are you sure you want to do that on a Sunday?"

"Of course. I'm going to be working, anyway."

"Then I'll come by. If I can find anything that helps even a bit, I'll be grateful. I'm spending half my life in the bathroom. I shouldn't complain, because I feel incredibly blessed to be pregnant and to have so much real love in my life with Brodie and all my friends."

"You're not complaining. No one wants to feel bad. And hopefully you're almost through the worst of it."

"That's what my doctor keeps saying. She's out of town right now, so I haven't had a chance to talk to her. The physician covering for her hasn't been that interested in giving me natural healing ideas. Hannah suggested I talk to Phoebe. She thought there might be some alternative methods that could help me."

She was happy to hear that Hannah had an open mind. Not that she was surprised. Hannah had always been forward-thinking. "There are lots of things you can try, including breathing exercises, meditation. There's a strong connection between the mind and the body."

Chelsea smiled. "I think Phoebe left her store to exactly the right person."

"I have nowhere near the knowledge she had, but I hope I can help you."

"I appreciate the effort. Shall we get dessert? I'm actually thinking I might eat some cake."

"Let's do it."

When they returned to the group, dessert was on the table and conversation was flowing fast and furiously. There were lots of inside jokes that Molly didn't completely understand, but it was easy to see the genuine love and friendship in the group.

She'd almost forgotten what it was like to feel part of such a close-knit group. She'd moved around so often in her life that friends came and went more often than they stayed. But many in this group had been friends for most of their lives, which seemed almost unbelievable to her. But that was Whisper Lake. It was a place where people were happy to spend their entire lives, something that also seemed unrealistic.

The group finally broke up around nine, and for the first time in hours, Adam actually looked at her.

"Are you ready to go?" he asked.

"Sure." She said her goodbyes, as did Adam, and then she got into the passenger seat of his gray Jeep.

She wasn't surprised he drove a rugged vehicle. It seemed to fit him, not that she knew him well enough to say that, but he seemed like a man of action, someone impatient, direct, and ready to go off-road if he needed to get somewhere. She smiled to herself. She'd done this her entire life, made up stories about people that probably weren't even close to being true.

"What are you smiling about?" Adam asked curiously as he started the engine.

"Nothing."

"It looks like something."

"Just thinking that this Jeep suits you, but then reminding myself that I don't actually know you."

"Well, it does suit me. And it gets me where I need to go."

"A practical car for a practical man."

He frowned. "Is that what you think of me?"

"I don't know what I think of you," she said candidly. "But what I do know is that you were uncomfortable with me being at the barbecue."

"I was surprised," he admitted. "I wasn't uncomfortable."

She didn't believe him for a second, but she wasn't in the mood to pick a fight. "It's a beautiful night. I'd forgotten how many stars you can see in the mountains." She peered out the window at the brightly lit sky. "What's the name of that place where everyone goes to stargaze?"

"I'm not sure what you're referring to."

"You get to it from the street behind the rec center. It's a couple of miles up some steeper hills and then at the top is a bluff. I think it's something with the word *peak* in it."

"Probably Carver's Peak."

"That was it. We had some teenage parties up there."

"That still happens in the summer, not so much this time of year."

She gave him a quick look as he suddenly changed lanes and made a right turn. "Where are you going?"

"Apparently down memory lane. Want to see if it's still the same? Or are you in a hurry to get home?"

His questions made her hesitate. She wasn't in a hurry to get back to Phoebe's apartment at all. She wanted to be a lot more tired before she tried to sleep in Phoebe's bed. On the other hand, spending more time with Adam was probably a bad idea. But maybe if they talked a little more, they could get past the awkwardness between them. "I'm not in a hurry," she told him.

"Then let's go see some stars."

CHAPTER SEVEN

LET'S *go see some stars—why the hell had he just said that?*

He should take Molly straight home, not to some remote mountain lookout, but the drive to her apartment had seemed far too short, and he was feeling far too restless to just go home. He'd been wanting to talk to her all night, even though he'd tried not to show any interest in her.

But here they were.

And maybe he was okay with it.

It took about ten minutes to get up the hills. When he turned onto the flat paved vista point next to a wide, grassy meadow, there wasn't another car in sight. In the summer, this place would be packed. But tonight, it was just them. That seemed both good and bad.

Molly was out of the car as soon as he parked. He followed more slowly.

When she reached the grass, she took off her shoes and walked a good twenty feet before she stopped in the middle of the meadow.

He impulsively grabbed a blanket from the back of his car. It was late summer, but here in the mountains, he'd learned to be prepared for anything. Though a starry night with a beautiful woman hadn't been on his radar until just this minute.

He walked over to join Molly. Her head was tilted up, her gaze on the sky.

"You need a better view," he told her as he spread the blanket on the ground. "There's only one real way to see the stars, and that's on your back."

She smiled at him. "Is that a line?"

"No. But is it a good one?" he asked lightly

"Well, it worked on me." She sat down on the blanket and then stretched out on her back.

He sat down next to her, but he was far more interested in looking at her than at the sky. Her face was beautiful in the moonlight, with her big eyes and wide smile. She had a face that made it impossible to look away from her.

"Do you know any of the constellations?" she asked.

He forced himself to look up at the sky. "Nope," he said.

"I think that's the Big Dipper. It looks like a kite to me."

"I don't see it."

"Really? It's right there." She pointed to the sky.

"You realize that I have no idea where you're pointing," he said dryly.

She turned her head to look at him. "You can't see the kite?"

"No, but I'll take your word for it."

She smiled, then looked back at the stars. "It is a beautiful sky," she said with a sigh. "I can't remember the last time I saw so many stars. It was probably the last time I was in Whisper Lake."

"Why were you here for just a couple of years?" He'd heard some bits and pieces of her history over dinner, but not enough to give him a complete picture.

"My mother was—is—" she corrected, "a wanderer. She could never stay anywhere for long. Something always went wrong, and then we'd leave. She brought me to Whisper Lake when I was fifteen. She'd gotten fired from a job in LA and her boyfriend had cheated on her, so it was time to make a change. A friend of hers offered her a job at a dance studio here, and she took it."

"So, your mom was a dancer."

"A dancer, a singer, an actress. Anything that put her on stage. But dancing was her first passion. She studied ballet from the age of three. And then she moved on to other styles. She eventually ended up on Broadway when she was eighteen. That's where she met my dad. They only dated long enough to accidentally get pregnant," she added with a dry note in her voice. "He left before I was born. Then we moved to LA, where my aunt helped take care of me while my mom worked. But once I got into elementary school, my mom started moving around. She'd go wherever the job was, and I went with her."

"Was she successful?"

"In the sense that we didn't starve, yes. But neither jobs nor money lasted a long time, not that I was completely aware of that when I was young. My mom would convince me that whatever move we were making was going to be exciting and wonderful and filled with possibilities."

"And did that always happen?"

"No. But then it was time to move again, so the dream started over."

"Your father was never in the picture?"

"No. I've never talked to him or heard from him."

"He should have been supporting you."

"He was a musician, and I don't think he made a lot of money. Are you bored yet? I'm probably oversharing."

"You're not."

"Anyway, I loved when we came to Whisper Lake. It was so clean. It felt far away from traffic noise and dirty city streets. The kids were nice to me. I also met Phoebe. She made a lonely teenager feel like there was magic just around the corner, like someone really cared to know what I thought, what I needed. When my mom started dating someone, I thought we'd stay here. I really liked that guy, too. He was so much better than everyone else. He would have been a good stepfather, but it didn't work out. My mom got an offer to work at a studio in New Orleans, and off we went."

"Where is your mom now?"

"New York. I called her before I came back here, and she had the oddest reaction to my news. She said Phoebe had told her when we left before that I belonged in Whisper Lake. That's where I'd be happy. My mother had been super annoyed by that comment, because she was determined to leave, and she wasn't going to leave me behind. She yanked me out of high school a month before graduation."

He frowned. "I probably shouldn't say this, but your mother doesn't sound that great."

"If you met her, you'd like her. She can be charming and fun. And aside from too many abrupt moves in my life, she treated me well. We were more like sisters than mother-daughter. We grew up together. Anyway, she wasn't happy that I came back here. She doesn't believe you can ever go back and recapture anything. She always tells me it's important to keep looking ahead, chasing my dream. That's what she did."

"Perhaps at your expense."

"Maybe. People are complicated—good, bad, and everything in between. I try not to judge. It doesn't get me anywhere. Not that I can help myself from having opinions."

"So, is your dream a career in health and wellness? To run a store like A Better You?"

"I've been in the wellness industry in some form for the last six years. I've worked for an herbal tea manufacturer, sold skin care products, and burned a lot of incense for a yoga retreat resort in the Napa Valley, but I haven't quite found the right niche. I think this store might be it. I've never wanted to do just one thing. I want to help people feel better in a lot of different ways. I believe stress is the most dangerous disease we have, and yet so easy to treat, with meditation, relaxation, sleep, exercise, and good nutrition. If I can further that cause, then I'll feel like

I'm doing something worthwhile. I've been drifting my whole life. I feel like I haven't left my mark anywhere. This is my chance to do that."

There was certainly passion in her voice, and he admired her goals. He just wondered how much of what she was selling was actually helpful.

"Anyway, that's my story," she said. "Let's talk about you. Lizzie and Chelsea told me a little about your family at dinner, how you were raised with a lot of values, like giving back to the community, protecting each other, but also making your own way in the world. Is that why you became a police officer?"

"Partly, yes."

"And the other part?"

He shrugged, not wanting to get into his past. "A story for another time."

"No fair. I just told you a lot."

"And you just reminded me I need to relax." He stretched out on his back.

A moment later, she said, "Do you do this often?"

"I've never done this."

"Really? Why not?"

"I don't usually slow down long enough to look at the stars."

"It's nice to just be, isn't it? Phoebe was always telling me to slow down, to be present, but it's a battle I continue to fight. I always have too many ideas, and too much energy. I have to force myself to breathe more slowly."

He rolled onto his side, propping himself up on one elbow. "I also have a hard time slowing down unless I'm forced to. But I have to admit, I like this…present."

She turned her head to look at him, then rolled onto her side to face him. "Do you like it? I thought you were annoyed with me tonight. You didn't like me being around your friends."

"It wasn't that. You took me by surprise, and I didn't like…" He searched for the right words.

"What?"

"I didn't like that I could still taste your lips on mine. I didn't like how much I wanted to kiss you again."

She sucked in a quick breath. "I never would have guessed that's what you were thinking behind that scowl," she said in a breathy murmur. "If you want to kiss me again, you can."

His pulse sped up at her offer, at her pretty face lit by the moonlight, her green eyes sparkling, her lips soft and so tempting. "It's a bad idea," he muttered, talking more to himself than to her.

"Why?"

"We're different."

"Different can be a good thing."

"Or very bad."

"You're a pessimist."

"I'm pragmatic. You're new here. You're starting a business, and your only friends are my friends. This could get complicated."

"It's already complicated. But…"

"But…" he echoed, feeling a desire he hadn't felt in a long time.

As they stared at each other, she said, "Do you want to draw up a pro and con list or do you want to just try it and see what happens?"

He grinned. "You think you have me figured out?"

"Am I wrong?"

"The pro and con list would be the smart thing to do, but let's go with your plan." He put his hand around her neck and covered her mouth with his. She tasted as hot and sweet as he remembered, her soft lips parting under his, unleashing a wave of desire within him.

He deepened the kiss, and she went along with him, her passion matching his, as they explored each other's mouths and moved closer together. But it wasn't close enough. He pushed her onto her back, following her down, feeling her soft breasts under his hard body.

He felt more reckless than he could remember. He suddenly wanted everything. He wanted their clothes off. He wanted to touch and taste every inch of her. He wanted to take everything she would give him right here on this mountain, in this meadow, on a blanket under the stars.

And then the sound of a car penetrated his lust-filled kisses.

Headlights briefly swept over them.

He pulled back, feeling out of breath and far too close to being out of control. Sitting up, he looked toward the turnout. Another car had parked, a couple sitting inside. He sat up as Molly did the same.

"We have company," he said.

She looked at him with her beautiful eyes, her gaze sparkling with flecks of gold. "Bad timing." She gave him a searching look. "Or do you think it's good timing?"

"I think…I should take you home."

CHAPTER EIGHT

As they drove down the mountain, Molly's pulse continued to race. She was reliving every second of their passion and was torn between wishing they hadn't stopped and wishing they hadn't started. Because now she couldn't pretend that there wasn't an attraction, that she didn't want him, that he didn't want her.

It was going to get complicated. Not that she was scared of complicated. Her life had never been simple. But she suspected Adam preferred simple. He hadn't grown up like her, with no rules, no boundaries, no long-term plans. He was a man who liked to control his life, who usually planned ahead. He'd gotten caught up in the moment. But now the moment was over. Maybe she should be happy they hadn't gone further. She didn't need a distraction like Adam. She finally had a purpose in her life, something she was excited about taking ownership of, and the store needed to be her focus. She couldn't be like her mom and let a man distract her.

As she glanced sideways at Adam, she suspected the same thoughts were running through his mind. His jaw was set. His profile was hard, and he had a tight grip on the wheel. There was no trace of the impulsive, reckless man who had kissed the breath right out of her chest. He was taking back control. And she was sorry to see it.

It almost made her wonder why he needed the control. She couldn't trace the need to anything in his past. He'd had a great childhood, a loving family. He seemed to do a job that he cared about. *So why was he hanging on so tightly?*

Maybe the answer had something to do with why he'd become a cop. He'd told her that was a story for another time.

Which meant there was a story, and she was more than a little curious.

But he wouldn't tell her now. In fact, she was doubtful that he would speak again before they got to her apartment.

It was just as well. Sex and love often got tangled up for her, and she was not looking for love. Despite that thought, she felt on pins and needles all the way home, the tension increasing with the ongoing silence.

Finally, Adam turned in to the small parking area behind the store.

"Well," she said, as he came to a stop. "Thanks for the ride." At his stiff nod, she couldn't help but try to soften him up. She gave him a warm smile. "It was fun."

His stony expression cracked at her words, and the glitter in his eyes came back. "It was fun," he admitted.

"I'm sensing a but."

"It shouldn't happen again."

"Is that what you've been telling yourself all the way here?"

"Yes," he admitted.

"Me, too."

Surprise ran through his gaze. "Why?"

"I have a lot going on in my life. While I like to be spontaneous and impulsive and a live-in-the-moment kind of woman, I need to focus on my business. I have an opportunity to create something real for myself, something I can control, and I've wanted that for a long time. So, I'm going to put passion on the back burner."

"I can understand that. I like you, Molly. And I enjoyed tonight. But I'm not an impulsive, live-in-the-moment guy. Not usually, anyway. I like to plan ahead. I prefer to know what I'm getting into before I get into it."

"I guess we're on the same page then." She felt insanely disappointed, even though she'd been the first one to say they should call a halt to whatever was brewing between them. "Goodnight, Adam." She opened the door, eager to have the last word.

Thoughts of her mother always wanting the last word, especially when it came to men, rang through her head, bringing a frown to her face. She really hated to be like her mom. She shut the door and moved toward the building.

As she drew closer to the back door, she thought she saw a light inside the back room. She paused, her nerves jumping as she saw the glass on the ground from the window next to the door. Someone had smashed the glass and reached inside to open the door.

She turned toward Adam.

He opened his door. "What's wrong?"

He'd no sooner gotten the question out when the back door flew open, and a man came running right at her. He shoved her so hard she lost her balance and landed hard on her ass.

Adam swore, yelling at the man to stop, identifying himself as a police officer. He tried to give chase, but his walking boot was no match for the intruder, who disappeared around the corner before Adam got within ten feet of him.

"Dammit!" Adam pulled out his phone and reported the burglary.

As he got off the phone, he turned and hobbled in her direction. "Are you all right, Molly?"

"I'm fine," she said, getting to her feet. She rubbed the sting in her hip. "What's going on, Adam? Why does someone keep breaking in? Are they looking for something specific?"

"I don't know," he said grimly.

"I can't imagine there's anything of great value inside the store. Taken together, there's a lot of stuff that could all add up, but still not enough to keep coming back for. It doesn't make sense."

"No, it doesn't." Adam opened the door, then stepped inside, switching on the light.

She moved into the building behind him. Nothing looked overtly different than it had when she'd left. She stayed glued to Adam's back as they moved into the showroom.

"The boxes," she muttered. "Some of them were opened." At his questioning gaze, she pointed to three boxes that were by the cash register. "Those are from Caroline."

As she finished speaking, a strobe light lit up the front windows, and a police car pulled up out front. While Adam went to speak to the officer, she looked in the first box. There appeared to be a pile of tapestries. She pulled them out, one by one, laying them on the counter. They were beautiful, but probably not expensive.

She checked the next box and found books. Many of them were in different languages. They ranged in topics, from yoga poses to plants, and holistic healing.

The third box just held a couple of big throw pillows.

She turned around as Adam brought the other officer into the store. "This is Officer Kyle Drogin—Molly Trent."

Officer Drogin was a young guy, who appeared to be barely thirty, with a boy-next-door kind of smile. "Nice to meet you," he said. "Anything taken?"

"I don't know."

"Adam explained you're just moving in. I'll take a look around the neighborhood, but it's been quiet out there."

She had no hope he'd find anyone, but she would feel better knowing that someone wasn't lurking in the shadows.

As Kyle left, Adam said, "Do you have any wood?"

She blinked for a moment, surprised by the question. "Uh, I

don't know. There's a shed in the back by the garage. I haven't been in it yet."

"I want to cover the window until you can replace the glass."

"Oh, right." She led the way out to the shed and was happy to see there was some plywood stacked against the wall. "Will that work?"

"Yes, and you even have tools."

"Finally, something going right," she muttered.

"We'll figure it out," he told her.

She gave him a confused look. "You're suddenly the optimist?"

"Let's just say I'm confident."

"Why? I can't imagine what there is to be confident about."

"This isn't random, Molly. It's not about opportunity. Someone wants something. We just have to figure out what that is."

"There are literally hundreds of items in the store."

"But at least ninety percent of them are not valuable. We just have to figure out what is. But first, we're going to cover the window. Grab the toolbox."

She did as he ordered and followed him across the lot. It only took him a few minutes to cover the broken glass. Then they went back inside. The door lock still worked. But she put on the extra dead bolt before leading Adam upstairs to the apartment, since he wanted to check that out.

The apartment could be reached from a stairwell in the hall next to the back room or from a separate front door outside the building. That door was still secure. So was the door to the apartment, which she had also locked just in case.

"Anything different up here?" Adam asked as he followed her into the apartment.

She took a sweeping glance of the room. "No. It looks the same." She blew out a breath. "I need some tea. Do you want some?"

He hesitated. "I'm not a tea guy."

"I didn't know there were tea guys and non-tea guys. But suit yourself."

"I'm going to check out the bedroom."

"Okay." She walked into the small kitchen while he did that. The ritual of filling the kettle with water, turning on the stove, and selecting just the right tea helped calm her nerves. Phoebe had told her there was peace in rituals and her breathing was starting to slow down. She just wished Phoebe were here, that she could tell her what she might have that someone would want.

But she would have to figure that out herself. And she would. The store was hers now. She needed to protect Phoebe's legacy, and that included everything that belonged to her.

As the kettle sang, she turned off the heat and poured the water into a mug. On impulse, she pulled out another tea bag and a second mug and did the same.

When Adam stepped into the kitchen, she handed him the mug. "Just in case you want to see what being a tea guy is actually about. Unless you really don't want it."

"I think I can handle it," he said dryly.

She sat down at the kitchen table and sipped her tea, savoring the calming flavors.

"It's good," Adam said, a note of surprise in his voice.

"I knew you would like it," she said, as he took the seat across from her. "It's one of my favorite blends. I actually told Phoebe about it a few years ago. She became a huge fan."

"What's in it?"

"Ginseng, cardamon, chamomile, orange, lavender, and some other herbs. Maybe you'll become a tea guy," she teased.

His expression turned wry. "You're not going to let me forget that, are you?"

"Depends on how many more times I hear you say you're not a something kind of guy. Do you really want to restrict yourself from life experiences like that?"

"Fair point." He set down his mug. "I've been thinking about you staying here. In fact, I just got off the phone with Lizzie, and she has an open room at her inn that you can use for as long as you need."

"You called Lizzie?" she asked in surprise. "It's almost eleven."

He shrugged. "She's a night owl."

"You shouldn't have bothered her, Adam. I'm going to stay here."

"Why? You told me earlier that you didn't feel comfortable sleeping here, and I would bet that feeling hasn't gone away now."

"I have felt uncomfortable, because when I'm here, I feel like Phoebe should also be here. I appreciate the offer, Adam, but I need to stay. Phoebe left me her business, her life, and I should do what she would do. I don't think she'd leave her home because of what happened."

"Probably not. From what I knew of her, she was very stubborn."

"I can be stubborn, too." She infused the words with as much passion as she could, needing to convince herself as much as him. "I'll be all right. I'll lock the door, and there's no glass to break through. It will be okay, won't it? He's not going to come back tonight."

"Well, so far, he doesn't seem interested in breaking in when someone is on the premises," he said slowly.

"So, that's good."

"I can't make any guarantees. You'd be safer somewhere else. But if you're going to stay, I want you to know you can call me—day or night. If you hear something, see something, whatever, pick up the phone. You don't have to worry about waking me up."

Adam had gone into full-protector mode. She sensed it was a comfortable place for him to be. He seemed less uncertain now than he had earlier. This kind of relationship worked for him. She appreciated his concern, and it felt nice to have someone want to take care of her.

"Thanks," she said. "You should go. It's late."

He nodded and set down his tea.

She got to her feet and walked him to the door. "Do you think you'll be able to catch the guy?"

"Honestly, I doubt it. He was wearing a hoodie and gloves, so no prints to match. Neither of us got a look at his face. We already know there isn't a working camera on this building. You need to get one installed." He paused, frowning. "What about the alarm system? Why wasn't that on?"

"I guess I didn't set it," she said, feeling like a fool.

"You need to be vigilant, Molly."

"I know. I've been putting it on at night, but I was in a hurry to meet Chloe. I realize that's a poor excuse. I'll be better."

"I can help you look into security cameras as well."

"That sounds expensive."

"But probably necessary. I will check with the other merchants tomorrow to see if any of their security cameras caught your intruder."

"Maybe one did," she said hopefully.

"We'll find out." He opened the door, then paused, his gaze meeting hers.

The memory of their make-out session on the mountain came flooding back into her brain. She wanted to kiss him again. But it wouldn't stop there. And she had enough danger in her life.

"I hate to leave you here alone," he murmured.

"I'll be fine. And right now, I'm looking to calm down. If you stay, that won't happen."

A small smile played around his lips. "That's true. One for the road?"

"Goodnight, Adam." She gave him a gentle shove into the hallway and followed him back down the stairs. When he'd left the building, she locked the doors and set the alarm and then returned to the apartment. She headed straight for the kitchen. She needed more tea, so she could hopefully calm down enough to sleep. Despite her bravado with Adam, she was not looking forward to the night ahead of her.

Rituals, she reminded herself. She'd act just like she had when she was a little girl: finish her tea, brush her teeth, change into PJ's, play some calming music, and maybe leave the lights on like she'd done when her mom was out late at night, when she was alone and the shadows seemed like monsters. Unfortunately, the burglar was real and far more dangerous than an imaginary monster. She needed to figure out what he was looking for, and she needed to do that soon.

CHAPTER NINE

ADAM DIDN'T SLEEP at all Saturday night, waking up Sunday in a bad mood. He'd felt out of sync since he'd gotten injured, but it was Molly's arrival that had really thrown him off. He needed to stay away from her. She was sexy. She was beautiful. She kissed like a goddamned dream, but she was not for him. She was too impulsive, too reckless, too into woo-woo stuff that he didn't believe in.

When he'd dropped her off last night, he'd told himself to say goodbye and mean it, but then someone had crashed through her back door and made it clear that Molly had real trouble on her hands.

How could he walk away from her when she needed help?

Someone was after something, and he needed to figure out what that something was before Molly got hurt.

While the intruder had been happy to break in when no one was in the shop, the level of desperation might increase as Molly upped the level of security. There was a small window of time where the shop was still vulnerable, and that provided the best opportunity for another run at the store.

He got up, took a shower, and dressed. He wasn't in a real

rush since Drew was hiking this morning, so he didn't have to worry about getting breakfast for anyone but himself. As he was about to head down to the kitchen, his phone rang. It was Brodie. "Hey, what's up?"

"I was going to ask you that. Drew was supposed to be here at eight-thirty. It's eight-fifty. Is he coming?"

"Damn! I thought he left awhile ago. I told him to leave by eight. Hold on."

He walked down the hall and threw open the door to Drew's room. The kid was fast asleep, sprawled diagonally across his bed, his computer open beside him. Judging by the empty energy- drink cans on the floor, he'd been up half the night on his computer. There was no way Drew was going to make the hike.

He turned his attention back to the phone. "Sorry, Brodie. He's still asleep."

"No problem. We'll catch him another time."

He slid his phone into his pocket, then kicked the door shut behind him, enjoying the startled groan that Drew let out. He followed up by opening the curtains and letting the sun hit Drew right in the eyes.

"What the—" Drew put up a hand against the bright sunlight. "What are you doing?"

"It's morning, Drew. You were supposed to meet my friend Brodie for a hike, remember?"

"What time is it?"

"It's almost nine. I made an effort to get you a spot on the trip, and you bailed. That's not cool."

"I forgot to set my alarm," Drew grumbled. "It's not a big deal."

"It *is* a big deal. You agreed to go. You made a commitment."

"So, what? Are you kicking me out? Sending me home? Your duty is done?" Drew challenged, anger now burning in his sleepy eyes.

He had a feeling Drew wanted him to say yes, that he wanted to be kicked out, that he needed someone to blame. "Is that why you didn't set your alarm?" he challenged. "Because you could have just said no to the hike."

"Dude, I just forgot. Why are you being such a hard-ass?"

He blew out a breath of annoyance. He was being a hard-ass, and he was annoyed with both Drew and himself. "I'm going to make breakfast. Why don’t you take a shower and then join me?" He didn't wait for an answer.

As he headed to the kitchen, he wasn't completely sure Drew would join him for the meal, but he needed to do something productive. He also had to try to talk to Drew. They had yet to have any kind of conversation that hadn't turned antagonistic. They couldn't spend the next two months like this. Maybe he could find a way to communicate over pancakes. From what he'd seen so far, the best time to get Drew's attention was when he was stuffing his face.

An hour later, Drew entered the kitchen. He had showered, but he still had a sullen expression on his face.

Adam was sure he'd taken as long as he possibly could, but hunger had probably provided the final impetus. He pulled the food out of the oven where he'd been keeping it warm and set it on the kitchen table. He was actually starving, but he'd wanted to wait for Drew. Thankfully, he'd shown up before lunchtime.

For several minutes, they just ate. He wanted to have a conversation, but he didn't want to do it while they were both hungry. When he'd finished his pancakes, he set down his fork and said, "I want to apologize, Drew. I was disappointed that you'd missed the hike. I thought you would have enjoyed meeting people your age."

Drew shrugged. "There will be other hikes."

"You're right. You'll have plenty of opportunities to get into the mountains, but I did go out of my way to get you a spot."

"I didn't ask you to do that. It was your idea."

"True. So, let's make a deal. Aside from getting a job, which is non-negotiable, I'll offer suggestions of things you might enjoy. If you don't want to do something, just say no. If you say yes, make it happen. Can we agree to that?"

"Fine," Drew said shortly. "Are we done?"

"Not yet. What about the job? Can I help connect you with anyone?"

"I already got one."

He was surprised to hear that. "Where?"

"Some store."

"What store?"

"It's called A Better You."

His stomach clenched at that unexpected piece of news. "You're working for Molly Trent? When did this happen?"

"I started yesterday."

"You started yesterday?" he echoed. "Why didn't you tell me?"

Drew shrugged and then swigged down his glass of orange juice.

"I didn't think Molly was hiring anyone yet," he muttered, wondering why Molly hadn't told him she'd hired Drew. Maybe she didn't know Drew was connected to him. "Why would you want to work there?"

"It's good enough. You told me to get a job. I got one. End of story."

"Wait," he said as Drew pushed back his chair. "Let's talk."

"About what?"

"Whatever you want—school, your dad, friends…"

"I'm not in school. My dad sucks. And my friends are not here." Drew paused. "I only came to Whisper Lake because I didn't want to stay at my dad's house. But you can't fix me, and you can't fix your guilt. You should stop trying." With that, Drew left the table.

He let out a breath, Drew's words resonating deep within

him. There was truth in what he'd said, especially the part about getting rid of his guilt. He knew nothing could change the past, but it wasn't about his guilt; it was about helping Gina's brother, because she wasn't here to do it herself.

Gina had adored Drew. She'd been like a second mother to him. She'd skipped parties and ski weekends to watch Drew in a school play or to cheer him on when he came up to bat at a Little League game. They'd been tremendously close, and when she'd died, Drew had lost his biggest fan besides his parents. That loss had intensified when Drew's mother's illness got worse, and his father, Steven, had had to be there for his wife, leaving Drew on his own. It was a guilt that Steven carried now, a guilt he shared, even if it was in a different way.

Adam had wanted to stay close to the family, to Gina's parents, to her brother, but Steven and Teresa Kilborn had not wanted him around for a very long time. He couldn't blame them. He was the reason their daughter was dead.

He could hear Gina's voice in his head, telling him that wasn't true. But he knew it was.

Getting up from the table, he grabbed the empty plates and took them to the sink. Then he cleared the rest of the table, filled the dishwasher, and wiped down the counters.

He'd become much more of a cleaner after Gina died, needing everything in his life to be neat, to be organized, to be right.

But as he finished, Drew's words rang through his head: *he couldn't fix his guilt and he should stop trying.*

He didn't know how to stop. Having Drew around had brought everything back to the forefront of his mind. The kid was right about another thing. He had made a big mistake in inviting Drew to spend the next two months with him. He had spent years trying to put the worst night of his life behind him, and now it was back.

Molly spent Sunday morning getting the apartment organized. She wasn't sure what she could do about the persistent burglar or the hot police detective she couldn't stop thinking about, but she could get her living situation straightened out.

Putting her emotions about intruding on Phoebe's personal space aside, she made up the bed with clean sheets and a blanket. Then she stuffed Phoebe's comforter and throw pillows into a large garbage bag and put it into the back of the closet. She moved into the bathroom next, clearing out several drawers with a ruthless energy. She couldn't stop at every item and think about Phoebe's favorite lipstick or her perfume, or she'd never get through it. What was used or empty, she tossed away. Items that could be donated she put into a separate bag.

Phoebe would want her things to be recycled, to be used by those who needed them, and she wanted to honor that. Once she had made some space, she unpacked some of her things, feeling better to have accomplished that much.

After a quick lunch, she went downstairs, feeling nervous as she checked the front and back doors. Everything was still securely locked, and the board over the window was still in place. She blew out a breath and debated where to start. The boxes in the front room called to her. They had recently been sent to Phoebe and were the most likely place to find something of real value.

As she moved through the back room, her gaze caught on a bag on the table in the area where Drew had been cleaning the day before. Chelsea's name and phone number were written across the front of it. She looked inside the bag and found a blend of tea, a couple of herbal tinctures, a lotion, and a book. She smiled to herself. The book of poetry was one of Phoebe's favorites.

Pulling the book out of the bag, she opened the cover. There was an inscription on the first page.

. . .

Dearest Chelsea,

I always feel peaceful when I read these beautiful verses. There are some who say that morning sickness comes from mothers and babies seeking to find harmony together. You'll probably laugh and think I'm a crazy old fool, and you might not be wrong. But take this book and enjoy it.

With much love, Phoebe

Smiling to herself, Molly pulled her phone out of her pocket and called Chelsea. "It's Molly. I found the package that Phoebe put together for you."

"That's wonderful," Chelsea said with excitement. "Can I come and get it later?"

"Anytime. I'll be here all day. Just text me if I don't answer the door. I'm keeping things locked until it's time to reopen."

"It will probably be in an hour or so. I'm helping Lizzie with some event planning for next weekend's Harvest Festival."

"Chloe mentioned something about that last night."

"If you'd like to volunteer, no one would say no."

"I'm not sure. I have my hands full with the store, but maybe I could do something. I used to love the Harvest Festival. Chloe said it has changed a bit."

"Well, I wouldn't know how it has changed from when you were here, but it is a very fun weekend event. We can talk about it when I come by."

"See you soon." She slipped the phone back in her pocket and set the bag down. She'd leave it right where it was so she didn't lose it before Chelsea arrived. Then she headed into the front room and opened a box from Caroline.

It was filled with more books. Apparently, Caroline and Phoebe had both been big readers. But after pulling out a couple of books on holistic healing, she found a large photo album. She took it out and set it on top of the counter.

The cover was blank, but on the first page was a bright pink scrawl with the words: *This Was Us.*

Intrigued, she turned the page and looked at a black-and-white photo of two little girls with ice cream smeared across their faces. They were probably six or seven at the time of the photo.

The next few pages held similar photos. Phoebe and Caroline had clearly spent a lot of time together. As she made her way through the album, the girls slowly aged, with big life events noted: first day of high school, homecoming dance, and then a photo of Caroline and Phoebe standing by a car with a trunk filled with suitcases. Very few of the photos had been captioned, but this one said: The Last Day.

That must have been when Caroline went to Hollywood.

Caroline had a pensive expression on her face. *Was it fear of the unknown or sadness at leaving her friend and her home?*

Molly contemplated that question. Then her phone buzzed. She took it out, her heart jumping at the sight of Adam's name and number.

His text was simple but stirred her blood once more. *I'm out front. Can you let me in?*

Walking quickly to the door, she opened it. He hobbled inside, using only one crutch with his walking boot.

"I didn't hear you knock," she said.

"I didn't want to scare you in case you were up on a ladder."

His small smile sent a rush of warmth through her. Adam didn't smile a lot, but when he did, the heat ironically made her shiver.

"No ladders today. Not yet anyway."

"How are you doing?"

"I'm okay. I didn't sleep much last night. I jumped at every little sound, but it's a new day, and it's time to get answers."

"How are you planning to do that?"

"Clean until I find something of value. I didn't say it was a great plan, but it's something. So, why are you here?"

"I wanted to check in with you."

"Everything has been quiet."

"Good. The shop next door is closed until tomorrow. I'll stop by there in the morning and see if your intruder was caught on their camera."

She frowned. "I'm not sure alerting Mrs. Hunt to my intruder is a great idea. She already thinks my store will draw the wrong crowd. What about any of the other stores on the block?"

"I called my friend Jamal who runs the dry cleaners across the street, but he's out on the lake today. I probably can't get anyone at the bank around the corner until tomorrow, either, but I left a message with the manager."

"It's probably a long shot that the cameras caught anything, isn't it?" she asked with a sigh. "We saw the guy, and neither of us can identify him."

"If he got in a vehicle, that would help us ID him."

"Good point. That's why you're the detective."

"I also came by to talk to you about Drew. Did you know he's staying with me?"

"Oh, yes. He did mention that. Is there a problem? I can only hire him for two hours a day, so it's not a full-time job, but he seemed eager to help."

"Only two hours a day, huh?"

"It's all I can afford until we open. I told him there might be more hours down the road, but he didn't seem worried about it."

"He wouldn't be worried. I told him he had to get a job, and he got one. I didn't specify how many hours it needed to be. I would just rather see him working at a place where he could meet people his age."

"Is that really why you're not happy about him taking this job?" she asked, giving him a sharp look. "You think Drew working here gets me more entangled in your life, and you don't want me in your life, so that's the problem. Am I right?"

"Not completely," he said slowly.

"What's the deal, Adam? Who is Drew to you? He said something about you being a family friend. He told me you owed him and his father something."

Adam's gaze darkened. "What else did he say?"

"Nothing. I have to admit it made me curious. I had no idea Drew had any relationship to you when I hired him. I just thought he was a bored, aimless teenager who needed to make some money and have somewhere to go. I was that kid when Phoebe hired me. I thought I could return the favor."

"I don't know that he's the best worker. Drew has a huge chip on his shoulder."

"He was very helpful yesterday, and he said he could work this afternoon for a few hours."

"All right. I hope he doesn't let you down, but I have to warn you it's likely he will."

"I like to think the best of people until they force me to think otherwise. I should get back to work." She paused, glancing toward the window as someone knocked on the door. "It's your sister."

"Great," he muttered. "What is Chelsea doing here?"

"I have something for her." She opened the door. "Hi, Chelsea. Come on in."

"I really appreciate you looking for the package," Chelsea said as she entered the shop. She stopped abruptly, frowning when she saw her brother. "Adam. What are you doing here?"

"Just giving Molly a little help," he replied.

Chelsea's gaze sharpened suspiciously. "That's nice of you."

"What are you doing here?" he countered.

"I'm picking something up. Phoebe pulled some things together she thought might help my morning sickness, and Molly found the package this morning. Don't judge, Adam," she warned.

"I'm not judging, but I'm concerned. Some herbs are dangerous, and nothing is regulated."

"These are very mild," Molly interjected.

"Do you know that for sure?" he challenged. "Do you know exactly what's in the formulas that Phoebe put together? Let's not forget that she liked to push the envelope, and her ideas could be way out there."

"Adam, stop," Chelsea said. "This is between me and Molly. You're not involved."

She could see the frustration and concern in his eyes. "You don't need to worry, Adam."

"I'm not sure you can tell me that."

She wished he could trust her, but, clearly, he did not. "Why don't we go in the back room?" she suggested to Chelsea. "I'll show you what Phoebe left for you, and you can decide if anything is of interest."

Chelsea followed her into the back room, an annoyed look on her face. "I hate when Adam gets all big-brotherly. He always thinks he knows better than me."

"He's just trying to protect you."

"It's irritating."

"It's sweet. I always wanted a big brother or sister, someone to look out for me. You're lucky."

At her words, Chelsea's eyes filled with tears. "You're right. The hormones are making me bitchy."

"It's okay. I didn't mean to make you cry."

"The hormones do that, too." Chelsea sniffed and gave her a watery smile. "Just ignore me."

She handed Chelsea the bag. "This is the care package. I checked the herbal preparations. They're very mild, but please feel free to show them to your doctor."

"I'm not worried. Phoebe and I talked about my reluctance to try anything too strong. She said she'd take care of me." Chelsea looked through the bag, giving her a questioning look as she pulled out the book. "Poetry?"

"That was Phoebe. She had her own ideas about mind and body connections."

"Well, Adam and Brodie can't worry about me reading poetry," she said dryly. "I'll try anything."

"I hope you feel better soon."

"Thanks. Now, about the Harvest Festival. I know you're super busy here, so I won't pressure you to volunteer at the park, but I wanted to let you know that a lot of the local businesses are doing a sidewalk sale on Saturday. Many of the vendors on this street will be participating, so if you're up and ready to go by then, you might want to give people a chance to see what you're all about now that you've taken over."

"That would be great. That gives me five days to get my act together. It will be close, but I'll make it happen. It would be a great opportunity for me to show off the store." She just hoped she could pull everything together by then. "I better get to work."

"I won't keep you," Chelsea said.

When they returned to the showroom, she saw Adam looking through the photo album on the counter. She was a little surprised he'd stayed.

Chelsea held up the book of poetry as Adam gave her a questioning look. "Phoebe wants me to read some poems."

Adam raised a brow. "You're joking."

"It's part of the care package, along with tea, an aromatherapy candle and herbs, which I will check with my doctor," Chelsea added. "I appreciate your concern, Adam. Molly reminded me I'm lucky to have a protective big brother, so I'm sorry I snapped at you."

Adam looked surprised by Chelsea's apology. "No problem."

"I'll see you both later." Chelsea gave them a mischievous smile. "Have fun."

As the door closed behind Chelsea, Adam said, "That's the first time one of my siblings has apologized to me in I can't remember when. What did you say to her?"

"That she was lucky. But she was already feeling bad about snapping at you."

"Which she would have kept to herself if not for you."

"Maybe I'm not such a bad person to have in your life."

His gaze darkened and the electricity from the night before was suddenly back. But it abruptly ended when the door opened once more, and Drew walked in.

Drew froze, anger flashing through his gaze. "Seriously, Adam? Are you checking up on me?"

"I was checking up on Molly," Adam countered.

"You knew I was coming here to work. Did you tell her to fire me?"

"No," she interjected, drawing Drew's attention to her. "He didn't say anything like that, Drew. Last night someone broke into the store. Adam came by to make sure there weren't any more problems today."

"Someone broke in?" Drew echoed. "What did they take?"

"I'm not sure they took anything, but as you unpack, you need to look for anything of value, something worth stealing. Because this isn't the first time someone broke in since the previous owner passed away."

"That's strange," Drew muttered.

"If you want to keep going in the back room, that would be great."

"Sure." Drew didn't give Adam another look as he left the showroom.

"I'm going to go," Adam said. "Drew needs to work, and he doesn't need me looking over his shoulder."

She followed him to the door. "I don't understand what's going on between you and Drew, but if you ever feel like talking, I'm here."

"I'm not very good at talking," he muttered.

She could believe that. "Well, I'm really good at listening…"

"I'll keep that in mind."

She smiled, but once he was on the other side of the door, she let out a sigh that was a mixture of relief and disappointment.

She wanted to know more about him. She wanted to understand the shadows in his eyes. She wanted him to tell her why he owed Drew, but Adam wasn't going to talk, and she needed to accept that. She also needed to accept that he was a complication she didn't need. But every time he left, she seemed to miss him a little more.

CHAPTER TEN

"WE MISSED YOU," Sergeant Louise Hopkins told Adam as he entered the police station Monday morning.

"Not as much as I missed you." He smiled back at the middle-aged woman who basically ran the station.

"I saw on the log that you called in a robbery in progress at A Better You Saturday night."

"Yes. Unfortunately, the guy got away. This bum foot of mine prevented me from catching him."

"That's the second time in two weeks," Louise said with a frown.

"I'm aware, and I'm looking into it."

"Let me know if you need help."

As she answered the phone on her desk, he moved down the hall to his office, nodding at several patrol officers in the hallway. The Whisper Lake police force had doubled in size in the past three years with thirty-six people, ranging from admins, patrol officers, evidence technicians, detectives, and other operational support, all under the leadership of Chief Robyn Rimmer.

He was one of five detectives in the department, a promotion he'd gotten a couple of years ago. While he sometimes missed being on the front lines, he very much enjoyed seeing a case all the way through to its conclusion.

His office was small, with two desks, one of which was used by Detective Jada Burton, who was currently on maternity leave. Sitting down in a worn, creaky leather chair, he felt better than he had in ten days. This was where he belonged. Work was what he was good at. Protecting the community of Whisper Lake was a clear-cut goal, and he liked having a defined purpose in his life. He also liked taking care of his family and his friends. This town had worked its way into his heart.

He'd originally come here for a change of pace, and to keep an eye on Lizzie and Chelsea, but since then, he'd become a part of the community. He knew most of the business owners in the downtown area. He knew the troublemaking kids, who were just on the edge of making one too many mistakes. He even knew some of the outliers, the recluses in the woods, the loners looking for peace and isolation. He also knew that despite the beauty of the resort town there were elements of crime and ugliness that were on him to find and to get rid of.

Getting onto his computer, he pulled up his email, pleased to see a digital file from Rob Jonas, the manager of the bank around the corner from Molly's store. He'd left a voicemail for him yesterday and appreciated the answer to his request.

As he looked through the video, his pulse sped up as the man who had been in Molly's store came around the corner. He hopped into a silver sedan and sped off.

Adam tapped in the license plate number. The car was a rental. It had been rented at the Denver airport Friday afternoon. Picking up his phone, he called the rental car company and identified himself. After working his way through several reps, the owner of the company provided him with the name, address and phone number of the renter: Ethan Mercer, who lived in Aurora, Colorado, a few miles outside of Denver. He dug a little deeper. Ethan Mercer worked as a bouncer at a club in Denver called Bogey's.

Picking up the phone, he called Bogey's and asked to speak to the manager.

"This is Stu Tompkins," the manager said a moment later. "What can I do for you, Detective?"

"I need information on one of your employees, Ethan Mercer."

"Ethan quit two weeks ago. Said he got a better gig."

"Did he say where he was going?"

"No. He bailed last minute, so we didn't have a conversation. He hung me out to dry on a busy Friday night."

"Can you tell me anything else about him? Was he married? Girlfriend? Friends at the club who might know where he ended up?"

"Maybe Tara could tell you something. She's a waitress here. They hung out."

"Can you give me her number?"

"Sure. Hang on." He rattled off the number and then said, "Is that it?"

"For now. Thanks."

He tried Tara's number, but there was no answer, just a voicemail. He left a brief call-back message without referencing Ethan Mercer. Hopefully Tara would call him back.

As he set down the phone, he thought about the Denver connection. Caroline had been living in Beverly Hills before her return to Whisper Lake three months ago. It seemed unlikely that there was a connection between her and Mercer. But there could be a connection between someone in her family or someone who had worked for her while she was in Whisper Lake.

He didn't know for certain that the break-ins were connected to Caroline, but it seemed likely. She'd traveled the world. She'd been rich. And she'd left a lot of her things to Phoebe. Phoebe had never had any trouble at the store before Caroline died.

He needed to learn more about Caroline. He looked up as

Brodie entered the office. He was in uniform today and was just getting ready to start his shift.

"You're back," Brodie said, with a pleased smile. "How does it feel?"

"Good."

Brodie sat down in the chair across from his desk. "So, what's going on with you and Molly?"

"Is that question coming from you or Chelsea?"

Brodie laughed. "Chelsea. And since she's pregnant and not feeling good, I couldn't say no when she asked me to find out what was going on."

"Nothing is going on," he lied. "I'm concerned that there have been two break-ins at the store since Phoebe passed away, the most recent one Saturday night."

"Wait, what?" Brodie asked, losing the smile as his gaze turned serious.

"When I drove Molly home, I dropped her off at the back door to the shop. Before she could enter, a guy came busting through the back door, knocking Molly off her feet. I tried to go after him, but this damned boot on my foot made that impossible. At any rate, I have managed to ID him from the bank camera around the corner. Ethan Mercer, out of Aurora, CO. He was driving a rental car, which he picked up at the Denver airport Friday night."

"Where's he staying?"

"I haven't gotten that far."

Brodie gave him a thoughtful look. "What is this guy looking for?"

"Molly believes it might be something in the boxes Caroline Montgomery sent to Phoebe, because nothing else in the store seems to have tremendous value. I'm inclined to agree."

"I remember the boxes. Phoebe was surrounded by them when she died. I'll keep an eye on the store while I'm out today." Brodie paused. "By the way, Chelsea said she ran into you yesterday when she went to pick up some herbs. You got on her case about taking them."

"I just reminded her they aren't regulated."

"I told her the same thing, but she checked with her doctor. They're apparently fine. And she had some of the tea last night while she took a bath with an aromatherapy candle, and she slept better than she has in weeks, and that was without taking the herb tinctures, so maybe she just needed to relax."

"Molly said something about the mind-body connection," he muttered.

"Well, if Chelsea can talk herself into feeling better, I'm all for it. It's been difficult to watch her suffer, but she's tough."

"And stubborn."

"That seems to run in your family," Brodie said with a laugh. "So, are you going to answer my question now?"

"I thought I already did."

"Are you into Molly?"

"I'm concerned about her safety."

"Bullshit. You couldn't even look at her Saturday night. And I know what that means."

"I looked at her. I gave her a ride home."

"And..."

"Go to work, Brodie. Tell Chelsea to mind her own business. Then tell yourself that."

Brodie got up. "We just want to see you happy, Adam."

"I'm happy. Now get out of here."

As Brodie left, he let out a sigh. His friends had only his best interests at heart, but since everyone had coupled up, they had love on the brain, and he didn't do love. He might like Molly. He might be attracted to her. He might even have sex with her. But he was not going to fall in love. He didn't make the same mistake twice.

Molly blew out a breath of relief as Drew took the last of Caroline's boxes up to the apartment late Monday afternoon. She needed to go through them, but she also needed to get the store ready to open by Friday, so the boxes would have to be her nighttime project. It would be easier to go through them upstairs. Now she had room to breathe and she could see how she wanted to set up the store.

A sharp rap at the front door drew her attention to the window. A trio of women stood on the sidewalk. They appeared to be in their sixties or seventies and didn't look at all dangerous, so she opened the door and stepped outside.

"Hello, you must be Molly," the woman in front said. She had silver hair, bright-blue eyes, and a bright smile. "I'm Delores." She waved her hand at the other two women, one with brown hair, the other a platinum blonde. "This is Bea and Grace. We're friends of Phoebe, and we're in your Wednesday morning yoga class."

"Oh." She paused, surprised by Delores's words. "What do you mean, you're in my class?"

"You're going to keep the yoga classes going, aren't you?"

"Well, yes, at some point, but I don't have an instructor."

"Can't you teach the class? We're finally getting more limber, and we hate to lose the progress we've made. We already missed last week," Delores said.

"It's just an old lady's class," Bea put in. "I mean, Phoebe used to teach the class, so it's not like you have to do headstands or anything. She just talked us through the poses, especially the last few months when she wasn't feeling as strong."

"My husband says I'm so much nicer since I've been doing yoga, and if I keep it up, he'll take me on a cruise this Christmas," Grace said. "I really need the class and the cruise."

She looked at their pleading smiles and gave them the only answer she could. "All right. I'm a little rusty as a teacher, but I have taught yoga, so Wednesday it is. What time were you coming in?"

"At nine. Phoebe taught the class before she opened the store at ten. She was trying to get Elaine to come back and teach, but I don't know what happened with that," Delores added.

"Elaine?"

"Elaine Bascomb. She used to teach a bunch of classes here, but she had a baby a few months ago and took time off."

She made a mental note to check in with Elaine and see if she was ready to come back. "Well, until I can find another instructor, I will teach the class at nine on Wednesday. I'm not sure what equipment we have. I haven't had time to check out the studio yet."

"Oh, we all have our own mats, belts, and blocks," Delores said, dismissing her concern. "Thank you so much. I'm sure you have your hands full."

"I do. But I'm making progress."

"It was so sad about Phoebe," Delores added, her smile dimming. "She knew something bad was coming."

"What do you mean?"

"Our last yoga class was the day before she died. Phoebe was feeling down. She'd just lost her friend, Caroline, and she said that she felt like more trouble was coming." Delores paused. "She also called me that morning, around eleven. I didn't pick up the phone. I was at the market. She left me a voicemail, and she sounded shaken. She said she thought she might need some help. By the time I called her back, she was..." Delores's mouth drew into a tight line. "I'll regret that I didn't pick up that call for the rest of my days."

"There was nothing you could have done," Bea said. "Phoebe had a heart attack."

"Maybe because she was stressed about some problem," Delores said.

"But that's not on you," Grace told her friend. "Let it go."

"I'm trying," Delores replied. "But I can't get it out of my head."

And she couldn't get Delores's words out of her head. *Phoebe had known there was trouble coming? But what was the trouble?* It had to be tied to the break-ins.

"Phoebe was such a wonderful person, so kind and caring," Grace added. "She helped people improve their lives. I know she wasn't a witch, but she got the three of us to do yoga. I'm still not convinced she didn't put a spell on us." Grace paused as Jackie Hunt came out of her store and started down the sidewalk. "Uh-oh," she said under her breath. "Here comes the bad witch."

"What's going on? I heard there was another robbery," Jackie said sharply and loudly.

"A robbery?" Delores echoed, turning to Molly. "Someone broke in here?"

"Yes, but I don't think anything was taken."

"Or you just won't admit to it," Jackie said, sending her a suspicious look. "I know Phoebe was selling drugs."

"She wasn't selling drugs," Molly said firmly. "You need to stop spreading that rumor."

"Well, that's the second break-in since Phoebe died. You'd be wise to cut your losses and sell the store. I have a friend who's a developer. He'd like to talk to you," Jackie said, holding out a business card.

She reluctantly took it. "I'm not interested in selling. Phoebe wanted me to keep her business going."

"She's right, Jackie," Delores put in, then turned to her. "Phoebe would want you to keep it running, Molly."

"It meant so much to her," Bea said. "And the town needs this place."

"Don't be ridiculous," Jackie said. "No one needs this place."

"We do. We're taking yoga on Wednesday," Grace said. "You should try it, Jackie. It might calm you down."

"I am very calm," Jackie said hotly. "And I'm too smart to be taken in by Phoebe's snake-oil cures. I'm surprised the three of you don't have more sense."

With that, Jackie turned around and stormed back to her shop.

"She really should take some yoga," Delores said. "It might help get that stick out of her butt."

Molly smiled at her words.

Delores grinned back at her. "Just saying it like it is. Jackie is a well-known bitch with a nasty tongue and a dark heart."

"She's not that bad, is she?" Molly asked.

"Ever since her husband left her fifteen years ago, she's been cold and mean. Only the tourists shop at her boutique. Everyone else stays far away."

"Fifteen years is a long time. Maybe her anger is hiding grief and pain."

"Oh, you sound just like Phoebe," Bea said. "She always tried to see the good in people. In fact, she spent a lot of time trying to win Jackie over. I'm not sure she totally succeeded, but they called a truce at some point. They seemed to find some peace."

"I need to figure out a way to do that, too. I don't like to have conflict with my neighbors." She paused. "It sounds like you all knew Phoebe pretty well. Did she mention getting something valuable from Caroline, something someone might be willing to break in to get?"

"Is that what's happening?" Delores asked.

Seeing the curiosity across their faces, she was almost sorry she'd suggested it. She had a feeling these three were part of a much larger gossip network. "I don't know. There just isn't a lot of value in the store that would keep bringing someone back. I started thinking maybe Caroline left something to her."

"Maybe," Delores said. "They were very close. Caroline had a lot of money, so I wouldn't be surprised if she didn't leave Phoebe something special. Have you looked through all of it?"

"Not yet."

"Maybe the trouble Phoebe was hinting at had to do with Caroline's death," Delores said. "She said something about how people don't show up until you're dead. Perhaps there's a long-lost relative with a claim."

She thought about that. "I would think if that was true, there would be a lawyer involved, but I haven't heard from anyone."

"Not if whatever the item in question had been stolen or something like that," Bea suggested.

Delores rolled her eyes. "You have got to stop reading so many books, Bea. Why would Caroline Montgomery need to steal anything?"

"It's not such a far-fetched idea," Grace put in. "Maybe not the part about Caroline stealing something, but she could have had something in her possession from one of her husbands that wasn't purchased legitimately. Don't you think that could have happened, Molly?"

"It's possible," she murmured, pausing as a young woman, who appeared to be in her late teens, joined the group.

"Grandma, are you ready to go?" the girl asked Delores. "I have to meet my friends in a half hour."

"Oh, I'm sorry Cassie. We got to talking."

Cassie let out a sigh. "What else is new, Grandma?"

"This is the new shop owner, Molly Trent," Delores said. "My granddaughter, Cassie."

"Hello," Cassie said politely.

"It's nice to meet you, Cassie," she replied.

"You should join us for yoga," Delores said.

"I'm not very flexible," Cassie said.

"That's why you do it," Delores told her. "To get flexible."

Molly smiled as Cassie searched for an excuse. Fortunately for her, their conversation was interrupted by Drew, as he came through the door.

"Hey," he said, giving the group a confused look. "I'm going to take off, Molly..." His voice trailed away as his gaze met with Cassie's. He was clearly dazzled by the pretty blonde with the golden-brown eyes. "Hi," he said.

"Hi," Cassie echoed.

Delores cleared her throat. "Who's this handsome young man?"

Since Drew couldn't seem to take his eyes away from Cassie, she answered for him. "This is Drew Kilborn. He's helping me here in the shop."

"Drew, this is my granddaughter, Cassie," Delores said.

Drew and Cassie both said hi again.

"Drew is new in town," Molly said. "Maybe you can tell him the hot spots for people your age, Cassie."

"Well, there aren't a lot of hot spots, but there are some. Where are you from?" Cassie asked.

"Denver," he said. "But I've been going to school in Santa Barbara."

"California? Wow, that's amazing. I want to transfer to California next year, if I can. I'm at the community college right now."

"I can tell you whatever you want," he mumbled.

"I have to take my grandmother and her friends home," Cassie said. "But some of us are going to get pizza at Giovanni's around eight, if you're around, and you want to come by."

"Sounds good," Drew said. "I gotta go, too."

"Grandma?" Cassie asked as Drew headed down the sidewalk. "Are you ready?"

"Yes, we're ready. See you Wednesday, Molly."

"See you then."

She smiled to herself as she went back into the store. She'd learned a lot in the past few minutes, and Drew might have gotten himself a date. Things were looking up. She just hoped they'd stay that way.

CHAPTER ELEVEN

MOLLY OPENED the door to the yoga studio with some trepidation. It was the one room she hadn't been in yet, and she was mentally preparing herself to see another sea of boxes, but it was shockingly empty. The floor was shiny, the mirrors clean, and there was a sound system set up on the one table in the studio. Phoebe must have wanted to keep the studio in shape for her classes.

She walked over to a bulletin board on the wall. It was a class schedule for the month. But Phoebe had canceled all the classes except the Wednesday morning one that was labeled as gentle yoga. Without Elaine, she must have been too busy with Caroline and her own ailing health to keep up with the class schedule.

Elaine's phone number was on the sheet. Impulsively, she took out her phone and punched in the number.

"Hello?" a woman said, a baby crying in the background.

"Elaine?"

"Yes."

"This is Molly Trent. I'm taking over the wellness store for Phoebe."

"I heard that. I'm still so upset by Phoebe's death. It was so sudden."

There was genuine pain in Elaine's voice. "It was tragic," she agreed. "I'm trying to make sense of her business, and a couple of ladies dropped by and told me you used to teach yoga here."

"I did until three months ago when I had my baby. I needed some time to just be a mom, and Phoebe was very understanding. She was also busy with her friend moving back so she didn't have time to pay attention to her business."

"I'm beginning to realize that," she murmured. "Would you have any interest in teaching again?"

"Actually, I would. I had just told Phoebe I was ready to come back, and then she died. I didn't know if you would still need a teacher."

"I do. I probably need a week or two to pull things together."

"That would be perfect. I need to set up some babysitting with my mom, but I know she's happy to do it," Elaine said.

"That's great. Let's talk next week." She felt a sense of accomplishment as she finished the call. She'd finally gotten something done. She wanted to celebrate with a break. It was after five and the beautiful late summer weather called her name, so she locked up, and then strolled down the street.

Her block was a mix of retail and small businesses. The center of the downtown area was a few blocks away. That's where the action really began with restaurants, bars, boutiques, and other shops. The town had really grown in the years since she'd lived here. There was more of everything, including people. It was the off- season, but still the streets felt busy.

As she turned a corner, she had to quickly sidestep as she almost ran into someone. It wasn't Adam this time, but as she looked into the man's face, her heart stopped. The short crew cut, the scar over one eye, the dark hair, and the warm brown eyes all added up to Neil Loeffler, her mother's former boyfriend, the man she'd once picked to be her stepfather.

He'd aged in the last decade. He had to be in his fifties now, with silver strands of hair in his sideburns.

He stared at her with the same surprise. "Molly?"

"It's me." She felt a wave of mixed emotions. She'd been angry with Neil for letting her mom go, for letting her go without a word, not even goodbye. But she'd also cared a lot about him at one point.

It suddenly felt like way too much. She was overwhelmed. She couldn't handle everything that was literally coming at her.

"How are you, Molly?" he asked.

"I—I have to go." She broke into a run as she pushed past him. She jogged down the street, turning another corner, and once again almost running into someone. But, of course, this time it was Adam.

"Whoa," he said, grabbing her arms. "You never walk slowly, do you?"

She stared back at him in confusion, still lost in her thoughts, and in the past. "What?"

His gaze narrowed. "What's wrong, Molly?"

"Nothing. Sorry. I'll walk slower."

As she moved past him, he fell into step alongside her. "What's going on? You look like you saw a ghost."

"I did. I just ran into Neil Loeffler, my mother's ex-boyfriend, the one I thought might be my stepfather."

"How was that?"

She stopped to look at him. "Well, I ran away from him, so not good." She let out a breath. "Seeing him again brought back a lot of feelings, and I couldn't handle them all, so I bolted. He must think I'm crazy. Maybe he always knew that. That's why he let both of us go." She was rambling, and she felt even more off-kilter. "Sorry. Go do whatever you were going to do."

"I was going to get something to eat at the Red Sombrero. Do you want to join me?"

"The Red Sombrero?" she asked doubtfully. "That's quite a name."

"The food is excellent."

She hesitated. "I thought you wanted to keep your distance from me."

"Well, the universe seems to have other plans," he said dryly.

"You don't believe in the universe having plans," she pointed out.

"True. But we're both here, and the restaurant is across the street, so…what do you say?"

She hesitated. "I am hungry. But are you meeting someone?"

"No. I was hoping to have dinner with Drew, but he just texted me he's meeting up with some kids. I'm not sure that's true, but it's clear he wants to spend as little time as possible with me."

"Actually, it is true. I was with him when a girl invited him to meet up with her and her friends at Giovanni's Pizza tonight."

"Seriously?" Surprise ran through his gaze. "Where did this happen?"

"In front of the store. Cassie was with her grandmother, Delores, and two other women, Grace and Bea. Cassie is very pretty and apparently goes to the local community college. Drew was quite taken with her, and she seemed interested in him, too."

"I guess that's good," he said doubtfully.

"It is good. You want him to make some friends, right?"

"Yeah. But I don't know Cassie. And a beautiful girl could cause more problems."

"Well, she was picking up her grandmother, so she seems like a nice girl. But I can get more information on Wednesday."

"What's Wednesday?"

"My yoga class with her grandmother and a couple of other older women. They told me that Phoebe's yoga class changed their lives, and I must keep it going. One woman said yoga had literally saved her marriage, giving her a place to de-stress, so I couldn't say no. I wasn't planning to start classes for another few weeks, but they were very persuasive."

"Do you ever say no?" he asked with a wry smile.

"I can say no, but I'm trying to build a business, and I need to keep Phoebe's customers happy. I actually learned something from talking to the ladies. Delores said that the day before Phoebe died, she was feeling down and worried about something at their yoga class. The morning she passed away, Phoebe left Delores a voicemail saying she was concerned about trouble heading her way and she might need help. I think her uneasiness had to do with the break-ins that happened after she passed away."

"That's possible. Let's keep talking, but how about we do it over drinks and food?"

"I'm in." Now that the shock of seeing Neil was waning, she felt hungry again.

They crossed the street and entered the Red Sombrero, which was decorated, not surprisingly, with a multitude of red sombreros. The tables had colorful tile tops, and delicious smells wafted across the room from the open-air kitchen. They were given a seat by the French doors, which led onto a greenery-filled patio, where a large party was celebrating a birthday and mariachi music was playing.

They ordered margaritas, chips, and guacamole to start, followed by two taco platters. While they were munching on chips, Adam asked her what else Delores had had to say.

"Not much. One of the other women suggested that someone in Caroline's family might have been unhappy with Phoebe being the recipient of so many items from the estate, but she was just speculating."

"It's not a bad theory. I just need a link between Ethan Mercer and someone in Caroline's extended family."

She raised a questioning brow. "Who is Ethan Mercer?"

"The man who broke in Saturday night. The bank around the corner caught the guy getting into a car. I traced the vehicle, and it was rented to Ethan Mercer at the Denver airport Friday night."

"Where is the car now?"

"The rental agency located the vehicle in a parking lot on the north shore. It hadn't been driven in several hours. I suspect it was abandoned there."

She thought about that. "So this Ethan guy didn't go back to Denver?"

"It doesn't appear that way. I started looking into Caroline's life. She had three husbands. She married Vince Jaeger, a Hollywood actor and one of her leading men when she was twenty-seven years old. They were media darlings. Their marriage lasted ten years, no kids. Caroline then married Ron Gregory when she was forty-four. Gregory was an investment banker. He was fifteen years older than her and had a grown daughter, Patty Gregory, who apparently didn't like that her father was marrying a woman only four years older than her."

"I can see how that would be strange."

"Ron and Caroline were married for eight years before he passed away. Her third marriage was to film director Charles Weatherly, who had two adult sons, Richard and John. Caroline was sixty-two when they tied the knot, and he was sixty-four. They had worked together on several films before they married. They separated last year, shortly before she moved back to Whisper Lake. They were not officially divorced at the time of her death."

"That's interesting. Maybe there was some property in dispute."

"They did have a prenup when they married."

"You did a lot of research," she said, impressed with his progress.

"Some of that was easy to find. Caroline was a public figure, and she married men who were also well-known. I didn't have to dig that deep. I also put in a call to Caroline's attorney, Ava Washington, but she was out of the office." He sipped his margarita. "What I didn't find was any connection to Ethan Mercer. But I'm not done looking. What do you know about Caroline's family background?"

"Not much. There might be information in the photo albums she left to Phoebe, but I haven't looked through all of them."

"Phoebe never talked about Caroline when you lived here before?"

"She did." Molly paused. "I think that Caroline's parents divorced when Caroline went to Hollywood. Her mom wanted her to be a star. The dad didn't. I'm pretty sure he stayed behind. Phoebe said something about Caroline being better off without her father in her life. It was all very vague."

"I need to look into her family background next."

She was touched by his persistence. "I appreciate you doing this, Adam."

"It's what I do, Molly. I take it you didn't find anything worth stealing today?"

"No. I saw some tapestries and vases that could be valuable, but I'm not sure. I haven't lived a wealthy life. Maybe some items are worth more than I think they are. To be honest, I didn't open more than three boxes. I had Drew take them up to the apartment so I can focus on the store. With the Harvest Festival this weekend, I'm planning a soft opening on Friday followed by the sidewalk sale on Saturday. I basically have three more days to get everything up and running."

"That's fast."

"I think I can do it, thanks to Drew."

He raised a brow. "Seriously? He's being that helpful?"

"Yes. It turns out that Drew knows a lot about computers. Apparently, Phoebe had a software system installed, but she never used it, probably because it takes some manual labor to first enter all the inventory. Drew is doing that for me. He also said he can build me a website." She could see the surprise in his eyes. "You didn't know he had those skills?"

"No. From what his dad said, it sounded like he had no real skills or interest in anything academic or professional."

"Sometimes parents are the last to know."

"I have tried to talk to Drew, but I get little more than grunts, shrugs, and one-word answers."

"Sounds about right."

"But he talks to you," Adam muttered with a frown.

"I am paying him."

"I doubt that's the only reason."

"I'm not a threat to whatever image he's trying to portray. We have no emotional baggage. And, frankly, I think Drew feels a little superior when it comes to some of the business stuff. I am really good at teaching yoga and meditation, putting together herbs, and promoting wellness, but I don't have a lot of math or computer skills. I'm not great with numbers. I'm more of a guesstimate kind of person."

He smiled. "That doesn't surprise me."

"Anyway, if Drew can do everything he says he can do, I'll owe him more than minimum wage."

"I wouldn't worry about the money. Drew isn't broke. I just wanted him to work so he could find some purpose in life."

"Well, he seems to be into helping me at the moment. But now that he has set his eyes on a beautiful blonde, who knows how long that will last?"

"Women are always a distraction," he muttered.

She looked into his ruggedly attractive face and said, "Men can be, too."

The electricity sparked between them. She wanted to lean in and take a kiss. She thought he was thinking the same thing, but then the waiter appeared with their entrees, and they both sat back, forcing smiles onto their faces.

"This looks good," she said, the heady aroma of spices making her remember how hungry she was.

"This restaurant is one of my favorites," Adam said. "I come here at least once a week."

"Does that mean you don't cook?"

"I can cook. My mom made sure that all of her children could take care of themselves."

"You're the oldest, right? What was that like?"

"Mostly good. I had to do a lot of babysitting, which, when it involved my two younger brothers, was more like refereeing an MMA fight."

"They were fighters?"

"From the time they were toddlers, they were always wrestling. Grayson usually won. He was tactical and better at finding his opponent's weak spot, whereas Nathan just came in like a bull in a china shop. No strategy, just a full head of steam."

"What do they do now? Or are they making their money in a ring?"

He laughed. "No. Grayson is an orthopedic surgeon. He's into fixing people, not breaking them. Nathan is a wanderer, and he seems to do a little of everything except stay in one place."

She knew that feeling. She was more like Nathan than Adam. "How do you think your brothers would describe you?"

"Rigid, controlling, know-it-all."

"Would they be right?"

He gave her an unapologetic shrug. "I have always looked out for my siblings. I was raised to do that. I can't tell you how many times my parents told me to watch out for my brothers and sisters, to make sure that they didn't make any bad mistakes. That's what I tried to do. Sometimes, they didn't appreciate it. They thought I was judging them, but I always had their best interests at heart. I only came down on them when they were being stupid."

"I have a feeling their version of stupid differed from yours."

"Possibly. But I had the wisdom of my years." He smiled again, his features warming as he did so. "Now I sound like an old man."

"Not old, but kind of a know-it-all," she said dryly.

"Why shouldn't I try to stop someone from making a mistake when I can see they're heading down the wrong path?"

"Because your experience isn't everyone else's."

"I realize that. But if I have experience in an area, I'm going to share it." He paused. "Did Drew tell you I was a know-it-all?"

"He hasn't said anything about you."

"I'm not sure if that's a good or a bad thing," he murmured. "I really do want to help him, Molly. I know a little about what he has gone through, and I want to talk to him, but I don't know if he'll hear me."

"There's more between you than you're telling me."

"Yes." He paused as the mariachi music grew louder. "But we should eat before it gets cold."

She was disappointed to leave it there, but she'd wait for a better opportunity. For now, she was just going to enjoy a delicious meal and a little more time with Adam before he pushed her away again.

CHAPTER TWELVE

EVEN THOUGH HE ate at the Red Sombrero often, this dinner was better than any he remembered, which was, of course, because of Molly. She was one of the most interesting women he'd met. Talking to her was so easy—almost too easy. It bothered him how easily he opened up to her, but that was part of her charm.

"I'm stuffed," Molly said as they walked out of the restaurant. "But it was worth it. Best tacos I've had in years, Adam. Thanks for introducing me to this place. I will definitely be back."

"I'm glad you liked it."

She paused on the sidewalk. "I should go. There are a lot of boxes waiting for me."

Her halfhearted words echoed the feeling running through his head. They should both go to their respective homes. They should call it a night, but he didn't want to.

"Or we could take a walk, burn off some of the food," he suggested. "The lake isn't far from here."

"I haven't actually been down to the lake yet."

"Let's do it."

They walked in silence for a few minutes, but every time he thought about breaking that silence, he stopped himself. In fact, he was questioning the wisdom of even going to the lake with her. Every minute they spent together made him like her more.

Throughout dinner, he'd had to work hard not to stare at her beautiful face, at the riotous brown waves of hair that fell loosely around her shoulders. He'd also had to work hard not to kiss her in a crowded restaurant, so taking her down to the lake, which was probably deserted at this hour of the night on a Monday evening, was going to make that work even more difficult.

But he was committed now. He dug his hands into his pockets, and that's where they were going to stay.

They entered the park and then moved down a path to the beach. The moon was full and sparkling off the gently rippling water. They would have only another six weeks or so before the lake would turn wild with winter waves, the tree branches would be laden with snow, and the sand would glitter with icy crystals. But all that seemed a long way off on this warm September evening, the temperature in the low seventies, the sky filling with stars, reminding him again of what had happened between them on another star-studded night.

As they reached the beach, Molly kicked off her shoes, and carried the heels in one hand as she let the sand slip through her toes.

"You like to go barefoot, don't you?"

"As often as possible," she said with a laugh, as she kicked up some sand. "It feels great. Just as soft as I remembered." She paused and looked out at the water. "I always loved this view. I should have come here sooner. I got so caught up in the store and all the work that I forgot to take a minute and just breathe in this beautiful sight."

"You move so fast. I have a feeling you forget to take a minute quite often."

"That's why it's even more important that I force myself to do it. I can move too fast and get bogged down by all the details of life that lead to stress, unhappiness, and feeling overwhelmed."

"I thought we cured some of that stress with margaritas and guacamole."

She laughed again, sending another wave of warmth right through him.

"We did. I am still riding high on all that, but this view is a bonus." She headed to a nearby picnic table and sat down on the bench. "My sixteenth birthday party was on this beach, a little farther down from here. Chloe organized it. She got everyone at school to come. I think they probably came more for her than for me, but it was amazing. It was the first birthday party I ever had."

"Seriously? You never had a party before sixteen?"

"Not with a bunch of kids. My mom would always buy me a cupcake for my birthday. She said it was more special because it was a cake just for me, but I think it's because she didn't like to eat cake, and she didn't want me to realize that there was no one else around to eat cake but me." She sighed, then shook her head. "But it wasn't bad. I don't mean to imply that. She always got me a present and the special cupcake and sometimes a paper tiara to wear. It might have been just the two of us, but it was still fun."

"She should have let you invite your friends and had a bash, even if it was just at a park or something."

"I never had that many friends because we moved a lot. One time, she did let me invite this other girl in the apartment complex. Her name was Terri. My mom took us to the movies and out for pizza. I guess that counts as a party."

He frowned. "Only if your bar is very low."

"Well, I guess it is. And I guess you had big birthday bashes."

"Birthdays were a big deal in my family," he admitted. "My mom loved nothing more than a birthday party. In fact, I'm having a birthday party on Sunday. Lizzie and Chelsea are throwing a barbecue at the lake for me. You're welcome to come."

"That sounds like fun."

"I'm sure it will be." He stopped, seeing a shadow of pain flit through her eyes. "I'm glad Chloe made sure your sixteenth birthday was good."

"Seventeen, too. She was really great." Molly let out a sigh. "Anyway, it's a beautiful night."

"It is."

"You don't do this a lot, either, right? I know you said you never go stargazing, so I'm thinking evenings at the lake are also not high on the list."

"I live by the lake, so I do a fair amount of sitting by the water. But I should take more time to appreciate where I am. I'm generally just too busy. My work doesn't always stop when the day ends. Sometimes, that's when it's just getting started."

"Did you always want to be a police officer, Adam? Was it a childhood dream?"

"Yes, it was. But there was a time in my late teens, early twenties when I wasn't as sure. Then I was."

"How did you become sure? Did something specific happen?"

He hesitated as she closed in on a part of his life he didn't really want to talk about. "Just an aggregate assortment of things."

"That's vague." She turned sideways to look at him. "Why do you owe Drew?"

"I don't want to talk about that."

"Maybe you should talk about it. Keeping things inside is not good for your mental health."

"How would you know that?"

"Everyone knows that. You're only as healthy as your secrets."

"That sounds like something I'd read on a tag in a fortune cookie."

"You can make fun, but I'm not wrong, Adam. You bottle things up, and that's how you get ulcers." She paused, giving him a pleading look. "Just give me a little something. I'd like to understand you better. I'm working with Drew. I might be able to help you with him if I knew more about the basis of your relationship."

He let out a sigh. "I don't think you can help me."

"I could try."

She was definitely an optimist. "I don't really talk about it," he said slowly, realizing he was going to talk about it, and that shocked him. But he couldn't seem to resist the pleading smile in her eyes.

"All right," he said in surrender. "I was involved with Drew's older sister, Gina, when I was in my early twenties. We went out for about two years. Drew was eight, and Gina adored him. We spent a lot of time with him on the weekends. Drew and Gina's mother had a chronic illness, so Gina filled in for her mom when it came to Drew."

"I feel like this story has a bad outcome," she said quietly.

"It does." He drew in a breath. "I was different then. I was like everyone else—breaking rules, pretending I knew everything, that I was invincible because I was young. Gina was the same, even more so. She had a reckless, daring spirit, and she brought out a side in me I hadn't seen before. I was supposed to go into the police academy, but I kept putting it off, because I just wanted to spend time with her. One night, Gina and I went to a club in a bad part of town."

His mind drifted back to the night. They'd come out of the club to get some fresh air. They were a little drunk and out of control. They were kissing in the alleyway when the cars pulled up, when the shooting started. He drew in a shaky breath.

"What happened?" Molly pressed.

He looked out at the lake as the terrible images filled his head. "There was a drive-by shooting. One minute I was kissing Gina, and the next minute, she was sinking to the ground, and blood was coming out of her head. She stared at me in shock. She was frozen in that moment."

Molly's gasp drew his gaze to her.

"I'm so sorry," Molly whispered.

"I told Gina she was going to be okay. I'd get her to the hospital. She'd make it." He shook his head. "She didn't believe me. She told me to take care of Drew, to tell her parents she loved them. And she wanted me to know she loved me, too." He choked on the words, his lips drawing tightly together as he remembered her final moments. "And then she was gone." He got up from the bench and walked across the sand, his heart pounding against his chest with emotions he'd thought he'd put away a long time ago.

He stood there at the water's edge for several long minutes. When he finally turned around, Molly was standing right behind him.

"I shouldn't have pushed you to talk," she said.

"Well, you got it out of me. No more festering, ulcer-causing secret."

"I didn't know it was something so painful." She gave him a troubled look. "You blame yourself for what happened, don't you?"

"No one else to blame. And don't say Gina," he warned.

"If I was going to say anyone, I'd say it was the shooter. The person who pulled the trigger." She took a breath. "That's why you became a cop. You wanted to catch them. Did you?"

"No. But the shooter was killed about three years later by one of his friends, so he eventually paid a price. I just didn't make him pay it. I wish I had."

"Do you think it would have brought you peace?"

"I don't know," he said with a weary sigh. "I don't think there's ever peace. There's just living with it. Anyway, that's why I owe Drew, why I owe his father. I took Gina to that club. She'd be alive if I hadn't."

"It wasn't a dangerous activity, Adam."

"It was in a bad part of town. It wasn't a smart decision."

"Did she say no? Did she not want to go?"

"I told you not to blame her."

"I'm not blaming her; I'm not blaming you, either. You were in the wrong place at the wrong time. You know that kind of thing happens. I'm sure you've seen other people get into situations like that."

"It doesn't change it. Everything goes back to a decision that I made. And that she made," he added, seeing the fight in Molly's eyes. "I was older than her. I knew better. I should have been protecting her, even if it was just from herself. She wanted to party, to cut loose. She was scared about her mom. She just wanted to escape, and I wanted to make her happy."

"I think she was happy. She told you she loved you. She didn't die hating you, Adam."

"She didn't have time to realize…" He shook his head. "Her family blamed me, too. Her parents wouldn't talk to me for years. But last year, when Gina's mother realized she was dying, she reached out to me. She didn't want to die with this breach between us. I didn't know if Steven was on the same page, but he talked to me for a while after the funeral. Then, a few weeks ago, he asked me to help him with Drew."

"Drew thinks you offered to take him in because his dad put pressure on you."

"It wasn't exactly like that. There was no pressure, just a helpless request. Steven knew Drew was hurting, but he didn't know how to get close to him. He'd spent so much time taking care of his wife that he'd lost the connection with his son. He thought since I had straightened out my life that I could be some sort of example for Drew. But I don't think Drew sees it that way."

"Have you told him you didn't just ask him because his father made the request?"

"Not exactly."

"Not exactly? Or no?" she challenged.

"No," he admitted. "We haven't really talked. Drew is difficult to get into conversation. He came with a huge chip on his shoulder."

"And your first inclination is to knock it off."

"It's the way I dealt with my brothers."

"Drew isn't your brother. He's a kid who's hurting. He lost his sister and his mom. And he probably feels like he lost his dad, too."

"That's right. All he has left is the guy who got his sister killed," he said harshly. "Why wouldn't he hate me?"

"I don't even know if it's about that, Adam. It's probably more that he doesn't know you and he's lost in his pain. You said he got kicked out of school. What was going on there?"

"Apparently, a lot of partying and no studying."

"Did this happen after his mom died?"

"I think it started before that, but it definitely got worse after she died. I know he's lost, and he's trying to self-medicate. What I don't know is how to help him."

"You have to keep trying."

He frowned. "No pearls of wisdom beyond 'keep trying'? What happened to all your motivational quotes from a few minutes ago?"

"I can't think of any at the moment, but I know Drew isn't going to suddenly become your best friend and the greatest kid of all time. He's hurting. And he's alone. I know what that feels like. I also know what it feels like when someone keeps pushing to get to know you, to help you, to be your friend. Drew might not want to like you or your conversations, but I think he'll eventually respond if you keep at it."

"I did like him, Molly. We were friends when he was eight. I taught him how to throw a slider. I took him fishing. But that was all a long time ago. He's nineteen and I'm thirty-four. Plus, I'm a cop. I'm the picture of authority, the authority he wants to rebel against. I'm thinking I was the worst person Steven could have asked for help."

"You can reach Drew, but it won't happen overnight. People in his life disappear. And you're only set up to be his landlord for a couple of months. Why would he trust you? You have to find a way to make him realize that you really want to get to know him, to be his friend. It can't be fake. But if you don't want that, maybe you should back off now. Because the last person he needs in his life is someone he starts to like and then disappears."

At the passion in her voice, he suspected she wasn't just talking about Drew anymore. "Is that how you felt about someone?"

She started. "We aren't talking about me."

"We weren't, but maybe we are now. Why were you so rattled after running into your mother's former boyfriend?" he asked curiously.

"It just surprised me."

"That's not it. You said before that you liked him, that you thought Neil was stepfather material."

"I did, but he wasn't. My mom thought he would ask her to marry him, but he didn't. When she told him she was leaving because their relationship wasn't going anywhere, he let her go."

"And he let you go."

"Yes. I realized that our relationship had probably been fake, something he was doing just to be with my mom. It wasn't real. So, maybe I was thinking about that when I said you shouldn't lead Drew on. When you've lost people before, you don't let yourself trust too easily, and when you do, it hurts even more when it ends."

He thought about that, about her wandering life with her mom, about the lack of stability in her life. He was starting to understand why she moved so quickly, why she didn't always practice what she preached. On one hand, she probably wanted to stay in the moment, but on the other hand, she was afraid the moment wouldn't last, and she didn't want to be there when it ended. So, she moved on.

"Why are you staring at me like that?" Molly asked, a suspicious gleam in her eyes.

"Like what?"

"Like I'm a puzzle you're trying to figure out."

"Maybe I am trying to figure you out."

"Why?" she challenged. "Didn't you tell me we're not going to be anything?"

"I did say that," he admitted. "I don't have relationships anymore. I don't have it in me."

"Because of what happened to Gina? That was a long time ago, Adam."

"It's not only that," he said defensively. "I'm just better on my own. I can take care of more people if I'm single. I can give my life to the job."

"Do you really want to give your life to a job? Don't you want more than that?"

He should say no. But he couldn't quite get there. "Maybe someday I will, but not now."

"Then the real reason you don't do relationships is because you haven't met the right person. When you do, that will change."

"You sound confident."

"I can be a know-it-all, too," she said with a smug smile. "I've also seen it happen a lot. People don't want to get married and then suddenly change their mind when they fall in love. People who swear they don't want kids end up with three. People who think they'll never be able to touch their toes in yoga are suddenly putting their hands flat on the floor because they've fallen in love with how good they feel."

She might be right, but she wasn't going to be that person. He'd learned his lesson with Gina. If he was going to settle down, it would be with someone stable, someone who wasn't reckless or unpredictable or impulsive. Damn! That sounded boring as hell. *What was wrong with him?*

He knew the answer to that question. He was far too attracted to Molly. He enjoyed talking to her, even though he didn't want to believe half the things she said. But she was interesting and passionate, and she made him feel… He couldn't define how she made him feel, except that it was too good and also too risky.

"What about you?" he said, turning the conversation around. "Why aren't you in a relationship? Why were you so free and single that you could drop your entire life within a day and move to Whisper Lake and start over?"

She frowned. "I've had relationships. Just not recently. And when Phoebe passed away, I was at a crossroads in my own life. I was ready for a change."

"Aren't you always ready for a change?"

"What does that mean?"

"You said you're like your mom. You like to keep things fresh, new, different."

"I said I was afraid I was like my mom. I actually try not to be like her."

"But you do like change."

She sighed. "Sometimes I think I like it because it's my way of adapting to the change. I tell myself how great it will be so that I can do it. I can leave one life behind to start another. It has become a pattern, but I'd really like to break the pattern. I'd like to stay in one place, build a life, a circle of friends, like you've done. But I don't know if I have it in me. There are times when I think I'd like to find out."

She might want to find out, but he didn't want to take that ride with her. If he was going to get in a relationship with someone, it would be with a woman who was definitely going to stay, because this was his home now. He didn't want to live somewhere else. And he didn't want to fall for someone whose moods changed with the wind.

He frowned, feeling like he was suddenly becoming all the negative things anyone had ever said about him: too rigid, too unwilling to take risks, too predictable. If Gina had met him now, she probably wouldn't have given him a second look.

Here he was, sitting with a beautiful, sexy woman, trying to convince himself that he didn't want her, when all he really wanted to do was kiss her again.

"You know what I want to find out?" he asked.

Her eyes sparkled. "Whether it gets better every time we kiss?"

"Are you a mind reader now?" he grumbled right before he covered her mouth with his.

She tasted salty and sweet like the fruity margaritas they'd had earlier, and he felt like he could get drunk on her kiss, on her. The heat between them created a warm, cozy cocoon in the chilling evening air. One kiss led to two, then three. Each time he broke away, he went back for more. Each time he gave her a questioning look, she answered with her lips eagerly seeking his. He'd felt attraction before, but nothing so blinding, so filled with desperation and need and all the emotions he didn't want to feel.

Molly was a whirlwind. And she was knocking him over again. *How the hell was he going to keep getting up if he didn't put a stop to the madness?*

Finally, he let go of her, only realizing then how tightly he'd wrapped his arms around her.

She gave him a sweet, sexy smile, her lips full from his kisses, and he had to fight to keep away from her. He slid off the bench and forced his hands back into his pockets.

"I'll walk you home," he said.

She got up. "Well, at least we found out one thing."

"Don't tell me what it was," he warned.

"I don't have to. You already know. You might not want to want me, Adam, but you do."

"It will pass."

"Like a bad sunburn, huh?"

That wasn't the worst comparison. He'd definitely gotten too close to the sun. "I don't want to hurt you, Molly."

She gave him a thoughtful look. "I think you mostly don't want to hurt yourself, but we can play it your way. Don't worry about it, Adam. I don't have any expectations. I specialize in not expecting anything."

He wanted to tell her that wasn't the right way to live, but she was walking away, and he'd already made a mess of what he'd been trying to say, so maybe it was time to just shut up.

CHAPTER THIRTEEN

HER FEELINGS for Adam were going to pass, Molly told herself a dozen or more times between when he dropped her off Monday night to when she went downstairs to set up her yoga class on Wednesday morning. She'd hoped that more than twenty-four hours without an Adam sighting would have dimmed his image in her mind, but he was still there, and he was way too bright and vivid. She probably needed this yoga class as much as her students. She needed to forget about Adam, forget about all the things she still had to do for work, and just breathe in and out for an hour.

Her phone buzzed, and she smiled when Chloe's name flashed across the screen. "Hi, Chloe. How are you?"

"I'm good. You?"

"Better than I was. I've cleaned out most of the store. I'm now organizing the products that I want to sell, and I'm going to teach my first yoga class this morning. Phoebe's friends insisted they couldn't miss another class."

"Phoebe's friends?"

"A trio of older ladies, but they seem quite lively: Delores, Grace, and Bea."

Chloe laughed. "I know that group, and they are fun. I'm not sure I can see them doing yoga, though."

"Apparently, it keeps them sane and less bitchy toward their husbands."

"Wow. I didn't know yoga could do that."

"It can work miracles. I'm looking forward to an hour of calm before I get to work. I'm going to open the store on Friday for a soft opening and then hopefully be ready for the sidewalk sale on Saturday."

"That should be great. You'll get a lot of traffic both days."

"I hope so."

"So, you're probably too busy, but I wanted to invite you to Lizzie's inn tonight."

"Oh, what's the occasion?"

"We're having a bonanza baking session in the kitchen to prepare lots and lots of desserts to sell at the festival this weekend. We've done it for the last two years, and it's really fun. We drink wine and ice cakes while Lizzie's actual chef does most of the baking, but we're good for decorating, packaging, and chatting. We also do a little sampling."

"That sounds fun and fattening. I'm in."

"Great. We're starting at six. All the girls will be there."

A girls' night was just what she needed. "Should I bring anything?"

"A bottle of wine would be great."

"That's easy. I'll see you tonight." She ended the call and then walked out of the studio and into the shop. Drew was sitting on a stool at the counter, his gaze focused on the computer screen.

"You're in early." She'd given him a key the day before, after he'd spent hours working on the inventory and sales software that had completely baffled her.

"I've almost got this running," he said. "I just have to add the rest of the inventory today and tomorrow, and then you should be good to go by Friday."

"You're amazing, Drew, a lifesaver."

He gave an awkward shrug. "It wasn't that difficult."

"It was for me. I owe you so much more than I'm paying you. As soon as I bring in some cash, I'm giving you a bonus."

"It's fine. Don't worry about it."

"Well, I am worried about it, because you deserve to be paid for your time."

"I'm going to work on the website after I get this finished," Drew said, changing the subject. Clearly, he wasn't comfortable talking about money. "That will take longer. I can code, but I'm not great at design."

"One of my old friends does website design. I can ask her if she can help us out."

"Well, maybe you just want to have her do it then. Whatever."

Despite his careless *whatever,* she could see that Drew really wanted to build the site, and she already knew that Gianna had more business than she could handle. "She told me she was swamped, so I'll ask her about design only, or if she could give us some tips."

He shrugged, his gaze on the screen. But when the doorbell chimed, he immediately looked up, and then he stood up.

She went to open the door, welcoming in Delores, Grace, and Bea, who were followed by the beautiful Cassie.

"My granddaughter is going to join us, and her friend Jeannie, too. She should be here shortly," Delores said. "If that's all right with you, Molly?"

"Of course. The more the merrier. You can all head back to the studio."

As the older ladies moved toward the studio, Cassie lingered by the front counter. "Hi, Drew," she said.

Drew's eyes glittered as he smiled at her.

The kid actually smiled. Molly was shocked to see something other than a scowl cross his face. He had that in common with Adam.

"Hey," Drew said, as the two continued to stare at each other.

"I'm going to my friend's birthday party on Friday night," Cassie added. "Do you want to come?"

"Yeah, sure."

The front door opened, and another pretty girl walked in. "Sorry I'm late," she said.

"You're fine," Cassie told her, then looked at me. "We're not late, are we?"

"No. I'm going to go in the studio and get everyone warmed up. Just head on in when you're ready."

As she left, she heard Cassie introduce Jeannie to Drew. She smiled to herself, wondering if the real reason Drew had come in so early was to run into Cassie. Well, it was nice to see him happy and interested. After hearing about his mom and his sister, she thought he more than deserved some attention and happy times.

She walked into the studio where the ladies had their mats and blankets laid out and various pieces of apparatus, including blocks and belts. There was a good energy in the room. The women were excited to practice yoga, and so was she.

"Thank you again for doing this," Delores said. "We know you have a lot going on."

"Actually, I want to thank you for suggesting I start the class this week, because I need it, too. We're all going to de-stress together." As she moved to the table to turn on the music, Cassie and her friend Jeannie joined the group. She dimmed the lights and then moved to the front of the room. "We're going to start with some warm-up poses. Please go at your own pace. If something is uncomfortable, let me know. There is no pain in yoga. It's all about flexibility, strength, and stretching. We relax the body, and we relax the mind. That's where you find peace."

She just needed to practice what she preached, she thought, as she led them through a series of breathing exercises.

All of her problems, including the sexy detective, were on hold for the next sixty minutes.

He'd been put on hold. Adam tapped his fingers impatiently on the phone. He'd spent the past few days trying to track down Nina Williamson, the former manager of A Better You, and he thought he might be close. But now he was waiting again.

While he wasn't going to date Molly, he still wanted to help her. He'd had no luck tracking down Ethan Mercer. Nor had he found a connection yet between Mercer and anyone in the families that Caroline had married into. But he wasn't going to stop looking. There hadn't been another break-in yet, but he wasn't convinced there wouldn't be, and that worried him, especially since Molly lived just above the store.

He'd gone to Nina Williamson's apartment complex and had discovered a few things about her. One, she had not been planning to move to Florida until next year but had shocked everyone by leaving the day after Phoebe died. One neighbor had suggested that Nina might have been running from a man, someone who seemed to be arguing with her the day prior.

That fact bothered him. It could be completely unrelated, but the timing was odd. He'd managed to get a little more information out of the neighbor, which had led him to a massage spa in Miami, where Nina apparently worked as a therapist. When he'd called, he hadn't identified himself as a police officer, just said he was a client of Nina's. He was afraid she wouldn't get on the phone if she knew the police wanted to speak to her.

Finally, a voice came over the phone. "Hello, this is Nina," she said. "Who am I speaking with?"

"Detective Adam Cole." He heard her quick intake of breath.

"What can I do for you, Detective?"

"I want to talk to you about Phoebe, about the store."

"I'm working right now. I don't have time."

"It won't take long."

"I have nothing to say. It was tragic what happened to her. I still have nightmares about it, but I'm not there anymore. There's a new owner, and whatever questions you have should be directed to her."

"Why did you leave the day after Phoebe died? Your neighbors said you packed in a rush. You left your furniture behind. Why, Nina? Why did you need to get out of town so quickly?"

"I was shaken by Phoebe's sudden death. I'd been wanting to leave for a while, and it just seemed like a sign that I should go immediately."

"One of your neighbors said you had an intense conversation with a man outside the building the day before. She thought you were afraid. Who were you talking to?"

"I—I don't remember arguing with anyone."

"If you're in trouble, Nina, I can help you."

"I'm not in trouble; I'm in Miami, and I'm starting a new life. There's nothing you can help me with."

"Tell me about the day Phoebe died. Where were you?"

"I was out for lunch. When I got back, I found her. I really can't talk any longer."

"Here's the thing, Nina. I believe you know more than you're saying. Maybe you even got involved in something you shouldn't have. I'm going to find out what it is. I'm not going to stop until I do, whether you're in Miami or you're here in Whisper Lake. And I am really good at my job. You need to tell me what you know, and if I can help you, I will."

Silence followed his words. Finally, she said, "A man came to the shop the day before Phoebe died. He wanted to know where the boxes were, the ones from Caroline Montgomery. I told him they hadn't arrived yet. They were supposed to come that afternoon. He told me that there was something in the boxes that wasn't supposed to go to Phoebe, and he needed to retrieve it."

"Did he say what it was?"

"No. I told him that Phoebe would not hang onto something that wasn't meant for her, but I was pretty sure she was going to look through everything Caroline had left her before giving anything up. He said he couldn't wait that long, and he offered me a thousand dollars to let him into the shop that night. I refused. I went home, but he followed me, and he threatened me. When that didn't work, he upped the offer to two thousand dollars in cash. My husband left me last year with no money and a lot of debt. He only wanted to take something back from Caroline, so in the end, I gave him a key. I told him that if he went there at night, the alarm system would be on. Phoebe always put it on at night. If he went in the next day, Phoebe and I would be gone from noon to one for lunch."

"But Phoebe was there."

"Yes. She was supposed to meet me at a volunteer lunch, but she didn't show up. I don't know what happened with the guy. I don't know if he went in and found her dead or…"

His pulse sped up. "Or what? He killed her?"

"I don't see how. The paramedics said she had a heart attack. So, I think that was it. I don't know if she even saw him."

"How long did you stay at the lunch?"

"Until one. When I got back, I found her. I should have left the lunch the minute I realized she wasn't coming. I did call her, but she didn't pick up. I feel terrible."

He didn't much care about her guilt. "You were her friend, and you left her alone in a store that you knew someone was going to enter, someone who wanted something Phoebe had."

"I thought he'd leave when he saw her there. He didn't seem to want to run into her. He wanted to go in when no one was there. Maybe that's what he did. I heard someone broke in after she died, so maybe he saw her and left."

He could see she desperately wanted to believe that. "There was another break-in a few days ago."

"I didn't know."

"What is he searching for, Nina?"

"He didn't tell me."

"What did this guy look like?"

"He was tall, white, with brown hair and eyes, and a beard. He was probably in his forties."

"Did he have any tattoos? Did he give you a name? Was he driving a particular car?"

"I didn't see any tattoos, and he didn't tell me his name. He was driving a white SUV."

He sat up straight at that piece of information. The white SUV didn't match the vehicle Ethan had been driving Saturday night, but it was a white SUV that had almost run him and a little girl down about a block away from Phoebe's store. *Was it the same car? Were the two incidents related? Had Ethan been driving a different car that day? Had he panicked when he got into the store and found Phoebe dead on the floor? Or had they had a confrontation?*

"What's going to happen to me?" Nina asked, drawing his attention back to her. "How much trouble am I in, Detective?"

"I'm not sure yet."

"You said you'd help me if I talked to you."

"I will do what I can. I'm going to ask you one more time. Do you have any idea what the guy wanted from Caroline's possessions?"

"No. He just said it didn't belong to Phoebe. It belonged to her family, and he had to get it back."

"Her family? What family?"

"He didn't say."

"All right. Don't disappear again, Nina. It won't go well for you, and we will find you."

"I really didn't mean for anything bad to happen. It wasn't like he was robbing Phoebe; he was just taking something back. I have to go. I have a client waiting."

"I'll be in touch." As he set down the phone, he thought about what Nina had told him. She had let Ethan Mercer into the store. It had to have been him. Her description matched the photo ID he'd seen of Ethan. Ethan had been driving a sedan on Saturday night, but it had been rented. The white SUV they'd traced to an elderly man on the north shore, who hadn't realized his car had been stolen. That had to have been Ethan, too.

He drummed his fingers restlessly on the desk, his mind trying to put the puzzle pieces together, but they weren't fitting.

He'd never considered that the speeding driver had been connected to Phoebe's death. But it made sense. He just didn't know if Phoebe's heart attack had been triggered by Mercer's arrival, or if she had died before he got there. Obviously, Mercer had not gotten what he wanted that day or the next time or the time after that. But he was determined to reclaim something that belonged to the family.

Which brought him back to Caroline's three husbands and their assorted children.

Or…maybe he needed to dig into Caroline's first family, her mom and dad. He knew the mother had died, because he'd seen photos of Caroline at her mother's funeral, but he hadn't researched the father yet.

He looked up as Brodie came into his office with two coffees.

"I stopped by Java Blast," Brodie said. "Thought you might need an afternoon caffeine hit."

"Definitely." He accepted the cup with an eager hand. "Thanks."

"What are you working on?"

"It appears that two of my cases are now connected."

Brodie raised a brow. "Which ones?"

"The car that almost ran me over was driven by the same man who broke into Phoebe's store—Ethan Mercer. Mercer was probably at her store either before or after she died. It's possible he might have caused Phoebe's heart attack."

"How do you figure that?" Brodie asked in surprise.

He related what Nina had told him about the key and the payoff.

"There was no evidence of a struggle or a robbery at Phoebe's store," Brodie said. "I was the first one on the scene. There was no blood, no bruising, and the ME confirmed she died of a heart attack."

"I'm just wondering if Mercer scared Phoebe into that heart attack."

"I suppose that's possible."

"I also wonder what the hell he's looking for and how he's tied to Caroline's family. She was married three times, so I'm not even sure which husband or stepchild or whoever he's referring to."

"I'm happy to help. I need to get back out on patrol now, but why don't we get dinner after work?" Brodie suggested. "Chelsea is doing that baking thing at the inn with Lizzie, so I'm free. Let's get some food, talk about the case, and then we can hit up the inn for dessert."

"You got it." As Brodie left, Adam jumped back on the computer. He needed to find out more about Caroline's family members, starting with her father. The man had appeared to be out of her life after she went to Hollywood, and he'd be quite old now, probably in his nineties, so it was doubtful that he'd be involved, but he needed to check his name off the list.

CHAPTER FOURTEEN

"Too much icing, Lizzie," Chelsea complained.

Molly smiled, watching as Lizzie put several large dollops of whipped vanilla cream on a cupcake.

"Are you an expert on icing now?" Lizzie retorted. "If I wanted to be judged on my decorating skills, I would have asked Adam."

"He would definitely tell you less is more," Chelsea said.

Molly enjoyed the back-and-forth between the sisters, which had gotten livelier as the evening had gone on. Chelsea wasn't drinking, but Lizzie had had a couple of glasses of wine, as had Chloe, Gianna, and Hannah. She'd stopped at one, knowing she had to drive home and also work the next day.

"I disagree," Hannah interjected. "Less is never better when it comes to cupcakes or sex," she added with a mischievous smile.

Chelsea grinned. "I can't argue with that. In fact, I'll drink to it." She lifted her glass of water.

"No fair," Gianna complained. "You can't keep making toasts when you're not drinking alcohol, Chelsea. I've already had far too much wine. It's a good thing Zach is picking me up. And if anyone else needs a ride, he can take you home, too."

"Good to know," Hannah said, as she topped off her glass.

They were sitting around the vast island in the middle of the kitchen at Lizzie's inn, with dozens of baked goods in various stages of completion. Thankfully, most of them were done, since their skills were disintegrating with the amount of wine being poured.

"How's it going at the store, Molly?" Chloe asked. "Are you ready for the sidewalk sale on Saturday?"

"Not quite, but I'm getting there. I'm having a soft opening on Friday, so if anyone needs anything, feel free to stop by. You can test out my selling skills," she said.

"I'm going to need more of that tea you gave me," Chelsea said. "It has worked wonders on my nausea, along with everything else you gave me, including the book of poetry."

"You're selling poetry?" Hannah asked, a questioning gleam in her brown eyes.

"No, but Phoebe left a book for Chelsea," she replied. "Phoebe thought it would help calm her mind."

"I have to say I thought it was silly," Chelsea said. "But the poems are beautiful, and they really were calming. They also made me feel creative, and it has been awhile since I felt that way. The baby has been sucking all the creative juice right out of me. But after having my tea and reading the poetry, I started working on a new song, and I didn't feel like throwing up."

"I'm so glad." She was pleased that she'd been able to help Chelsea, which reminded her that the benefits of the store to the community could be huge. "I know you've been having a rough time."

"Worse than I thought it would be," Chelsea admitted. "But I keep telling myself it will be worth it."

"It will be worth it," Chloe put in. "As the mother in this group, I can attest to that. Leo has changed my life in so many wonderful ways. He just needs some little friends to play with, so the rest of you need to get on it."

"I'm barely married," Hannah complained.

"Well, then Gianna and Lizzie need to speed things up."

"Right now, my baby is this inn," Lizzie said. "But one day, I hope to have a couple of kids. I grew up in a big, loving family, and I want to create that with Justin. I also have to admit that Chelsea getting pregnant has made me want to speed up the timetable. I'm starting to get baby fever."

"You should speed up," Chelsea said. "It would be great to have kids close in age."

"We'll see," Lizzie said. "What about you, Gianna?"

"I'm still working on being a good stepmother to Hailey," Gianna replied. "But Zach and I have been talking about it. We both feel good about where we are right now and we would like to give Hailey a sibling, so maybe this time next year I will not be drinking the wine. But in the meantime, I have a design business to manage. I never thought working from Whisper Lake could be so lucrative. I thought I would miss out by not being in LA or in another big city, but it turns out that it doesn't matter where I am."

"Speaking of your design business," she cut in. "I have a teenager who's helping me with computer stuff, and he's come up with a template for a website, but he would love some input on design. It sounds like you don't have time, but—"

"I can make time," Gianna interrupted. "For my friends."

"I wouldn't ask you to do much, just an opinion or a few suggestions. He's good at building all the background stuff but isn't as confident about the look. I want the store to feel like it's a version of both me and Phoebe."

"That makes sense," Gianna said. "But what do you mean exactly?"

She had to think for a moment. "Phoebe was this wild, eccentric, quirky woman who was bigger than life, with her red hair and her mystical ways, and I'm not that. I believe in wellness products that create harmony between the mind and the body, but I'm certainly not a witch. I won't be reading tarot cards or tea leaves, and I definitely won't be having séances in the store like she used to do."

"The séances!" Hannah snapped her fingers. "We went to one with you, Molly."

"I didn't go," Gianna said.

"Well, I don't know where you were," Hannah continued. "But I was there with Molly."

"And me," Chloe put in. "I was a little terrified of what was going to happen."

"What did happen?" Lizzie asked with interest.

"There was a really cold breeze." Hannah's eyes lit up with the memory. "We were sitting around the table in Phoebe's back room. It was the three of us and Genevieve Robinson and her sister Julie."

The scene flashed through Molly's head. "That's right. Genevieve and Julie wanted to contact their father, who had passed away when they were children."

"What happened?" Lizzie asked. "Did the spirits speak to you?"

"There was an odd breeze," Chloe said, echoing Hannah's earlier remark. "It was weird because the windows were closed. But we all felt it. I remember shivering."

"Me, too, and I didn't even think I believed in that stuff," Hannah said.

"It was strange," Molly added. "It was cold and then it was hot. I almost wondered if Phoebe had played with the temperature controls to make it feel different. But she never got up from her chair."

"She had a faraway look in her eyes," Chloe continued. "Like she could see into another world."

"Did the other world talk back?" Chelsea asked impatiently.

Molly smiled at the rapt interest on the faces of those who had not been there. "Phoebe closed her eyes and then she opened them and looked straight at Genevieve. She said her father was there, and he was worried about his girls. He wanted them to stop hiding things from their mother."

"That's right," Chloe said. "Then Julie cried and told Genevieve they should have told Mom."

"We still didn't know what they were talking about," Hannah said.

"Genevieve looked at Phoebe in shock and wonder," Molly continued. "She asked Phoebe to tell her dad that she was sorry, that she wouldn't take the car again without asking first. Phoebe closed her eyes and mumbled a bit, and then she looked back at Genevieve and said he knows, and he loves you and your sister very much."

"Do you think Phoebe was just guessing that they'd done something like that?" Lizzie asked.

"Hard to say. But clearly they had kept a secret from their mom."

"Looking back, though," Hannah continued, "it seems like an obvious thing—that a teenager might keep something from her mom. Phoebe could have just been guessing."

"Maybe," she agreed. "But after you all left, I cleaned up our snacks, and Phoebe sat at the table for a long while. She had her eyes closed, but her lips were moving ever so slightly, like she was talking to someone. It was the strangest thing. And then she got a call on her phone. It only vibrated, but it seemed so loud. She opened her eyes and smiled. She answered the call and said, 'Caroline. I was just thinking about you.'"

"Caroline—the film star, the one who left her so much stuff?" Chelsea asked.

"Yes. I didn't hear any more, because she told me I should go home."

"I wish I had the power to make someone call me," Hannah said.

She smiled. Hannah had never realized how much power she actually had simply by the force of her personality.

"Phoebe seemed to be connected to the present and the past and the future all at the same time," Chloe interjected.

"That's true. It felt like Phoebe's mind was very fluid, like she saw more than anyone else. She often knew exactly what I was thinking. But then, I probably wasn't as complicated as I thought I was. I'm sure it wasn't that difficult to figure me out." She paused. "I miss her."

"Phoebe was something else," Hannah agreed, lifting her wine glass. "Let's drink to Phoebe."

She couldn't resist that one as she clinked glasses once more and sipped her wine.

"How's it going with your neighbor?" Chloe asked. "Jackie Hunt was in the café the other day with one of her friends, and she was on a rant about you selling drugs next door."

"I don't know why she's stuck on that when it's not true."

"She's just a bitter, angry woman," Hannah said.

"That's kind of sad," she murmured. "Maybe I need to be kinder to her, try to build a friendship. She and Phoebe were able to peacefully coexist. I need to figure out how to do that, too. In fact, I'm a little confused about why she wasn't doing all this ranting when Phoebe was alive. Or perhaps she was."

"Maybe Phoebe put a spell on her," Hannah said with a grin. "Didn't she used to have a big book on her counter that she called her bible, and we used to joke that she kept her magic spells in it?"

"Yes," she said, startled by the reminder. "I have not seen that book, not in the store anyway. It could be in her apartment. I need to find that."

"So you can cast a spell on Jackie?" Chloe asked. "That might be more effective than kindness."

"I'll try anything. Phoebe always told me a problem is the perfect opportunity to grow and be better."

"Sometimes a problem is just a problem, and sometimes it's unsolvable," Hannah said.

"Thanks for the downer," Lizzie said, rolling her eyes.

"Sorry, but I work in medicine, and not every good person survives a bad problem."

"Okay, I need a cupcake," Chelsea said.

"I'll stop," Hannah said, putting up an apologetic hand. "I didn't mean to bum anyone out. Let's talk about something else. Anyone want to complain about their man?"

"Yes," Gianna replied. "Is it really that hard to take off your shoes and socks in one place? Do the socks have to be left ten feet away from the shoes?"

As Gianna and Hannah started grumbling about small spousal irritations, Lizzie checked on the next batch of cupcakes while Chloe stepped into the other room to call her babysitter.

Chelsea turned to her with a smile. "I wish I'd gotten to know Phoebe better. She sounds fascinating."

"She was an interesting person and very nurturing. She listened to whatever I had to say without judging. Of course, she also gave me a lot of unsolicited advice. But she was generally encouraging and inspiring. She urged me to reach for the stars and to not get bogged down with my mother's life and my mother's problems. That was easier said than done, because my mom was all I had, and she always had drama in her life. Whenever the drama got too much for her, we left. She liked starting over."

"How did you handle that?"

"I learned to like starting over, too. Some moves were easier than others. I didn't always like where we'd landed, so I was okay to move on. The worst move was the one from here. I loved Whisper Lake. I loved all these girls. I felt a part of something for the first time, and I really didn't want to leave, but my mother got into a failed romantic relationship, and she insisted we go."

"You couldn't refuse?"

"No. And I wouldn't have refused even if I could," she said honestly. "Because then my mom would have been alone. I always felt like I needed to take care of her, maybe even more than she felt she needed to take care of me. We were more like sisters than mother and daughter. She was really young when she had me, so we grew up together."

"Are you still close?" Chelsea asked.

"Yes, but she moved to New York last year, so we haven't

seen each other recently. When I told her I was coming to Whisper Lake, she was not thrilled. She doesn't believe in do-overs. Once she's been somewhere, she doesn't go back."

"Well, that's her and not you."

"Sometimes I'm not sure how different we are. Part of me has always longed for roots, but then a part of me thinks that might be too boring, like maybe I'm made to wander, to always be trying something new."

"It's funny how it takes so long to really understand ourselves," Chelsea said. "I've had to do a lot of soul searching in the past five years. I made some decisions that I thought would be safer choices, but they didn't make me happy. I had to really look at myself, at who I am, what I want. Brodie was a big part of that self-discovery. I'd gotten caught up in my image, what everyone else in the public thought about me. I was trying to live up to impossible expectations. Finally, I realized it didn't matter what anyone else thought or what they wanted for me. I have to be who I am, flaws and all."

"That sounds like an interesting story."

"Someday, I'll give you all the dirty details. Or you'll probably hear them from someone else—maybe Adam," she added, giving her a speculative look. "He seems to be spending time with you."

"He's looking into the break-ins at my store."

"Is that all he's doing?"

She hesitated. "We're…friends."

A gleam entered Chelsea's eyes. "I saw the way Adam was looking at you the other night. He didn't have friendship on his mind. He was interested in you."

"Maybe reluctantly. But I'm not his type, and he has been very direct about not wanting a relationship."

"Because he's so damned stubborn," Chelsea said with annoyance. "Adam lost someone close to him a long time ago, and ever since then, he's been gun-shy."

"Maybe he never got over her."

"I don't even know if it's that. But he changed so much after Gina died. He became a different person."

"How so?" she asked curiously.

"He lost his fun side. He was always the most serious, the most determined, the most do-the-right-thing kid in the family. He took his job as a role model to heart. But he could also be funny. When we were young, Adam liked to party and tell jokes and dance. He was open to new ideas. After Gina died, he just shut down. Then he became a control freak. He would grill me and Lizzie more about our dates than our dad would. He was hard on my brothers, too. He treated us like we didn't have brains in our heads. It was coming from a place of love, but it was irritating. Sometimes, I think he became a cop just so he could make people do the right thing."

Chelsea's comments answered some of the questions she'd had about Adam. Unfortunately, her words only reinforced the idea that the fun Adam probably wasn't going to reappear. She'd seen bits and pieces of that guy, but there was always a point where he shut down, where he regained control. "What was Gina like?" she asked.

"Always smiling. She was happy, friendly, and fun-loving. She took nothing seriously. She loved going out to clubs. That's where she died. She was caught in a crossfire."

She nodded. "Adam told me."

Chelsea's brow shot up. "He told you about Gina?"

"Yes."

"Wow! He does like you. He doesn't talk about Gina to anyone."

"Don't get carried away," she warned. "I gave Drew a job. I didn't know his relationship to Adam until after he started, and then Adam told me about Gina and why he feels responsible for Drew."

"That's interesting. How is Drew working out?"

"It's going really well. He's a whiz on the computer. He set up my entire store inventory and sales system and is building a website now."

"That's great. I wonder if Adam is doing as well as Drew," Chelsea said, a concerned frown on her face. "I worry about Adam having Drew here. I feel like it's going to drag him back to the past. I don't want him to have to relive that terrible time in his life. But he thinks he owes this kid something, and when Adam sets his mind, there's no changing it."

"He does seem like a stubborn person."

"That's for sure. But he's also a really good man. He has fierce loyalty and love for his friends…for the entire community, really. Just in case you're at all interested," Chelsea added with a sly look.

She didn't really know what to say to that. Of course she was interested. She'd never been so physically and emotionally attracted to a man, but she didn't know where her life was going to go. She and Adam would probably drive each other crazy, and not always in a good way. It was better if they just kept things platonic.

Fortunately, her conversation with Chelsea was interrupted.

Unfortunately, it was interrupted by the man they'd just been talking about.

She sat up a little straighter as Brodie and Adam entered the kitchen. Just seeing Adam made a mockery of her wanting to keep things platonic. Her body was tingling all over, her heart was racing, and he'd only given her a brief smile. *How on earth was she going to stay just friends with this man?*

CHAPTER FIFTEEN

Of course, Adam had known that Molly would be at the inn. Even if Brodie hadn't told him she was going, he would have guessed that the women would have included her in their annual drunken bake-off. Not that they called it that, but in his experience, there was usually more wine than cake decorating.

But knowing she'd be there still hadn't prepared him for the instantaneous reaction he got every time he saw her laughing smile and sparkling green eyes. She was always lit up. Whatever she was doing, she did it with more than a hundred percent effort. She lived enthusiastically and in the moment. He envied that ability. He'd been like that until the moment Gina died.

Then he'd realized that thinking ahead resulted in fewer mistakes and was infinitely safer. It might be argued that he had a little less spontaneous fun these days. But he'd made that trade a long time ago, and he didn't see that changing.

But Molly was going to test that resolve. She'd literally knocked him over when they first met, and she'd been metaphorically knocking him over ever since.

Which was why he should have said no to coming to the inn with Brodie. He'd briefly considered that option, but his desire to see her had overridden his desire to play it safe. He'd rationalized his decision by telling himself he needed to fill her in on what he'd learned so far. It wasn't the real reason, but it was the one he was going with.

"So, what's good?" he asked, surveying the array of desserts that were still unwrapped.

"If you like lots of frosting, Lizzie's cupcakes are for you," Chelsea said dryly.

"Or if you want a tiny speck of icing that will barely coat your lips, go for Chelsea's," Lizzie returned.

He shook his head in bemusement. "My God, you two have been fighting over how to ice cupcakes since you were little kids."

"That's because Lizzie refuses to do it right," Chelsea said.

"I just don't do it your way," Lizzie retorted. "And they're delicious, Adam." She held one out to him.

The heavy dollop of icing was not that appealing. "I'm thinking about one of those lemon bars instead."

"Oh, well, that figures. Molly made those," Chelsea said with a laugh.

"All I did was sprinkle the powdered sugar," Molly said. "The rest was the work of Lizzie's pastry chef."

"Where is Shannon?" he asked, referring to Lizzie's pastry chef.

"She left like an hour ago," Lizzie said with a hiccup at the end of her sentence, which turned into a laugh. "She packaged most of it up before she left. We just have to do the rest." Another hiccup punctuated her sentence.

"I see the wine has been flowing."

"Would you like some?" Gianna held up the half-empty bottle. "I think there's also beer in the fridge."

"There's always beer in the fridge," Lizzie said. "Justin's drink of choice."

"Where are Justin and Zach?" he asked.

"They said they were going to walk through Justin's new offices to go over what still needs to be done, but I think they were also getting dinner somewhere," Gianna said. "They should be here soon. Zach is going to give me a ride home."

"That seems like a wise idea. I hope you all have rides home."

"I actually might need one," Hannah said. "Jake had to go down to Denver to check out some new skiing equipment, and I did drive, but then someone kept refilling my glass."

"I can give you a ride," Chloe said. "I'm sober. And if you need one, Molly, I can take you home, too."

"I'm okay. I've only had one glass."

He was surprised. He would have expected Molly to cut loose. "How did you manage that?"

"She keeps saying she has a lot of work to do," Chelsea said, answering for Molly.

"Which I do." Molly put a lemon bar on a plate and handed it to him. "Here you go. If it's great, I will take credit for it."

"Fair enough." He took a bite. As he'd expected, the lemon bar was absolutely delicious. "It's perfect."

"Well, I'm taking one of Lizzie's cupcakes," Brodie said.

"I knew you were my favorite brother-in-law," Lizzie said.

"I'm your only brother-in-law," he retorted as he took one of her cupcakes.

"But not my favorite husband," Chelsea chided. "Traitor."

Brodie gave Chelsea a kiss. "Sorry. My sweet tooth won out. But Lizzie is my favorite sister-in-law."

"Lizzie and I need some sisters-in-law," Chelsea declared. "But our three brothers seem determined to stay single." Her gaze swung to him. "You really should go first, Adam. You're the oldest."

"That doesn't matter."

"Mom says it does."

"She does not say that." As he bickered with Chelsea, he caught sight of a wistful smile on Molly's face, and it reminded him how lucky he was to have siblings. They could all be a pain in the ass, but they always had his back, no matter what. Molly hadn't had that. She hadn't had a lot of things.

But he was impressed that she hadn't let it get her down. She was a positive person. Even with all the bad in her life, she saw the good, which was the opposite of him. In fact, the longer he worked in law enforcement, the harder it became to see the positive side of life. He felt tired just thinking about it. But he was also weary of feeling tired, of being jaded. Maybe he needed to change his perspective.

"Well, I should go," Molly said, as she slipped off a stool.

He couldn't help but notice how pretty she looked in a short, colorful skirt and a sleeveless, tantalizingly sheer top that kept drawing his eyes to her full breasts. He drew in a quick breath, dragging his gaze back to her face, but her soft mouth and sparkling eyes weren't going to stop him from staring. In fact, he thought he could probably look at her for hours on end and it wouldn't be enough time.

"Thanks for coming," Lizzie told Molly, getting up to give her a hug.

"No problem."

He watched as Molly made her way through the crowd's series of hugs, noting that she seemed endearingly and awkwardly touched by the affection.

When she got to him, he didn't hug her, he just said, "I'll walk you out."

He was pretty sure he heard Chelsea mutter something under her breath, but he ignored her and everyone else. He didn't care what they thought.

He followed Molly out of the inn. As they stepped onto the porch, he shut the front door behind them.

She turned to face him. "My car is right there. You don't have to walk me anywhere." She tipped her head to the light-blue Prius that she'd apparently driven from San Francisco. "You should go back and join the party."

"I want to talk to you, Molly."

She looked at him in surprise. "Really? I thought we were trying not to talk to each other."

"This is different. This is business."

Her expression turned wary. "Business? Okay. What's going on?"

"Quite a bit, actually. I spoke to Nina, Phoebe's former manager. She was followed home from the store the night before Phoebe died. A man approached her, threatened her, and then bribed her to give him a key to the store. She told him the alarm system would be on at night, but if he went the next day during lunchtime, both she and Phoebe would be away. They never put the alarm on during the day. Phoebe had a change of heart about lunch and didn't go, which meant she was in the store when Ethan Mercer entered."

Molly stared at him in astonishment. "You're saying that he killed Phoebe?"

"I'm not saying that. I don't know if she saw him or not. But there is a scenario where her heart attack was the shock of their encounter. Or it's possible she died before he arrived."

Molly gave him a long look as she processed that information. "Nina sold the key to Mercer? How could she do that? Did she talk to him again?"

"Nina said she was desperate for money and that she never saw him again. But she was terrified that he might have done something to Phoebe or that someone would figure out what she'd done, so she ran to Florida. She said that Mercer told her he was looking for an item that should never have been sent to Phoebe, because it belonged to the family."

"Which is what?"

"She didn't ask. He didn't say."

"This is unbelievable. I just thought Phoebe's heart gave out, but maybe it was shock or fear or both."

"There's one other detail Nina gave me that doesn't affect you or Phoebe, but it affects me. The day Phoebe died was the day I was hit by that car, saving that little girl's life. It was a block away from the store. Nina described the car Ethan was driving when she saw him, and it matched the one driving away from the hit-and-run."

Surprise made her shake her head. "That's crazy. It's all tied together. But what are they looking for? And who is Ethan Mercer? Is he working alone? Is he working for someone in the family?"

"That's what I still need to figure out. I haven't been able to reach Caroline's attorney yet. I'd like to know what happened to the rest of her estate. I learned from a local Realtor that the house Caroline was living in was co-owned with Caroline's husband, Charles Weatherly. The Realtor has heard that Mr. Weatherly will probably put the house up for sale. But I don't know what happened to the rest of Caroline's estate. She had other properties: a house in Beverly Hills, a condo in Miami, and an apartment in Paris. She also had money and probably jewels and art. I'm hoping to get a list from the attorney."

"That might help us pinpoint what's missing. If it is Charles Weatherly who's behind this, it seems like he might be willing to say what he's looking for."

"I doubt he'd own up to three burglaries. And it may not be him. He's in his seventies now, and he was not divorced from Caroline, so any property in dispute will probably end up with him."

"That makes sense."

"Charles does have two adult male children in their forties. I need to figure out their story." He paused. "I also discovered something else that was interesting. Caroline's father, Elliot Peterman, died ten years ago, but he left behind two kids, a son and a daughter. They were apparently his stepchildren. His second wife, Janet Kenney, passed away twenty years ago, but the kids, adults now, Ray Kenney and Kim Collins live here in Whisper Lake. Ray is an auto mechanic on the north shore. Kim lives here in town. She works as a stylist at the Main Street Beauty Salon."

A gleam of excitement entered her eyes. "So these two people are Caroline's step-siblings."

"Yes. They were thirty years younger than her, though. Caroline's father was twenty years older than his second wife. He didn't marry her until he was in his late fifties. Ray is forty-two and Kim is thirty-eight."

"We need to talk to them. Or have you done that already?"

"I haven't. I just figured all this out a few hours ago. I'll talk to Kim tomorrow."

"Can I go with you?"

"No. This is police business."

"It's also my business."

"We need to tread carefully. We don't know who is involved. I need to see if I can find a link between Ethan Mercer and either Kim or Ray or anyone in the Weatherly family. I don't want to show my cards before I'm ready. So, let me take care of this."

"All right," she said. "It's not like I don't have a million other things to do. I put all of Caroline's boxes up in the apartment, or rather, Drew did. I haven't had time to look through them. I need to get ready to open on Friday, so it's probably going to be this weekend. But I did talk to the security company who told me you sent them over."

He shrugged. "You need to update everything."

"I don't disagree, and I appreciate your help. I should be in good shape once they put in a better system that includes cameras. They're also going to change the locks again and put some bars over the back window once it's replaced. I should be secure."

"Maybe you should stay here until that's done. I'm sure Lizzie has a room. It's the off-season."

"I don't want to impose."

"You wouldn't be. This is an inn. People stay here."

"I know, but I have to stand on my own two feet, Adam. I can't run scared."

"It's fine to be independent, but you don't know what you're up against."

"It's been a couple of days, and nothing has happened. Maybe Ethan Mercer gave up, or maybe he found what he was looking for."

His gut told him that hadn't happened, but he didn't want to scare her, even though a part of him didn't think she was scared enough. "I don't think he's given up. Don't make the mistake of getting too comfortable."

She gave him a disgruntled look. "I don't think I'm ever going to be too comfortable with you around."

"I'm not trying to make things worse."

"I know. I just can't deal with any more problems right now. I'm beginning to realize what a huge undertaking I've accepted. I don't want to blow it. Phoebe entrusted her baby to me. I can't let her down."

"I don't think you'll let her down."

"I hope not."

"I'm going to follow you home. I'll just make sure you get in safely."

"It's only eight-thirty, Adam. It's not late."

"It's dark, and these aren't ordinary circumstances."

"I'm sure you'd rather hang out here with your friends."

"I got what I came for," he said with a smile. "I was dreaming about one of Shannon's lemon bars."

"They are dream-worthy. I had one when I was sprinkling the sugar."

"You have a little sugar on your nose," he said.

She gave a self-conscious smile as she dabbed at the end of her nose. "Did I get it?"

"Yes," he said, wishing he'd been the one to kiss the sugar off. "Did you have fun tonight?"

"I did. It was so great to be with all the girls again. Lizzie and Chelsea are awesome, too. I don't know their men very well, but I've liked what I've seen so far."

"It's a good group."

"You're lucky to have so many friends."

"I am." He fell into step with her as she walked toward her car. "How is Drew doing, by the way? He seems to work far more than two hours a day, or else he's just staying away from my house."

"He's been at the store from morning until night. I owe him big time, Adam. He has put the entire software system together, all the inventory, the financials. He is amazing with numbers."

"I guess he just didn't care about his college courses."

"Well, I don't know how he does in school, but in the real-world, he's very focused and sharp. He's going to build me a website next. I don't think I could have opened the store without him."

"I had no idea he was doing so much. But then he barely grunts in my direction when I ask him a question. What about the girl? Does he talk about her?"

"No. But she took my yoga class this morning with a friend of hers, and she chatted up Drew before and after, so I think there's some interest both ways."

"I don't know if that's good or bad."

"Pick good. You want Drew to make friends and be happy, right?"

"Yeah, but a girl could complicate things."

She smiled. "You and your complications," she said, rolling her eyes. "And guys can be problematic, too. Maybe the risk has to equal the reward." She opened her car door. "You really don't have to follow me."

"It's not a problem."

He drew in a breath, fighting the urge to kiss her again. It wasn't easy, but somehow, he managed, mostly because she got in the car and shut the door.

He hurried over to his vehicle and slid behind the wheel, then followed her out of the parking lot. When they got to her shop, he parked and followed her up the stairs to her apartment, insisting on checking out her place before he left.

There was no one inside, and with the multitude of boxes in the living room, the apartment looked much more crowded than it had the last time he'd been in it. But it was also starting to feel more like Molly than Phoebe.

"Do you want something—to drink?" she asked, as they faced each other in the middle of the living room.

"I don't want a drink, but…"

"But what?" she challenged. "Do you even know what you want, Adam?"

He knew they weren't talking about drinks anymore. "I want you, Molly, but…"

"It's complicated. I'm complicated. You're complicated. It's all too big of a risk. I get it. But…"

He grabbed onto her half-finished sentence like a drowning man who had just been tossed a lifeline. "But what, Molly? Can you finish that sentence?"

"I can, but I shouldn't."

"Just say it."

"Fun. It could be fun," she said helplessly, looking into his eyes. "Not everything has to mean something, Adam. In fact, most things don't, when you come right down to it."

"I don't like your low expectations."

She looked at him in surprise. "You should love my low expectations. It lowers your risk of me wanting more from you than you want to give."

She was right. But he didn't like that she didn't want more for herself. He also didn't like that she could read him so well. It felt like she was in his head. And he didn't let anyone into his head.

Molly moved to the door and opened it. "You should go, Adam."

He walked over to her and gave her a long look. "What if I wanted to stay?"

She gave him a steady look. "When you know the answer to that question, you won't have to ask."

His lips tightened and then he stepped into the hall, knowing she was right again. He didn't like it. He didn't like anything about this. So he left, and he cursed himself all the way home.

Why hadn't he just taken what she was offering? Why couldn't he just choose fun?

For the first time in a long time, he found himself questioning his decisions, especially his decision not to spend the night with Molly. He could handle a fling. Most of the women he dated were flings. Sex was easy. Intimacy was another story.

The truth was that he wasn't afraid Molly would want more than sex from him; he was concerned that he would want more from her.

CHAPTER SIXTEEN

Molly didn't think she'd ever worked so hard in her life. Thursday had passed in one long blur of activity. Now it was Friday, and the store would open in fifteen minutes. She wasn't quite ready. There were still products that hadn't been unpacked and a few sparsely decorated shelves, but it was almost time to officially kick off her new life as shop owner, health and wellness adviser, and yoga teacher.

A knock drew her attention to the door. She could see Chloe on the sidewalk holding a platter of cookies. She opened the door. "What is all this?"

"Cookies! Happy opening day," Chloe replied. "I thought you could put them out for your customers."

"This is so sweet of you." She took the tray out of her hands. "Do you want to come in?"

"I'll come by after lunch. I need to get to the café. I just wanted to wish you luck. I know what it's like to run a business —part exciting, part terrifying."

"So true. And today, the terrifying part is taking over."

"You'll be good. All our friends are planning to stop by at some point."

"That's great. I'm a little worried that after all this work, no one will come, and I'll just be here alone."

"That won't happen. But if it does, just stand behind the counter, go on your computer and look busy. That's what I do."

"I can't believe the café is ever not busy."

"You'd be surprised. We get lulls and it always makes me nervous. But it usually passes quickly, and then I wish I'd taken advantage of the quiet time."

"I will keep that in mind." As she waved goodbye to Chloe, an older man strode down the sidewalk, his gaze on her.

She gave him a wary look. He was dressed in a gray suit, and he didn't look dangerous, but he did have an intense expression on his face.

"Miss Trent? Molly Trent?"

"Yes."

"I'm Lance Baylor."

"Should that mean something to me?"

"I'm Charles Weatherly's attorney."

She stiffened. She'd had zero time to look into Caroline's family. "What do you want?" she asked.

"Can we talk?"

She glanced at her watch. "I have a few minutes before I open." She waved him into the store and relocked the door. She set down the tray of baked goods on the counter and said, "What can I do for you?"

"It has been brought to our attention that Ms. Montgomery might have inadvertently given away something that didn't belong to her."

"You mean something that someone tried to steal three times now?"

He gave her a wary look. "I'm not aware of any theft attempts."

"Well, if you talk to the police, they can make you aware."

"All right. I will do that, but you can rest assured my office has no knowledge of any attempt to retrieve the diamond."

"The diamond?" she echoed. "There's a diamond?"

"It was a gift from Caroline to her husband, Charles, valued at three million dollars."

She gasped. "Seriously?"

"Yes, and it's missing. We think you might have it."

"I haven't seen any diamonds in the boxes that Caroline sent to Phoebe. Wouldn't she have kept something that valuable in a safety deposit box or a private safe? In fact, if it was a gift to Charles, why doesn't he have it?"

"He believed it was in a safe at the house. But upon checking the safe, it was discovered that the real diamond had been replaced with a copy."

"I don't know what to say, except that I don't have the diamond."

"Mr. Weatherly would like to send someone over to take a look through the items that Caroline sent to Ms. Haller. He can have that individual here this afternoon."

"No. I'm sorry. I'm busy today with my grand opening, and the Harvest Festival this weekend. I promise to take another look, and I will consider your request for possibly one day next week."

The lawyer didn't look happy with her response. "This is a very valuable diamond. We need to find it as soon as possible."

"Why didn't Mr. Weatherly send you last week? Was it because his thugs couldn't do the job for him?" she challenged.

"I'm offended by your implication. We don't employ thugs. We only ask for your cooperation to retrieve what rightfully belongs to Mr. Weatherly. As for the timing, we only recently discovered that the real diamond had been replaced."

"Well, I'm going to need to check with Ms. Montgomery's lawyer, and Phoebe's lawyer. And then I'll get back to you. I have no problem turning over something that wasn't meant for Phoebe, but I'm not just taking your word for it." She glanced at her watch. "And that's all the time I have." She opened the door and motioned for him to leave.

He gave her a speculative look and then handed her his business card. "Please call me as soon as possible. We'd like to get this resolved. If someone else is trying to get the diamond, time is of the essence."

She didn't say anything, just watched him walk down the street.

Was Charles Weatherly the one who had sent someone to steal the diamond? Or was that someone else?

A familiar Jeep pulled up in front of the store, and Adam got out, holding a vase of flowers. Her heart skipped a beat. He bypassed his crutch to simply hobble over to her.

"What is this?" she asked in surprise, taking the vase out of his hand.

"A little something to celebrate the big day."

She was touched by the gesture. "This is so sweet, Adam."

He shrugged uncomfortably. "It's not a big deal."

"It's a big deal to me. Thanks."

"Was that a customer you were just talking to?"

"No, it was a lawyer. Can you come in for a minute?"

"Sure." He followed her inside the store. She put the flowers next to the cookies.

"I see someone else dropped by," he said.

"Chloe. Would you like a cookie?"

"No, thanks." He looked around the store with surprise and admiration. "You have transformed this place. I barely recognize it."

"I divided the shop into sections: nutrition, sleep, mental health, physical fitness, with subcategories within each section," she said, waving her hand around the space.

"No crystals?" he teased.

She smiled. "They're in the section under mental health. Some people really do believe in them."

"I know." He turned back to her. "Tell me about the lawyer."

"Lance Baylor is his name. He's representing Charles Weatherly. Apparently, Caroline gave Charles a diamond worth three million dollars. It was supposed to be in a safe in the house, but they discovered it had been replaced by a fake. Baylor and, apparently, Mr. Weatherly believe the diamond was inadvertently given to Phoebe."

Awareness entered his gaze. "So that's what everyone is trying to steal."

"Yes. But I haven't seen a diamond. I would have noticed. It has to be huge for that amount of money?"

"I would think so. Is the diamond in a ring?"

"I didn't ask if it was set in a ring or just loose. Anyway, Mr. Baylor wants to send someone over to look through what came from Caroline. I told him it would have to wait until I had a chance to talk to Caroline's attorney. Plus, I'm swamped today and tomorrow." She paused. "At least, I hope I'll be swamped. There's not exactly a line waiting to rush through the door."

"The customers will come. I'm glad you told Baylor you need to check with Caroline's attorney."

"I don't know when I'll have the chance to do that."

"She's out of the office until today. I already have a call in to her. I'll ask her about the diamond."

"That would be great. What happened with Caroline's step-siblings?"

"I went up to the north shore yesterday and spoke to Ray Kenney. He owns an auto shop. He's married, and his wife, Erica, works in the office. They were both friendly. Ray said he only saw Caroline a few times in his life. She was rarely around and so much older than him that she didn't seem like a sister. Nor did she apparently act like one. Although, he did say that she'd left both him and his sister a significant cash inheritance, which they were excited about."

"Did he say how much?"

"No, but I'll find out when I talk to the attorney."

"Did Ray see Caroline when she moved back here? Did he meet Phoebe?"

"No to both, but he said his sister Kim had visited Caroline and knew Phoebe. I'm going to head to the salon when I leave here."

"It doesn't sound like you think Ray is involved."

"My gut says no. He was forthcoming and didn't seem like he had anything to hide. But the one piece of the puzzle that keeps Ray in the picture for me is that Ethan left his rental car on the north shore. He also stole a car earlier, not far from that same location. I'll keep digging. You just concentrate on your opening."

"You're right. I need to stay focused." She paused as Drew came through the door. "Good morning."

He gave her a nod, then threw a stony look in Adam's direction. "Are you checking up on me?"

"No," Adam replied. "Not everything is about you, Drew. I brought Molly some flowers to celebrate."

"Oh, cool." Drew turned back to her. "Sorry I'm late."

"You're fine. We're only ready to open today because of you. I really appreciate your hard work, Drew."

He flushed a little, not looking her or Adam in the eye. "Do you want me to run the register?"

"Yes. And it looks like we have our first customers," she said, seeing two women looking through the window. "I hope they come in."

"You've got this, Molly," Adam told her.

She met his gaze. "I'm more nervous than I thought. I've worked retail before. I've worked in this store before, but this feels different. I have a lot at stake. I'm not used to having anything to lose."

"I understand. But you don't have to worry. It's going to be great."

"Thanks, Adam. I know you don't even believe in the efficacy of probably half the things I'm selling—"

"I believe in you."

"You do?" she asked with surprise.

"Yes." He opened the door and smiled at the two women. "The shop is open. You should come in and check it out."

She didn't know if the women were eager to shop or if they couldn't resist the sexy smile on Adam's face. But they entered the store, and she got to work on making her first sale.

Adam drove away with a smile on his face. He'd liked being able to send Molly's first customers into her store. He'd also liked how happy she'd been when he'd given her flowers. He might not believe in some of what she was selling, but he wasn't anti-wellness, and he'd already heard from Chelsea how much the tea had helped her morning sickness. He was just naturally suspicious, and he preferred products that had gone through some sort of formal regulation.

But Molly was also selling a lot of products that weren't medicinal. He'd seen books, yoga mats, exercise balls, mental brain-teasing games. She'd really expanded the idea of health and wellness, and she was just getting started. He was more than a little impressed and even a bit surprised at how organized the shop was. Molly seemed more like a wing-it kind of girl, but the store had a structure to it, and he appreciated that. He hoped she would be successful. She was trying to build something for herself, and that was never easy.

He also liked the way she'd stood up to Charles Weatherly's attorney, but he wasn't at all happy that there might be a missing three-million-dollar diamond hidden somewhere in Phoebe's belongings. That put a target on Molly. He didn't know if Weatherly had hired someone to get the diamond before trying a more legal approach, or if there were other individuals who also knew about the very expensive gem.

A short time later, he parked and walked down the street to the hair salon. A young woman greeted him as he entered.

"I'm looking for Kim Collins," he told her.

"Do you have an appointment?"

"No. I'm Detective Cole. I just need a few minutes of her time."

"Okay. She's in the back. I'll get her."

A few minutes later, the receptionist returned with a blonde woman, who, despite the warm weather was dressed all in black. She was very thin, with a hard edge to her face.

"I'm Kim Collins," she said. "What can I do for you?"

"Can we speak somewhere private?" There were only a couple of people in the salon, but he knew how fast gossip flew around Whisper Lake.

"Will outside work?"

"Sure." He followed her out to the sidewalk.

"What's going on?" she asked.

"I understand you're related to Caroline Montgomery."

Her gaze shifted. "This is about Caroline?"

"Yes. I spoke to your brother yesterday. He mentioned that you saw Caroline more than he did."

"I saw her once after she moved back here, but I wasn't there long. She wasn't feeling well. I didn't realize at the time that she'd stopped all treatments, and she would die soon after our conversation. She didn't talk about that at all."

"What did she talk about?"

"Nothing in particular. She said she was divorcing her third husband, Charles. I had gotten a divorce last year, so we commiserated about that. We weren't close, but we were tied by her father and my stepfather."

"What was Caroline's relationship with her father?"

"She didn't like him at all. She thought he was selfish and demanding. I can't say she was wrong. He and my mother didn't have the happiest of marriages, but there were problems on both sides. Why are you asking me these questions?"

"There's a very large diamond that seems to be missing from Caroline's estate. Have you heard anything about that?"

Her eyes widened. "No. What do you mean, missing?"

"Just what I said."

"I don't know anything about a diamond. Caroline left me and my brother twenty-five thousand dollars each. It was a very generous gesture. We weren't blood relatives, and we weren't close. I was surprised she left us anything."

"That's a significant amount of money."

"It will really help me. My husband left me with a lot of debt."

Was that a motive he'd just heard?

"I knew my husband was loose with money when I married him," Kim continued. "Thankfully, with this gift from Caroline, I'll be able to finish cleaning up his debts and go forward with a fresh start."

"Is there any chance your brother might have felt that twenty-five thousand wasn't much considering how much wealth Caroline had accumulated?"

"No. He was incredibly grateful." She paused. "I heard that Caroline left a lot of her personal things to her friend, Phoebe. I know Phoebe passed away shortly after Caroline did, but maybe the diamond is in her belongings."

"That seems to be the theory, but Phoebe's heir has not found it."

"Well, I don't know what to tell you. If I had a diamond worth millions of dollars, I wouldn't be cutting hair. Is there anything else?"

"That's it for now. Thanks."

As Kim entered the salon, he wondered if she'd told him the truth. Maybe Kim and Ray were just keeping up the pretense of being working class people who were grateful for the crumbs that Caroline had left them. That cynical thought was replaced by Molly's optimistic voice in his head, suggesting they could be innocent and genuinely happy about the unexpected inheritance.

It could probably go either way. He walked back to his Jeep and then drove to the station. When he got into his office, he contacted Caroline Montgomery's attorney again. Finally, this time he was able to get through to Ava Washington, who was based in Beverly Hills.

"How can I help you, Detective?" Ava asked. "I understand you've been calling about Caroline Montgomery?"

"Yes. There's apparently a three-million-dollar diamond missing."

"I've just been made aware of that by Mr. Weatherly's attorney. The diamond was supposed to be in a safe at Caroline's house, but I understand that there was a fake in its place."

"Who was supposed to get the diamond upon her death?"

"Well, the ownership of the diamond was in dispute during the divorce. Caroline had purchased the diamond. She was going to have it made into a ring and cufflinks for Mr. Weatherly. She told him about the gift on his birthday, but then they had a falling out, and she filed for divorce. He insisted that the diamond was a gift to him, and it should be in his possession. Until the judge ruled, it was supposed to be in the safe. Now that Caroline has passed away, the diamond will probably go to Mr. Weatherly."

That information made him doubtful that Weatherly would try to steal the diamond rather than go through legal channels. "Tell me about the items that Caroline sent to Phoebe Haller. Do you have an itemized list? Do you know who packed the boxes, or who might have had access to them?"

"I don't have a list of what went to Phoebe. Caroline told me that they were all personal items. The rest of her estate was to be distributed to various parties."

"Can you give me any more details on those parties?"

"The properties that were owned by both Mr. Weatherly and Caroline, including the house in Whisper Lake, will go to Mr. Weatherly. Caroline owned two other properties that will be sold. The money received, in addition to her personal investments, will be donated to a foundation that Caroline supported. She was a world traveler, and she wanted her money to support a variety of charities dedicated to animals and the environment."

"What about her previous husbands and her stepchildren? Did they inherit anything?"

"No. Caroline wasn't close to her previous husbands or any of her stepchildren. She wasn't involved in raising any of them, and I know she didn't particularly care for Charles's two sons. She thought they were spoiled and entitled. However, she did leave some money to her step-siblings." Ava paused. "Are you suggesting that someone stole the diamond because they didn't get an inheritance?"

"It's a theory. I know Caroline was sick, so it seems doubtful she packed the boxes that were later sent to Phoebe."

"Her housekeeper, Rebecca Pierce, handled that under Caroline's supervision. She had most of the items packed before Caroline passed away."

"What can you tell me about Rebecca Pierce?"

"Rebecca worked for Caroline for over twenty years. I believe she returned to Los Angeles after Caroline passed away." Ava paused. "I have her number." She rattled off the digits. "She would certainly be able to tell you about what was in the boxes."

"Would she have had access to the safe where the diamond was supposed to be?"

"I don't know. It's possible. As I said, she was a longtime friend and employee of Caroline's. She worked for Caroline for many years and was devoted to her."

"Did Rebecca get an inheritance?"

"Yes. It wasn't huge, but it was enough that she can retire if she wants. She's in her late fifties, so I think that's probably what she'll do."

"All right. What about other employees? Do you know who else was with Caroline when she moved to Whisper Lake?"

"There were no other full-time employees. Hold on one second." She paused for a long moment, then said, "Rebecca hired a woman named Brenda Dunn to come in once a week for heavier housecleaning. She lives in Whisper Lake. She also hired a gardener, Reuben Cardoza, who handled the landscaping."

"Anyone else?"

"There were hospice workers and a nurse who went into the house. I don't have that specific information. I can have my assistant look into it. I'll also have her send you the contact information for the individuals I just mentioned."

"I'd appreciate that."

"No problem. I would like to resolve the issue of the missing diamond, so whatever I can do to help..."

"I'll let you know if I need anything else." After ending the call with Ava, he punched in Rebecca's number. It didn't connect. A feeling of unease ran down his spine. The only person who knew what was in those boxes had changed her number. That wasn't good.

Ava said Rebecca had gotten an inheritance. Maybe it wasn't enough. Maybe she'd decided to swap out the diamond and/or steal it. Rebecca was probably the person who had had the most access to Caroline and to the diamond. He needed to find her.

CHAPTER SEVENTEEN

"NOT A BAD FIRST DAY," Drew said as Molly turned the Open sign to Closed Friday evening.

"It was better than I thought," she admitted. "Thanks for all your help, Drew."

"I didn't have anything better to do."

"I saw Cassie come in this afternoon. Are you two seeing each other?"

"We're hanging out," he said carelessly. "She's cool. She plays guitar and sings."

A beautiful, guitar-playing singer. Drew was a goner. "Have you met her friends?"

"Some. We're meeting up tonight at the festival."

"That sounds fun, and you deserve it."

"Yeah, tell that to Adam," he grumbled.

"I'm sure he's just trying to watch out for you."

"I'm nineteen years old; I can take care of myself. And it's not like he did a great job looking out for my sister." Drew stopped abruptly, looking a bit shocked that he'd said the words out loud.

She frowned. "Do you blame Adam for what happened to your sister?"

"Did he tell you about it?"

"Yes."

Drew hesitated. "I don't know. I did blame him for a while, mostly because my parents did. But after I grew up, I thought about it more, and I realized that Adam didn't know what was going to happen that night. It was random."

She was relieved to hear that. "Have you ever told Adam that?"

"No. We don't talk about my sister."

"Why not? You have her in common."

"Because we don't. Nobody in my family talks about her, either."

"What was Gina like?" she asked curiously.

"Why do you want to know?"

"Because I do. If you don't mind telling me."

Drew thought for a moment. "She was pretty. She laughed a lot. She liked stupid jokes, or maybe she just laughed when I told her stupid jokes. I can't really remember. She liked baseball. She always came to my games. And she'd yell so loud from the stands. It was embarrassing, but kind of nice, too."

"That is nice. I never had anyone in the stands for anything I did."

"Why not?"

"I was raised by a single mom. She was usually working whenever I was having a game or a recital, and I didn't have any siblings."

"My mom was sick all the time. She wasn't around much. She felt bad about it. I'd go into her room and sit on the side of her bed after a game and tell her everything that happened. But it wasn't the same as her being there. Now, both she and Gina are gone."

"That sucks."

"Yeah." His lips tightened. "And my father sent me away to get my act together, even though he's sure that's not going to happen."

"Is that what you let him think?"

He gave her a sharp look. "What do you mean?"

"Adam and your dad seem to believe you're nothing but a partier, but that's not who you are. You're incredibly smart, and you're a genius with computers and math."

"I'm only a genius compared to you."

She smiled at that. "Good point. But you still have a very sharp mind, and you think ten steps ahead. I barely think about the step I'm on. If you didn't have your act together in school, then there's a reason that you haven't told anyone, because I know you can handle school."

"I just didn't see the point. Gina died before she could finish college. My mom died before I could graduate. What am I even doing at school?"

"Maybe that's why you needed a break, to find out what you really want to do. Because I know you're not going to lay around and smoke weed, drink beer all day and do nothing. You could be doing more of that here, but you're not. You're working for me."

"I told you—I had to get a job."

"I know. But I've seen how hard you work." She paused. "I was like you once, Drew. I first came to this store when I was fifteen. I was mad because my mom had moved me here from LA. I didn't want to start over again in a new high school. All the kids from Whisper Lake would have known each other forever. I wasn't going to fit in. And my mom was busy with the job she'd gotten, so she wasn't even around to complain to. That's when I saw the sign in this window and asked Phoebe if she could give me a job. She gave me a lot more than that. She made me feel like I had someone in my corner. She was kind of crazy, and some people thought she was a witch, but I saw a woman who was kind and very caring. Anyway, if you need someone in your corner, I'm available."

"Do you tell Adam what I tell you?" Drew asked, his sharp gaze raking her face.

"You haven't told me much, so, no."

"Are you dating Adam?"

"Why would you ask that?"

"Because he keeps coming around, and the way he looks at you."

She cleared her throat. "We're friends. We know a lot of the same people."

"But you like each other."

"Maybe, but we're not going to do anything about it."

"Why not?"

She had to think hard to come up with a reason, because she really thought they should do something about it. But there was one reason staring her in the face. "I don't know that Adam has ever gotten over losing your sister."

"That was a long time ago."

"I don't think time changes love. But there are other reasons, too. Anyway, you and I can have a friendship that doesn't include Adam. But I will say this. I know he's kind of gruff and serious, but I think he really cares about you."

"He took me in out of duty to my father."

"He did it for you, Drew. He wants to help you. Maybe you should try to talk to him. Open up a little. He might do the same. You're going to be here for a couple of months. Wouldn't it be more comfortable and fun if you got along better?"

"Adam doesn't trust me."

"Show him that he can."

"We'll see." He stood up. "I gotta go."

"Okay. Are you still on for tomorrow?"

"I'll be here all day."

"Great. Have fun with your friends."

After Drew left, she turned out the lights in the store and went up to her apartment. Kicking off her shoes, she flopped down on the couch and put her feet up on the coffee table. As she took her first big breath of the day, she heard the faint sound of music.

Getting back up, she walked over to the window to see the

lights from the Ferris wheel that had been set up in the middle of Lakeside Park. She'd planned to go to the festival tomorrow night, after her sidewalk sale, but as she compared her quiet apartment to the dazzling lights just a few miles away, she changed her mind. She could use a little fun, too.

Molly changed into comfortable jeans, flats, and a lightweight sweater and then headed down to the festival. It seemed like half the town had the same idea, and she was carried along by a lively crowd of tourists and locals all headed in the same direction.

When she reached the park, she hit up the food booths first. It was after seven, and she hadn't had anything to eat since she'd snuck one of Chloe's cookies around lunchtime. She knew some of her friends were working at the bakery booth and the cakewalk, but she needed some real food.

As she checked out her options, she felt a part of the excitement but also a little isolated. She tried to shake off the feeling. She was used to being a loner in the middle of a crowd, but she was tired of being that person. If she stayed in Whisper Lake for a long time, she would become part of the fabric of the town. She'd have a crew of friends. She'd have her own business. It was everything she wanted. *Wasn't it?*

Her mother's words rang through her head. "Change is exciting, Molly. If you're not changing, you're not living."

Her mother had certainly lived by that philosophy. *Did she want to do the same?*

She pushed the question out of her head. She didn't have to decide anything now. And she wasn't good at planning for the future. She was better at living in the moment. At this moment all she really needed was food. Her gaze lit on a stand selling hot dogs on a stick which reminded her of her first time at the festival as a teenager. She smiled. *Why not?* She was starving.

She moved toward the stand, but as she got caught up between a family with two strollers and a dog, she made a quick move to the left, only to collide with a man coming in the other direction. Of course, it was Adam.

He laughed as he steadied her. "We have to stop meeting like this."

"I don't think we can. I was trying to make a quick pass," she added, as the group in question moved past them.

"Why are you in a hurry?"

"I'm hungry, and that giant hot dog is calling my name."

He looked at the sign and then back at her, shaking his head. "You can do better than a hot dog on a stick."

"Dipped in mustard? I don't think so. I remember them as being yummy."

"How old were you then?"

"Sixteen."

"That explains why you liked the hot dog. You should check out the Falafel Hut. It's great."

"Is that what you're getting?"

"I was thinking about it."

"Well, how about I get two hot dogs, you get two falafel wraps, and we grab one of those picnic tables and see who made the better choice? Unless you're afraid of a hot dog?"

"I think I can handle it."

They split up by the two booths. She was happy to see no line at her booth and put in her order with the long-haired guy at the window. As she waited for her hot dogs, she couldn't help sneaking another look at Adam.

He wore jeans and a short-sleeve navy-blue polo shirt that showed off his broad chest and long legs. Even with the ever-present boot on his foot, he looked fit and athletic. As the cashier set down her hot dogs, she dragged her gaze away from Adam and reminded herself once more that she really needed to get over her attraction to the man. But that didn't seem like it would happen any time soon.

After getting small plastic containers of spicy mustard, she made her way to a table. Adam joined her a couple minutes later.

"What should we eat first?" he asked as he sat down across from her.

"I think we should start with the hot dogs. They should be eaten hot." She handed him a hot dog on a stick. As he took it, she added, "You need to dip it in the spicy mustard. That's the best part."

"Got it, but you go first."

She swirled her hot dog around in the mustard and took a big bite. At first, she thought it was pretty good, but as she chewed, there was an odd aftertaste, and she had to force herself not to show the distaste on her face.

Adam started laughing before she'd even swallowed. "You can spit it out."

She grimaced as she swallowed, the pepper in the sauce making her eyes water. "Oh, my God, that is literally the worst thing I've ever put in my mouth." She grabbed the soda she'd also purchased and took a long swig.

"Told you," Adam said with a smug gleam in his eyes.

Her gaze narrowed. "What did you know that I didn't?"

"Well…the hot dogs used to be made by Benjamin Halter, but he turned it over to his son Ricky last year, and let's just say that Ricky doesn't make the same mustard sauce."

"That's why there was no line."

"Everyone learned their lesson last year."

"How does the town let him sell something so disgusting?"

"It's the sauce, not the hot dog."

"You're right. It's the mustard sauce. What's in it besides pepper?"

"I think that's the main ingredient. But some people still seem to like it."

As she saw a group of teenage boys at the booth, she had a feeling she knew who those people were.

"So, falafel time?" he asked, handing her a falafel wrap. "I think this is going to be the easiest bet I ever won."

"Too bad there weren't any stakes." She bit into the falafel and immediately the delicious taste replaced the peppery mustard sauce. "You made a huge mistake, Adam."

"You don't like it?" he asked in surprise.

"Are you kidding? It's fantastic. You should have bet me something. You would have won easily."

"I couldn't do that in good conscience. I had insider information."

She took another bite and smiled. "You're very ethical, aren't you?"

"I try to be."

"Even when it comes to a silly bet?"

He shrugged. "It's just who I am."

"I really wish the hot dog had been as good as I remembered. But I guess nothing is ever like that. Our memories are better than reality."

He gave her a thoughtful glance. "Is that what you think?"

"I don't know. I just thought of it," she said with a laugh. "In case you haven't noticed, I don't always think before I speak. But upon reflection, that is what I believe…that our memories make things better than they were."

He nodded, his gaze suddenly far away. She realized she'd just sent him back into his own past—his tragic love story.

"I could be wrong," she said hastily. "I am often wrong."

"I don't know that you're wrong," he said slowly. "In fact, you might be right. When people say time heals all wounds, I wonder if they don't just mean time dims the memories of those wounds."

"You don't think healing is possible?"

He sighed. "I don't know. Let's get back to talking about hot dogs."

"We've already covered that subject."

"Then tell me how opening day went."

"Amazingly well. Thank you again for the flowers, for the encouragement. It was unexpected, and I was really touched that you thought of me."

"I want you to be successful, Molly."

"Why? Why do you care? You don't even like what I sell."

"I care because it matters to you."

She wanted him to say that *she* mattered to him, but he left it at that.

As if sensing things were getting too personal, Adam cleared his throat, and said, "I'm glad I ran into you, because I need to fill you in on what I learned today. I spoke to Kim Collins, Caroline's stepsister. Caroline left her and her brother twenty-five thousand dollars each."

"That's a nice chunk of money."

"Kim also had a conversation with Caroline shortly before she died. So, she was in Caroline's house."

"Are you implying that she had access to the diamond?"

"Just relating what I know. I also spoke to Caroline's attorney. Caroline was going to give Charles the diamond and had told him about the gift, but then they had a fight and split up and she wanted to keep it. The ownership of the diamond was in dispute at the time of her death."

"What happens now—if we find the diamond? Who gets it?"

"Charles. Which doesn't give him a lot of motive to try to steal it back from Phoebe. He has the law on his side, which is why he sent his lawyer to your door."

"That sounds logical. The person who hired Mercer, and I'm assuming we think he was hired, can't have any right to the diamond. But remember what Mercer told Nina—that he wanted to get something back for the family. Which brings us back to the family."

"Yes. Caroline's step-siblings, Weatherly's two sons, her former husbands and their children."

"Can we narrow it down?"

"That's the next step. There is one other suspect—Rebecca Pierce."

"Who's that?"

"Caroline's housekeeper who worked for her for twenty years and packed the boxes that were going to Phoebe. She also received a cash inheritance from Caroline. I don't know the amount, but I suspect it was similar to what Ray and Kim got. But here's the thing—her phone number doesn't work anymore. And I can't find her. I know she got on a plane to LA a few days after Caroline died, but after that, the trail ends. She lived with Caroline, so she had no other residence, but she hasn't shown up at any of Caroline's properties."

"What about the money? Can't you track her through her bank?"

"I haven't gotten that far yet. I'm also looking into some locals who worked at Caroline's house part-time. The attorney sent over contact information for a cleaner and a gardener. I left messages for both of them to call me back."

"You were busy today, Adam. You're really getting into this."

"It's a puzzle that needs to be solved."

"Maybe it doesn't. Maybe this is all over. Nothing has happened in the last six days. Whoever hired Mercer might have given up."

"That's an optimistic point of view," he said with a small smile.

"I'd rather be thinking of the glass half full than half empty. It makes life better."

"You can stay positive, but you also need to stay alert."

"I will."

"How did Drew do today?"

"He was amazing. He worked nonstop for eight hours. He barely took time for lunch. He's really a good kid, Adam. We talked a little after we closed. He said he was going to be at the festival tonight with Cassie, meeting some of her friends."

"I saw him before I came over here. He managed to get a couple of sentences out when I tried to talk to him."

"What did he say?" she asked curiously.

"Not much. But he did mention that he liked working for you and that he was coming to the festival."

"It's a start." She paused. "So, dessert?"

"Why don't we take a ride first?"

She looked at him in surprise. "You want to go on one of the rides? Really?"

"Yes."

"Like a pirate ship that goes almost upside down?" A grimace crossed his face, and she laughed. "No? But there's nothing better than turning your world upside down. It gives you a different perspective."

"Nothing better, huh? How about the Ferris wheel?"

"It's kind of slow, but I can live with that."

"Good. I don't really trust rides at pop-up parks like these. But I don't think there's much risk riding the Ferris wheel."

"Well, let's see what happens when we get stuck at the top," she teased.

Silver lights suddenly lit up his blue eyes. "What do you think is going to happen?"

"You never know, Adam. Not everything in life can be planned."

"Then why do I think you have a plan?" he countered.

She shrugged as she got to her feet. "I guess we'll have to see." She smiled to herself as they walked across the park. It was fun flirting with Adam, even if nothing would ever come of it.

And she did have a plan, if she had the nerve to carry it out.

CHAPTER EIGHTEEN

ADAM HAD NEVER FELT MORE excited to get on a Ferris wheel in his life. As they waited in line to board, he was shoulder-to-shoulder with Molly, and he had to fight the urge to grab her hand and wrap his fingers around hers. He didn't know why it was so difficult not to touch this woman. He had plenty of female friends. He didn't have trouble keeping his hands off them, but every time he saw Molly, he wanted to run his fingers through her hair, wrap his arms around all her sweet curves, and kiss her hot mouth.

He had no idea what would happen when they got to the top of the Ferris wheel, but he was dying to find out.

Molly looked up at him, a knowing gleam in her eyes. "I can almost hear you thinking."

"I hope that's not true," he said dryly.

She smiled and then stepped up to the platform. The wheel stopped to let a couple disembark, and then they got on. He slid as close to her as he could. The attendant snapped a metal bar down in front of them, and then they were off. But they didn't go far, only a few feet in the air. Apparently, another couple needed to get off.

"Does this count as the top of the Ferris Wheel?" he asked.

"No. And if we don't stop at the top, then…maybe nothing will happen."

"That would be disappointing."

"Would it? I thought you didn't want anything to happen between us."

"Let's just say I'm not thinking beyond this Ferris Wheel ride at the moment."

"Adam Cole, living in the moment," she teased. "I like it."

"Well, you should. You're responsible."

"Chelsea told me that there was a time in your life when you were all about the fun."

"Considering I'm several years older than her, and we didn't hang out together, I don't think she knows what she's talking about."

"You weren't fun in high school?"

"I didn't say that. I had a lot less to worry about back then."

"Where did you fit in at school? Were you a sports guy, musician, nerdy kid, or in the parking lot crowd?"

"I was into sports. I played baseball and basketball."

"And academically? Straight As, always did the extra credit, or kind of walked your way through?"

"I wouldn't say straight As, but I did a fair amount of extra credit."

"I figured you'd be an overachiever."

His heart sped up as the wheel lifted them higher. They made it up three more spots, before being stopped once more. "Uh, we're getting close."

"Not quite there." She gazed out at the view. "It's beautiful up here, though."

He supposed it was, but he was only looking at her. The Ferris wheel started once more. To his dismay, they reached the top and then kept on going.

"What the hell?" he muttered.

She laughed. "It could still happen," she said, as they continued their way around.

"Well, let me put it this way: we're not getting off until it does happen."

"I don't think they let you ride forever. That would be against the rules. And I don't believe you're a man who breaks the rules."

"You tempt me to break a lot of rules," he said, looking into her pretty green, sparkling gaze.

"I'm not trying to."

"I know. That makes it even more tempting."

"I like this rule-breaking side of you, Adam."

"Don't get too excited. It's not going to last longer than this ride."

"I know. That's okay, too. We need people like you to keep us all on track."

He frowned. "That's not what I want to be to you, Molly—someone who keeps you on track."

"But you also don't want me to be someone who takes you off track. So, where does that leave us?"

"Going around in a circle?" he said lightly.

"Good point," she said, as they moved past the beginning and started upward once more.

This time he was thrilled when they stopped at the very top of the wheel. "We're here, Mol—"

Her mouth was on his before he'd finished saying her name. And the kiss was everything he'd anticipated and more. She tasted so good, her eager lips parting, as he slid his tongue into the warm heat of her mouth and they got as close as they could.

Then their chair started moving once again, and she broke away. He put his hand around her neck and pulled her in for another kiss. And he kept his mouth on hers as they made their way around the circle.

He was breathing hard and so was she when their chair was stopped at the bottom, when the attendant pulled open the bar and motioned for them to exit.

For a moment, he wasn't sure he could stand.

But then Molly was holding out her hand, and he grabbed her fingers and followed her off the platform. She didn't stop walking, leading him toward a grove of trees. When they were in the dark shadows, she kissed him again.

He wrapped his arms around her, not wanting to let her go. The extreme weight of that thought almost made him let go. Because he couldn't do forever, and she was starting to feel like someone he might want to do forever with.

It was Molly who finally ended the kiss, her eyes glittering in the moonlight.

They stared at each other for a long, long minute.

"I wish…" she began.

"What?" he asked.

"It doesn't matter."

"Maybe it does."

She put a smile on her face, one that felt more forced than any other he'd seen. "The ride is over."

"It was over five minutes ago, but that didn't stop us from coming here."

"I just needed a little more time with you before I said goodnight. I have a busy day tomorrow. And like I said, the ride is over."

He didn't feel like it was over. He felt like he was still spinning around. "You keep knocking me off-balance."

"And you don't like that." It was more of a statement than a question.

"I'm afraid I like it too much."

She gave him a thoughtful look. "I'm afraid, too."

"Why?"

"Because I don't like to care."

"Back to your low expectations."

"Let's just call them realistic. This was fun, Adam. I like hanging out with you, but I need to go."

"I'll take you home."

She put up a hand. "No, I'm going to walk. It's not late, and it's not far."

"I just want you to be safe."

She gave him a small, somewhat sad smile. "The truth is, we'll both be safer if I go home alone. You know I'm right." She kissed his cheek. "Goodnight, Adam."

She was gone before he could stop her.

And he wanted to stop her, even though he shouldn't. It was safer to let her go, but he was getting damned tired of playing it safe.

By late Saturday afternoon, Molly was exhausted. The sidewalk sale had been a huge success. The street traffic had been constant all day long. She'd have to order more inventory on Monday, which seemed shocking considering how much she'd had to sell when she arrived.

It had also been fun to be part of the merchants who were selling their wares. At lunch time, she'd gone up and down the street and met her neighbors. Jackie had been her usual stuck-up self, but most of the other retailers had been friendly and interested in her business. The more she talked about the mission of the store, the more it became defined in her mind. She wanted to change things up a bit. She wanted to get away from the "magical witchiness" of Phoebe and focus in on more practical and modern methods of healing and wellness.

While manning her table, she'd also met a lot of Phoebe's customers and friends. Many of them had asked whether there would be a memorial at some point. They wanted to pay their respects, but they didn't know where to go. She needed to think about that. It still baffled her that Phoebe had left her ashes to her without any instructions on what to do with them, except a simple note that directed her to wait until she knew what to do.

Phoebe was confident she would one day know exactly where her ashes should go.

Well, she still had no idea what to do with the urn that was currently at the attorney's office. And she would have to decide soon, because the attorney had asked her to collect it on Monday.

She'd worry about that on Monday.

She looked up as Drew and Cassie came out of the shop. Drew had been working all day, and Cassie had come by at lunch and stayed for the rest of the afternoon, volunteering to help out.

Molly suspected Cassie just wanted to be with Drew, but she wasn't turning away any help she could get. Plus, Cassie's friends had also shown up and made some purchases.

"What else can I do?" Drew asked.

"If you could put the card table in the back of the store, that would be great."

As Drew left, she smiled at Cassie. "I'd like to pay you for your time, Cassie."

Cassie waved away her offer with a careless hand. "It's not a big deal. I didn't have anything else to do today. And Drew said you don't have much money yet."

"Well, I am just getting started. But how about free yoga classes for the rest of the year?"

"I'll take that," Cassie said with a smile so dazzling Molly had a good idea why Drew was smitten. Cassie looked toward the store where Drew had disappeared and then turned back to Molly. "So, Drew is pretty great, don't you think?"

"I do. He seems to like you, too."

"I know he's not here for very long. My mom and my grandmother aren't thrilled with me seeing someone who isn't local, but he's so cool, and it's not like I'm going to stay here forever. I want to go away to school next fall. Maybe California. What do you think?"

She was surprised by the question. "Well, I'm nowhere close

to being an expert on relationships, but I think sometimes we worry too much about the future that we miss enjoying right where we are."

Cassie nodded in agreement. "I like that."

"What do you like?" Drew asked, as he returned.

"Molly is going to give me free yoga classes for the rest of the year," Cassie said.

"That's nice." He looked back at her. "Do you want me to help you with this last table?"

"No, you two go and have fun. I can manage."

"I'll see you Monday."

"Actually, I'll probably see you tomorrow. Are you coming to Adam's birthday barbecue?"

"Oh, right, that thing at the lake. I'll probably stop by."

"You should. Bring Cassie."

"I'm up for that," Cassie said, throwing Drew another bright smile.

"We'll see you tomorrow."

She smiled as they walked down the sidewalk and Cassie slipped her hand into Drew's. They were cute together. She hoped they'd make it, but long distance was hard, and they were both very young. *Who knew where their lives would go?*

Grabbing an empty carboard box from under the table, she packed the last few remaining products. She was just about done when she saw a man walking toward her, and she stiffened. It was Neil Loeffler.

His steps slowed when he saw her, his eyes darkening with some emotion she couldn't decipher.

"Hello, Molly."

"Neil," she said shortly.

"How was your sale?"

"Very successful."

"I heard."

"From who?"

"One of my firefighters stopped by earlier, Shelley Dearborn."

"Oh, I didn't realize she was a firefighter."

"She's just about to come back from maternity leave."

"I met her baby. He was very cute."

As their pointless conversation came to end, she shifted her feet. "Don't let me keep you."

"How's your mother?"

She drew in a quick breath. "She's great. She's in New York. She's really happy."

"That's good. I'm glad she found what she was looking for. I wasn't sure she ever would."

Her gaze narrowed. "What does that mean?"

"She liked new over old, change over stability. I used to think she was running away from something more than she was running toward something, but she told me I was wrong. That the future called to her, that she couldn't turn away from the possibilities and just settle for what she already knew."

Something about his statement didn't jibe with what had happened between him and her mother. "I don't understand what you're saying. The only time my mother wanted to stay anywhere was here in Whisper Lake, but you didn't want to get married. That's why we left."

He shook his head. "That's not why you left."

"It is. She thought you were going to propose but you didn't. When she pressed you about the future, you said you didn't see anything long-term. She came home crying. We packed up a few days later. She was devastated by your breakup."

Neil stared at her in disbelief. "Molly, that's not what happened."

"Of course it happened. I was there."

"You weren't there when I asked your mother to marry me, and she said no."

His words were shocking. "That's impossible. She wouldn't have said no. She loved you. She wanted us to be a family. *I* wanted us to be a family. You were the only person I ever wanted to be my stepfather. But you pushed us away. You let us go."

"I can't believe she told you that," he said in shock.

He put out a hand to touch her arm, but she jerked away, her emotions reeling.

"My mother didn't lie to me. She was a lot of things, but she wasn't a liar. She would tell me when she wanted to leave somewhere. She didn't make up a story." The more she talked, the more desperate she became to convince herself, but seeds of doubt were growing in her mind.

"She made up a story that night. I proposed to her, Molly. I showed her a ring," Neil said forcefully. "I asked her to be my wife. She said no. She was sorry. She thought she could say yes. She thought she could settle down, but she couldn't do it. I never saw her again after that."

"Why would she lie?" she whispered, talking more to herself than to him.

"I don't know. Maybe it was easier for her to be the victim."

"Because I would have been angry," she said, answering her own question. "I wanted her to marry you. I wanted you to be my stepfather, and she knew that." She shook her head in bewilderment. "Why did she say no? She told me she was in love with you."

"Not enough to stay, Molly," he replied, a heavy note in his voice. "Like I said before, I didn't know if she was running away from something or toward something, but I knew she was running, and she couldn't stop. She couldn't stay in one place. She was afraid it would stop her from being who she was meant to be. It sounds like she's happy now. Is she married?"

"No. And I don't know if she's happy or if she's staying in New York. Nothing seems to last long with her. I guess she's just built that way."

He cleared his throat. "For what it's worth, I wanted to be your stepfather, too. I thought about you a lot after you left. I've actually been following you online."

"Seriously?"

"Yes, but not in a creepy way," he added hastily. "I just like to see what you're up to. I was shocked when I heard Phoebe left you the store. But then I remembered how close you two were." He paused, smiling to himself. "And now I understand why she told me a few weeks ago that eventually the people we love come back. I thought she was talking about your mom, but she must have been speaking about you."

"I don't think she knew she would die so suddenly and so soon, though. Although, she did read tarot card and tea leaves, so who knows?"

"Are you into all that, too?"

"No. I'm into health and wellness, but not the mystical stuff. I guess I just don't have that much faith in the universe. I prefer to call my own shots."

"I think that's wise."

She looked past Neil, startled to see Jackie Hunt bearing down on them, carrying what appeared to be two fast-food bags.

"These were left outside my store by your employees," Jackie said. "If this happens again, I will call the police."

Neil stepped between them as Jackie looked like she was about to toss the trash in Molly's face.

"What's going on, Jackie?" Neil asked.

Jackie stiffened. "Well, of course you'd be here, coming to her rescue."

Molly frowned. *What the hell did Jackie mean by that?*

Neil ignored her comment. "What's the problem?"

"The problem is this store is a scab on the block and it needs to go. She's selling nonsense and stealing people's money. I won't stand for it."

"I'm not going anywhere." She stepped around Neil so she could face Jackie. "This store is not a scab or a scam. That trash could have been left by your own customers or some random person walking down the street."

"I saw those teenagers who were working here earlier eating this food."

"They threw their bags away inside the store. But let me take care of that for you." She grabbed the bags from Jackie's hand. "Are we done?"

Jackie whirled around on her high heel and stormed back to her boutique.

"She's still a piece of work," Neil muttered.

"That seems like too nice of a description. She can't stand me or the store, as you just heard. I don't know how Phoebe tolerated her all these years. I've thought about trying to kill her with kindness, but I think she might kill me first. I wish she would just give me a chance to prove that I can be a good neighbor and I can show her exactly what I'm selling."

"I don't think that will matter. I don't know about her relationship with Phoebe, but her animosity toward you is probably not just about the store; it's also about your mother."

"What are you talking about?"

"I dated Jackie for a few months. I broke up with her shortly after I met your mother."

"I had no idea."

"She thought your mom stole me from her, but that wasn't true."

She stared at him in amazement. "Really? You dated Jackie?"

"I didn't realize when we first started going out that she was such an unhappy person. She had only been in town a few years then, and I didn't know her sad history."

"What was her history?"

"She lost a child. It was an accidental drowning. Her husband left her shortly after that. She moved to Whisper Lake to start over. Her sister lived here. That's how we met—through her sister. But it became clear that we weren't right for each other. I was going to break it off. Then I met your mother, and I knew I had to end it with Jackie. The two events weren't as connected as she might have thought, but they did happen fairly close together."

"My mom said something once about how popular you were. I didn't know that someone hated her guts for stealing you."

"I don't think that Jackie and your mom had much to do with each other."

"Did Jackie try to get you back after we left?"

"No. The only thing Jackie has more than anger is pride."

"Well, thanks for telling me. I need to figure out a way to get along with her, which doesn't seem likely, but I have to try. We're neighbors. I can't have her bad-mouthing me and the store to everyone in town."

"Your customers will counter that with their own rave reviews. I wouldn't waste too much time on Jackie." He paused. "Are you going to stay in town, Molly? Is this where you plan to be for a while?"

"I'm here for now. That's all I can say."

His gaze filled with shadows. "You sound just like your mother."

"I grew up with her. It's hard not to be like her. We moved around so much, she was the longest and strongest influence in my life."

"I understand. I'm glad you're back, for however long. If you'd ever like to get coffee or a meal sometime, I wouldn't mind hearing more about your life."

"Sure, maybe once I get things more settled."

"Whenever you're ready—and only if you want to. Take care."

She let out a breath as he walked away. *Had he told her the complete truth? Had her mother lied to her about the reason for their breakup, the reason why they'd left Whisper Lake?* Only one of them was telling the truth.

She'd put her money on Neil. He'd never lied to her, and while she'd thought her mom had been mostly honest with her, she also knew that her mother had a way of shading the truth to her benefit.

Taking the trash into the store, she threw it away, then returned to finish the last of her cleanup. When that was done, she pulled out her phone, debating whether or not she should call her mom.

Maybe Neil was the reason her mother hadn't wanted her to come back to Whisper Lake. Her mom hadn't wanted her to find out she'd lied to her.

She stared at her phone for a long minute and then put it back in her pocket. This was her life, her relationships, and they had nothing to do with her mom. She could see Neil again or not. She could stay or go. She could do whatever she wanted.

She just had to figure out what that was.

CHAPTER NINETEEN

SUNDAY MORNING, Adam hopped on the stationary bike in his garage and put in a good five miles. He would have rather been running outside in the mountains. That was his favorite thing to do on the weekends, but with his foot, he was still non-weight-bearing, so biking was his best option.

As he finished his workout, the door opened, and Drew came in.

"Hey," he said, grabbing a nearby towel. He let the bike slow down as he mopped the sweat off his face. "What are you up to today? Do you want some breakfast?"

"I'm going to meet Cassie."

"That seems to be going well."

Drew shrugged as he dug his hands into his pockets. But he didn't leave, and Adam found that surprising since Drew didn't seem to like to spend much time in his company.

"Something else on your mind?" Adam asked.

"I was just thinking…" Drew paused. "I mean I don't know for sure, but…"

"You're going to have to finish one of those sentences."

"What if I wanted to stay until after Christmas, or maybe even until June or next fall?"

"Well, you've only been here a week, and I guess I'd have to ask why you think you'd want to stay?" He actually already knew why, but he needed Drew to talk to him.

"It's better here than I thought it would be," Drew said. "I like the job."

"And you like Cassie."

"She has to stay here 'til June to finish her second year of community college. Then she's going to transfer, probably to California. And it's not like I need to rush back. I'm thinking I could just take this year off. I can stay out of my dad's hair and decide what I want to do next year."

He thought about what Drew was asking, fighting back the urge to tell him he was out of his mind to make decisions about his life based on a girl he'd met a week ago. But he sensed that wasn't the right approach. He thought about how Gina would have reacted. As her smiling face filled his mind, he knew exactly what she would have said. "You're welcome to stay here as long as you want," he told Drew.

Relief filled the kid's gaze. "Really?"

"Sure. As long as you keep working and don't break any laws, I'm happy to have you. You probably should talk to your dad, though."

"I'm saving him tuition for a year, and he won't have to worry about me, so I don't think he'll be a problem."

"Your dad does worry about you, Drew."

"How would you know?" he challenged.

"He told me."

"Because he wanted you to take me in."

"Actually, he told me after your mom's funeral. He couldn't fathom how you were going to handle all the losses you'd had to suffer, and he knew he'd been distant, that he'd been so distracted taking care of your mom that he hadn't been there for you."

Drew looked taken aback by his words. "He said that?"

"Yes. He felt guilty."

"Well, I'm fine, so it doesn't matter."

"I'm glad you're enjoying your life here, but I don't think you're fine, Drew. It's okay to still be grieving."

"It's pointless. It doesn't change anything."

"It's just a process. We all go through it when we lose someone. I mourned your sister for a long time."

"And where did that get you? You're alone."

"Well, I'm not alone because of that. I'm just happy being single."

"Yeah, right."

He frowned at Drew's disbelieving comment. "I have a busy job. And I'm not going to be alone forever. Not that I'm alone. I go out. I have friends. I have a great life." He suddenly wondered who he was trying to convince—Drew or himself.

"Whatever you say. But you don't seem anything like the guy who dated my sister. That guy laughed. He knew how to have fun. He broke the rules; he didn't enforce them."

"When Gina died, things changed. I changed. I had to act differently. I had to grow up."

Drew gave him a long look. "It wasn't your fault."

His gut twisted. "You don't know what happened that night."

"I know enough. It was just…random. And that's why it's so pointless to try to control anything, because anything can happen at any time. You should know that. You're a cop."

"I do. I also know that good decisions can prevent some of the bad from happening."

"My dad certainly believed that. He wouldn't let me do anything after Gina died. I had to stay safe. I had to live. They couldn't lose another kid. I never got to go anywhere. No high school trips, like Gina took. I had to be home by curfew every night. And that only changed when I left home to go to school. I picked California because I had to get away from my dad. I couldn't stand living under his rules. Then two years later, my mom dies, and I didn't spend hardly any time with her because I was away. If my dad hadn't made it so impossible to stay near home, I would have gone to school in Denver. I would have spent more time with my mom. But I couldn't take his constant worry about me being hurt. In the end, I got hurt anyway. My mom died."

Drew gave an angry, bitter shake of his head, then continued. "My dad couldn't stop that from happening, just like he couldn't stop Gina from dying. And he can't protect me whether I'm sitting right next to him or I'm far away." Drew blew out a breath, as if exhausted by the words that had just poured out of him. Then he said, "Go ahead, tell me I'm wrong. You're just like my dad. You're living your life like you think you can control it, but you can't."

"I can't tell you you're wrong because you're not. But I know how your dad feels. He couldn't protect Gina, so he had to protect you."

"And you couldn't protect Gina. So, what—you're protecting the whole world?"

"I can't take credit for the whole world, but maybe just Whisper Lake."

"Okay, Superman," Drew said dryly.

He smiled. "One day, you should tell your dad what you just told me."

"He doesn't want to hear it. He never thinks he's wrong about anything."

"That's probably true. Gina used to say that about him, too. But she also knew that he really loved his family, so his worry always came from a good place."

"I gotta go," Drew said.

"Are you coming to the lake this afternoon for the barbecue?"

"Yeah, I'm bringing Cassie."

"Sounds good."

As Drew left, he started pedaling once more. He needed to ride a few more miles while he thought about what Drew had said. He knew he had an issue with control. And if he was Superman, he definitely had his kryptonite—Molly.

He couldn't help wondering if she hadn't put some of Drew's live-in-the-moment ideas into his head. A lot of what Drew had said sounded like Molly, and they'd been spending a lot of time together.

But he couldn't blame Molly for whatever influence she'd had on Drew, because he seemed like a changed kid. Molly respected him and had built up his confidence, and Cassie had made him see the possibility of a future. That might end as fast as it had started, but maybe it was also just what Drew needed.

Which made him wonder why he was pushing away the one person he needed just because it might not be for forever. Nothing was forever.

He pedaled faster but he wasn't going to outride his feelings for Molly. Every time he pushed her away, he just wanted to go back and get her. Maybe one of these days, that impulse would win out.

As his phone buzzed, he slowed down to grab it. He didn't recognize the number. "Hello?"

"This is Brenda Dunn. I got a message from you."

He stopped pedaling. "Yes. I understand you did some cleaning for Ms. Montgomery before she died."

"I did. But I never saw Ms. Montgomery. I only saw her housekeeper, Rebecca Pierce. She told me what to clean and that's what I did."

"Were you involved in packing any of the boxes that were sent to Phoebe Haller?"

"No. Rebecca took care of that. You should be talking to her."

"I can't find her. Did you have any contact with her after she left?"

"The last time I saw Rebecca was the day before Ms. Montgomery died. Phoebe was there that day, too. She was crying when she came down the stairs."

"Did you know Phoebe?"

"Sure. I've lived in Whisper Lake my entire life. Why are you asking me questions? What's the problem?"

"We're looking for a missing diamond. It was supposed to be in Ms. Montgomery's safe, but it's not, and no one knows where it is now."

Brenda gasped. "Well, I didn't take anything out of that house," she said in indignation. "Is that what you think? Is someone saying I did? Because if anyone took anything, it was probably the gardener. He always seemed to be looking in the windows. I'd be making a bed and I'd look out and see him staring in the window. It was creepy."

"That's Reuben Cardoza?"

"I didn't know his name. I think he works out of the north shore."

"Was there anyone else around besides the gardener, Rebecca, or Phoebe?"

"She saw Kim Collins. Kim works at the hair salon. I think she might be related to Caroline in some way."

That confirmed what Kim had told him about her visit. "Anyone else?"

"Not that I saw. I hope I'm not in trouble, because I was just there to clean."

"Did Rebecca talk to you about Caroline, about their relationship?"

"Not really. She only said that Caroline was obsessed with her privacy. She didn't want anyone to get a picture of her. I had to leave my phone in the car when I cleaned. I saw her that one time, and she looked old and sick. I could understand why she wanted people to remember her like she used to be."

"Has anyone else been in touch with you? Anyone from Caroline's family?"

"As a matter of fact, I got a message from someone named Lance Baylor. But I haven't called him back yet. Who is he?"

"He's an attorney for Charles Weatherly. Don't call him back. If you happen to answer, and he's on the line, tell him to contact me."

"All right. I don't understand why everyone wants to talk to me, but I won't call him back."

"Thanks for your help." He said goodbye, then called Lance Baylor. The call went to voicemail. Not surprising, since it was a Sunday. He left a message with his name and number. He'd barely set down his phone when it buzzed. Molly's name flashed across the screen and anticipation raced down his spine.

"Hello?"

"Happy birthday!" she said.

"Thanks. Are you coming to the barbecue tonight?"

"I wanted to ask you what you thought about that. I'd like to come, but I don't have to. It's been a crazy weekend. I can stay home. It's not a big deal. I want your birthday to be the way you want it to be, with whoever you want it to be with."

"Are you done?" he asked, as her nervous ramble came to an end.

"I think so. I don't want to make things awkward for you, Adam."

"They won't be awkward. I want you to come. All your friends will be there. Even Drew and Cassie are coming."

"Oh, good. I was hoping Drew would agree to go."

"Drew and I had a chat this morning. It went deeper than any other conversation we've had recently. He's really taken with Cassie. He asked if he could stay here past Christmas."

"How do you feel about that?"

"I'm happy to have him, as long as he's working and staying out of trouble."

"He's really a good kid, Adam. I think he's smarter and far more together than his father gives him credit for. I'm glad you talked."

"Why do I get the feeling you encouraged that?"

"I say a lot of things. Most people don't listen," she said with a self-deprecating laugh.

He smiled to himself. "I bet you'd be surprised. How did your sidewalk sale go?"

"Really well."

"What are you doing today?"

"I just went for a walk and got some decadent pastries from the bakery. And then I'm going to start looking through Caroline's things. Any updates?"

He filled her in on his conversation with Brenda and that fact that Rebecca was missing.

"It's odd that the housekeeper has disappeared," Molly said. "It makes her look guilty. Maybe she told Caroline she was giving the diamond to Phoebe, but she kept it for herself. But I wonder who had the fake diamond made?"

"Could have been anyone, including Caroline," he said. "She didn't want Charles to get the diamond."

"That's true," she said. "I should go."

"So, I'll see you later?"

"You will. Bye, Adam."

"Bye," he echoed, as he let out a breath. Then he went to take a shower—a cold one.

Before Molly started unpacking the boxes, she decided to make a little room in the apartment for whatever she might find. She walked over to the antique and weathered desk that Phoebe had told her was one of the few things she'd kept from her parents' house after they'd been killed in a car accident. Phoebe had loved to sit at the desk and write letters or jot down notes in her bible, as she called it. *Which reminded her…*

She pulled open the first drawer and took out the two-inch thick, three-ring binder. Sitting down at the desk, she leafed through the pages. The first section was devoted to products, the second section to ideas that Phoebe had for creating her own herbal combinations, and the third section was about her customers.

Phoebe had written down notes about many of her regulars:

Phil Stanley always came in saying he was looking for vitamins, but what he really wanted was something to help grow his hair back. She smiled at that note, seeing that Phoebe had suggested other products that would make him feel better: a multi-vitamin, a skin cream for aging, a travel book. She'd also mentioned setting him up on a date, which had resulted in a relationship that was still ongoing.

Turning the page, she paused as she saw Jackie's name. Apparently, Jackie kept reporting Phoebe to the city for alleged violations that were basically nuisances, and she always seemed to be worse in the fall. Phoebe finally realized what was behind the seasonal bursts of anger. Jackie had lost her daughter in September. Every year, right after Labor Day, Jackie went into a funk. Phoebe had decided that instead of fighting with Jackie, she would try to make her life better.

She dropped off her special brand of tea designed to combat insomnia, as well as a lavender-scented eye mask. She'd also left candles and a blank journal in the hopes that Jackie might find a way to vent somewhere else. It had worked. She and Jackie had made a truce. She'd even talked to her about how important it was to get sleep. Jackie admitted that she rarely slept more than an hour or two. Phoebe had jotted down additional notes on other ways to help Jackie sleep better, especially in the fall.

Molly sat back in the chair, thinking about that. It was September now, and Phoebe had died two weeks ago. She'd been preoccupied before that with Caroline and her own health issues. She probably hadn't thought about Jackie at all.

Maybe she could do what Phoebe had done—find a way to get Jackie to sleep, so she wouldn't be so angry toward her.

She was a little surprised that Jackie had called her store a scam when she'd been personally helped by Phoebe and some of the products in the store, but then again, sleeplessness could lead to irrational behavior.

Setting aside Phoebe's bible, she made some notes on a blank pad, which made her think she should probably start her own notebook. But for now, she would just focus on Jackie. The boutique was closed today, so she would start her campaign to win Jackie over tomorrow. She'd put together a series of care packages, using some ideas from Phoebe and some of her own. It might not work, but it was worth a shot.

She got to her feet, let out a sigh, and opened the first box. But she really didn't want to go through it. She was tired of cleaning and organizing. She'd been running fast since she'd arrived, and it was starting to catch up to her. She went into the bedroom and stretched out on the bed. She'd just take a little rest.

It was after three when Molly woke up with a start. She'd slept for hours. It was worth it. She felt immensely better. After a quick shower, she changed into white jeans and a tank top and headed down to the barbecue. She felt a little guilty about showing up empty-handed, but both Chelsea and Lizzie had said not to bring a present. She was going to take them at their word.

When she arrived a little past four, the barbecue was in full swing. The group had taken over two grills and several picnic tables in Sweetwater Cove, which was a little off the beaten path, and it looked like they had the cove pretty much to themselves.

There was quite a crowd. All her friends were there: Chloe, Hannah, Gianna, and their spouses Jake and Zach. Lizzie and Chelsea were present, along with Justin and Brodie. And then there were another twenty or so people she didn't know.

As soon as she entered the area, Hannah grabbed her by the hand and started introducing her around. She realized then there was quite a representation from the police force, the fire department, and a basketball team that Adam apparently played on.

It was clear that he was a popular guy. She'd thought at first that Adam was gruff and too serious, but she'd seen a sexy, playful side to him as well, and that side was in full view tonight. He was smiling and laughing with everyone he spoke to. He was apparently a great friend, because everyone she met raved about him in one way or another. He was the best guy they'd ever worked with or played on a team with or played cards with. He was the guy they all counted on. He was the one they turned to for advice.

And then there were the women. There were several single ladies in the crowd, and they weren't shy about flirting with Adam. It was the first time she'd seen him getting hit on, and she didn't like it. In fact, she was a little shocked at the stabbing jealousy she felt. Adam wasn't hers, and she needed to get over that fast.

"Something wrong?" Hannah asked.

"What?" she asked distractedly.

"I know that look. You have a thing for Adam."

"I don't have a thing."

"Then why can't you stop staring at him?" Hannah challenged.

She dragged her gaze away from Adam. "I was just trying to figure out who everyone was. And it is his birthday, so he's the center of attention."

"I don't think he's interested in any of those women," Hannah said with a knowing smile.

"Why would you say that? They're all attractive. He seems into a few of them."

"Maybe he's trying to make you jealous. When I was introducing you around, I couldn't help but notice that Adam did not look happy when you met the hot guys from the firehouse."

"You're exaggerating."

Hannah laughed. "I'm not. Seriously, Molly, what's the deal with you two?"

"There's no deal. I like him. And I think Adam likes me more than he wants to. But we're different people, and I don't even know if I'll stay in Whisper Lake. That kind of uncertainty doesn't sit well with Adam."

"That's true. He is not a guy who just wings it. He always has a plan. But you know what they say about plans. When love comes in the door, plans go out the window."

"I've never heard that before."

"I might have made it up, but I think it's true. We all have plans and ideas for how we want our lives to go, but then you meet someone, and everything changes. Nothing matters except how you feel. Nothing is as important as love—not jobs or geography."

She put up a hand. "Whoa, slow down. I didn't say anything about love. I barely know Adam."

"So, get to know him."

"It might be pointless. And it might hurt more when I leave."

"Are you going to leave? You have your own business. You have friends. Why would you want to go anywhere else? You always said this was your favorite place to live."

"That's true, but I've never stayed anywhere longer than a couple of years. I don't know that I won't get bored."

"I think you're just afraid, Molly. If you don't want it, you won't be hurt if you don't get it. And it's not just Adam that falls into that mindset—it's probably the success of the store, too."

She looked into Hannah's perceptive brown eyes. "You might be right. I want to succeed, but I don't know if I will. And moving has always been the answer to a problem. In some ways I like goodbyes, because it means I'm going somewhere new, and in other ways I hate goodbyes, because I'm leaving people behind." She let out a sigh, confused by her own thoughts. "I don't know. I've made a lot of changes really fast, and to be honest, my head is still spinning."

"You don't have to decide anything tonight, or tomorrow, or even this year. I know you're not leaving that fast. You just got here. And I think you're going to fall in love—maybe not with

Adam, but definitely with Whisper Lake. You loved it once before, probably more than any of us who stayed."

"And that love broke my heart. I almost didn't come back because of that, but Phoebe forced me to take another look. She always thought I belonged here."

"Maybe you do. Look, I'm the last person to give relationship advice. It took me ten years to get over hating Jake enough to let him back into my heart. But I will say this: love is always a risk, and you love to take risks. You love to leap into the unknown."

"But Adam doesn't make moves like that. He's not about fun for the moment; he's about planning for the future. I don't want to hurt him. He should be with someone stable and solid."

"That sounds boring as hell."

She smiled. "Am I wrong? You know him better than me."

"I think he hangs on a little too tightly to predictability. And sometimes we all need a kick in the ass to change our perspective."

"I don't think he needs a kick in the ass on his birthday," she said dryly.

"True. Let's get a drink, and I'll introduce you to one of my friends from the clinic. He just moved here a few months ago. He's single and not nearly as weighed down with emotional baggage as Adam."

She could use a drink. She wasn't all that interested in meeting another guy, but maybe she should. She could at least look at someone else for a while and that would be a small victory.

CHAPTER TWENTY

ADAM FELT INCREDIBLY lucky to have so many people at his birthday party. It wasn't a party he'd wanted, but his sisters had, of course, gotten their way, declaring that big birthdays were always a Cole tradition, and he couldn't mess with tradition. He'd had no argument to that because they were right. Traditions were big in his family, and he liked the sense of continuity, of keeping things going from one generation to the next.

As the sun set, the food bins were emptied, all the drinks had been poured, and the party wound down. He said a multitude of goodbyes and gave a lot of hugs, until the only people left cleaning up were his sisters, their spouses, and Molly. He'd barely spoken to Molly. She'd always been on the periphery of whatever group he was in. He'd caught her staring a few times, and she'd caught him looking at her, too. They'd shared a lot of smiles but not a lot of words. And he wanted words. He wanted to talk to her. He wanted to spend the rest of his birthday with her, and he was glad she'd stuck around.

He walked over to the picnic table where she was pulling up the paper tablecloth. "You don't have to clean up, Molly."

"It's fine. Your sisters did so much work. I want to help."

"I never got a chance to talk to you tonight."

"You were very popular." Her smile didn't quite reach her eyes. "Lots of pretty, single women wanted your attention."

"Jealous?" he asked hopefully.

"No. You're free to do whatever you want."

"So are you. But that guy from the firehouse—Mark—not for you." He shook his head to add to his point.

She raised a brow. "Why would you say that? Mark was very nice. And fun-loving. He told me all about the six months he spent backpacking through Europe. He seems to have a real sense of adventure."

"He's into adventure, yes, but he's also into serial dating. He goes from one woman to the next, and he brags about his numbers."

"You mean like how many women he sleeps with?"

"Exactly."

"If he's such a jerk, why are you friends with him?" she challenged.

"He's on my basketball team. He's not a bad guy. Mark is fearless when it comes to fire. You just don't want to date him."

"I'll keep that in mind."

"Did he ask you out?"

"Is that your business?" she countered.

He frowned, wanting to make it his business. "If he did, you should say no."

"It's not your call."

"I'm just watching out for you, Molly."

"I don't want you to watch out for me. I'm not your sister."

"Oh, I know that, believe me," he said forcefully.

She flushed. "Well, I can take care of myself. I've been doing it for a very long time."

Lizzie came over to the table, interrupting their conversation. "Last call for trash?" She held open a half-filled garbage bag.

"This is all that's left," Molly said, stuffing the paper into the bag. "Sorry, I was just going to bring it over."

"No biggie." Lizzie turned to him. "Did you have fun, Adam?"

"Best birthday ever."

"You say that every year."

"Because you top yourself every year."

"I am a good party-giver," she said.

He gave her a smile. "Mom would be proud."

"Did you talk to Mom today?"

"Yes. I also spoke to Dad and Grayson. Nathan sent me a text. I even heard from a bunch of our cousins, including Hunter."

"I was hoping Hunter and Cassidy would be able to come. But they're taking a long vacation in San Francisco. Keira was sad to miss it, too."

"I also heard from her and Dante," he admitted. "Everyone checked in."

"Well, good. That's how it should be. It's your special day. I kind of hate that it ended so early, but it's getting too dark out here."

"It was perfect."

"I got a chance to talk to Drew," Lizzie continued. "He seems like a good kid. I think you're doing right by him. I wasn't sure it was a good idea, but maybe it was."

"I don't know why you always doubt me," he said. "I knew it would be good for him to come to the mountains, change his environment."

"I always agreed with that. I just didn't know if it would be good for you, bringing the past back into the present," she said pointedly.

"It's all good."

"If you say so. Anyway, I think we're done." She smiled at Molly. "Thanks for your help. I know it was a busy weekend with the festival and the sidewalk sale and this party, but you better get used to it, because Whisper Lake loves any opportunity to throw an event and bring everyone together."

"I'm beginning to remember," Molly said. "And you seem to be right in the middle of it all, Lizzie."

"I'm a social person, and events are good for my business. It keeps people coming back, even during the off-season. I hope you met some new people."

"I did. I'm not sure I remember everyone's names, but I'm sure I'll see some of them again, hopefully in my store."

"You will. We're all going to head out," Lizzie said. "Adam, do you need a ride? I couldn't help noticing how many drinks you had tonight."

"I'm not ready to go yet. Molly and I haven't had much chance to talk tonight."

"You should do that now," Lizzie said with a gleam in her eyes. "Have fun. And Molly, don't let him drive home."

"I can give him a ride," Molly said.

"Good."

As Lizzie left, following Chelsea, Brodie, and Justin to the parking lot, Molly gave him a pointed look. "Your sisters are going to get the wrong idea about us."

"What idea would that be?"

"That we're involved in some way."

"Is that really the wrong idea? We are involved."

"You keep telling me we can't be."

"I know. But here we are."

She gave him a thoughtful look. "Our relationship seems to be as complicated as you were afraid it would be."

"So, let's make it simple. I'd like to spend some time with you tonight. If you're up for it, we can walk out to the point. There's a cool cave you can see from there."

"That sounds like a line," she said with a smile.

"It does," he admitted with a laugh. "But the cave really does exist."

"Are you sure your foot is up for walking?"

"It's feeling much better," he said. "I don't even need the crutch anymore. But if I need a little support, can I lean on you?"

"I doubt you would ever admit you need support, so sure," she said.

"Well, I am feeling like I might need a little help getting through the sand. Maybe you should put your arm around me."

She gave him a suspicious smile. "Of course." She came around the table, sliding her arm around his waist.

He put his arm around her shoulder, and they took the sandy cement path as far as they could before carefully making their way over the rocks to the outermost point of land. He didn't really need her support, but he liked leaning on her. He liked having a reason to hold her and for her to hold him.

"So, where is the cave?" Molly asked when they got to the point.

"See those rocks?" He pointed to the left of where they were standing. "Where it looks like there's a door?"

"Oh, yes. That does look like a door."

"It's just a natural rock formation. The water doesn't go in very far, so you can wade into the cave. A lot of kids have carved their initials into the rock walls. In the summer, we actually board it up to cut down on the cave parties."

"And the local kids don't have their own cave parties in the off-season?"

"They all know that this area is patrolled heavily on Friday and Saturday nights."

"No one is around tonight," she said.

"I think the festival tired everyone out. And it's Sunday." He let go of her to take a seat on a large flat rock. He patted the spot next to him, and she sat down. "I'm glad you came tonight. I'm sorry that I didn't get a chance to hang out with you."

"You were the birthday boy; you had to make the rounds."

"I didn't expect such a large crowd. But I should have. I told you birthdays are a big deal in my family."

"You all definitely do them right." She let out a sigh of appreciation as her gaze moved across the lake and the majestic towering mountains. "This is another beautiful view, Adam.

There's no shortage of them here. The water, the mountains, the blanket of stars… It's peaceful and inspirational at the same time."

"It's nice in the winter, too, when the snow covers everything."

"I barely remember what it's like to live in the snow." She turned to face him. "I'm going to have to buy new boots and a heavy coat. It's so warm tonight. It's hard to believe winter is not that far away."

"You've got about six weeks. Right now, you just need to enjoy the last of the warm weather."

"I am enjoying it. In fact, I wish I had my bathing suit. The lake looks so inviting."

"Have you been in it yet?"

"I've been too busy. But I do want to feel that water." She gave him a mischievous look. "Have you ever gone skinny-dipping in the lake?"

"No. Have you?"

"Once, a long time ago. I did it on a dare with Hannah and Keira. Gianna and Chloe refused. Then they stole our clothes and we had to run to the parking lot stark naked."

He smiled at that image. "It sounds like fun."

"It was." She paused, a gleam entering her eyes. "Why don't we do it?"

His nerves sharpened at her words. "You want to strip down and go in the lake?"

"It's dark. There's no one around but us. And it's your birthday. You should do something bold on your birthday, celebrate another year around the sun."

"I…" He meant to say no. He needed to say no. He didn't skinny-dip. That wasn't him.

But he wouldn't mind seeing Molly strip out of her clothes and jump into the water.

No. He shook his head, feeling like he was going back in time to the worst place, the worst night. Gina had wanted to go to that club. He'd told her he didn't like the area, but she'd smiled at him, and he couldn't say no.

This felt like the same moment. The situation was different, but the lake could be dangerous. "It's not a good idea," he said. "You could get hurt. It's too dark to see the rocks."

"Well, I wasn't thinking of diving in, just wading out..." She paused, her brows drawing together. "What's wrong, Adam?"

"Nothing. I don't think it's smart. We can go in the lake when it's light out," he said, running a hand through his hair, his breath coming too fast.

"I'm not going naked in the lake when it's light out."

"So wear a suit," he said, his tone short and clipped.

"You're pissed off at me, now?" she asked in wonder.

"No." He blew out a breath. "I'm angry with myself. I want to stop the voices of caution from coming into my head, but they're always there, because...well, they're just always there."

"Were they always there? Or did they appear after Gina died?"

"They got a lot louder after she died."

"I get it."

They sat in silence for a few minutes. "Damn," he swore.

"What?" she asked warily.

"I hate this feeling."

"What feeling?"

"Being conflicted between what I want to do and what I should do." He looked into her eyes. "Logically, I know we won't get hurt if we go in the water. I'm being too careful, and I really want to feel fearless again."

"Adam, you are fearless. You threw yourself in front of a car to save a child's life."

"That was different. That was on the job. I can do anything on the job. I can also risk my own life without thinking twice. It's yours, Molly. I don't want to risk your life or the life of anyone I care about."

"That's a heavy burden to carry, Adam. You can't prevent

other people from getting hurt. You don't have that power. No one does. You can play it safe and be careful and maybe that will work, or maybe it won't," she said.

He gave her a warning look. "Don't try to tell me things happen for a reason. I hate when people say that. I don't think there was any reason for Gina to die."

"I wasn't going to say that. If there is a reason, I don't think we have the capability to understand it. So, it doesn't comfort me when people say that, either. It was my mom's favorite saying. Every time we moved, or we had to change something, she said, 'Everything happens for a reason, Molly. It will all make sense one day.' I don't think any of it has ever made sense."

"I feel the same way," he said, surprised they were on the same page.

"See, we do agree on something," she said lightly.

He gave her a small smile. "We do. And your mother sounds like a piece of work."

"A work in progress is what she always says." She paused. "I ran into Neil again at my sidewalk sale. We talked this time. He told me that he asked my mother to marry him, and she said no. That is not the story I heard. She always said he broke her heart, that he didn't want to get married, didn't want to be a stepfather, and that's why we had to leave. She couldn't stand seeing him anymore. But she lied to me. That wasn't the reason at all."

"Are you sure she was the liar? Maybe Neil—"

She cut him off with an emphatic shake of her head. "No. It was my mom who lied. I wanted to think it was Neil, but he was very convincing. And the thing is—his version makes so much more sense than hers ever did. It just makes me angry because I really liked it here. I had the best friends I'd ever had. I had Phoebe, who was my mentor and my friend, and I had an entire town of warm-hearted people who cared about each other. I lost all that when we left and went to New Orleans. But I was doing it for my mom. I wanted her to feel better. She didn't think about my feelings. And that has really been the pattern of our life. I don't think I've seen it as clearly as I do now."

"I'm sorry you got dragged around as a kid. That must have been difficult."

"I tried to make the most of it. She drilled into me the idea that every change was an opportunity for something wonderful to happen, so I embraced whatever we were doing, wherever we were. But sometimes, late at night, when it was dark, and I felt alone, it didn't feel wonderful; it just felt lonely."

"Maybe it's time to stay somewhere."

"Sometimes I think that I should stay here. But then I wonder if I'm built to stay anywhere. I did like some of our moves. It was fun to live in different places. I have an adventurous spirit like my mom does. Maybe I couldn't stay even if I tried. I've moved three times in my twenties, and they were good moves. I got to live in Boston, Las Vegas, and then San Francisco. I had experiences I wouldn't have had if I'd stayed in one place." She paused. "I don't know. I'm rambling on. I want it all. I want to have people in my life, but I also want the adventure. I don't know if I can have everything. If my mother is any example, it doesn't seem like I can."

"You need to separate yourself from your mother."

"She used to say that you can't fly if you have roots. You have to choose one or the other."

He didn't want her to choose to fly away from him. He wanted her to pick roots, but he could hear the indecision in her voice, and the yearning. That poked at him, awoke some of his old yearnings, ones he'd buried a long time ago when he'd chosen not just roots but to play life as safely as he could and avoid all chance of pain. He'd given up on having it all.

"I'm sorry, Adam," Molly said. "I'm bumming you out on your birthday. Let's talk about something else."

"I don't think we should talk at all," he said decisively.

"Oh, okay. I can drive you home."

He put a hand on her thigh as she started to get up. "I don't want to talk, and I don't want to go home."

She licked her lips. "Uh, well, it's kind of rocky here, so I'm not sure what you think we're going to do..."

He smiled. "I wasn't thinking that, but I like where your brain is going."

"Then what are you thinking? Tell me. Because I clearly cannot figure you out."

"I want to go skinny-dipping," he said, making a sudden decision.

She gave him a wary look. "You just told me you didn't. It's dark. It's dangerous. It's a bad idea."

"I changed my mind. I don't want all the adventures to be over, either." He grabbed the hem of his shirt and pulled it up and over his head.

"Oh, wow," she said, her gaze running down his chest. "You're really going into the water?"

"We're going into the water." He stood up and grabbed her hand. They walked off the rocks to the sand below. Then he took off his walking boot and his other shoe. "I'm not doing this alone," he said as she seemed to be frozen in place. "I take something off—you take something off. Unless you were just talking before? And you don't really have the guts to do it?"

A smile spread across her lips. "You know what I can never turn down? A dare."

"Then I dare you."

CHAPTER TWENTY-ONE

MOLLY TOOK off her tank top and tossed it on the ground, shaking out her hair. The long waves tumbled over the lacy blue bra she had on. "Keep going," she said, giving him a nod.

He realized he'd stopped abruptly as soon as she'd started taking off her clothes. "Sorry. You distracted me."

"It's only going to get more distracting."

He could only hope. He shoved his jeans and briefs down and stepped out of them.

She caught her breath as her gaze swept his body. "You must work out a lot, Adam."

"Some. Let's see what you've got."

"Not as many muscles as you." She pulled off her bra and then stepped out of her jeans and panties. She wasn't muscled, but she was all soft, sweet curves, and his mouth watered, his body hardening. He didn't want to take her into the lake. He wanted to lay her down on the sand and make love to her.

Molly sucked in a breath as electricity sparked between them. "Now or never," she said.

He thought he better get in the water before he couldn't walk. So, he turned and hobbled his way into the lake.

Molly came in right behind him, squealing as she splashed

her way into waist-high water. "It's freezing." She wrapped her arms around herself.

"I thought you liked to look at things positively. I'd say it's invigorating."

She laughed as she took in a breath and then dunked herself down to her neck. She popped back up, covering her breasts with her hands. "Oh, my God, it's cold. I think my heart stopped."

He moved through the water, eager to get to her. He felt cold and on fire at the same time. When he reached her, he cupped her face, gazed into her moonlit eyes, and took the kiss he'd been thinking about since the last time he'd kissed her.

The touch of their mouths created a blasting heat that washed over him. He wasn't freezing anymore. He was on fire—for her. He moved her hair to the side as he slid his tongue down her neck. She let out a sigh of appreciation and wrapped her arms around his body, pressing her breasts against his chest. He slid his hands down her back, cupping her sweet ass, wanting to get even closer to her than he was. But then she pulled away with a laugh.

"We're in the middle of the lake, Adam," she said breathlessly.

"I thought you wanted an adventure."

"Maybe one that's not so cold."

"Is it cold? I feel nothing but heat. Or I did, until you moved away."

"We should get out."

"Why? This is the most fun I've had…" He shrugged. "I can't remember when."

Her gaze met his. "I want to have the fun somewhere warmer."

"I can keep you warm, Molly."

"You want to have sex here in the lake where anyone could see us?" she challenged.

"I don't even know where we are right now, and I don't care."

"I think I've created a monster."

He laughed. "That might be true. You definitely unleashed something in me. I feel free."

"I don't want you to lose that feeling, but with skinny-dipping, you go in and then you get out."

"You go first. I want to watch."

"You are bad, Adam," she said with a grin.

"You haven't seen anything yet."

"I want to see everything." She licked her lips. "Maybe we should go back to my apartment."

"No maybe about it," he said with a promising look.

She ran through the water, heading toward shore. He followed more slowly, not only because of his foot, but because he didn't think he'd seen anything more beautiful than her naked body leaving the water under a bright moon.

She was halfway dressed by the time he got out. It wasn't quite as magical to put his wet body back into his clothes, but he wasn't going to let the practical side of his brain grab hold. He was living in the moment, and he wasn't ready to get out of it.

They made their way to Molly's car. As soon as she was behind the wheel, she turned on the heater full blast. Then she gave him a questioning look. "Where do you want to go, Adam?"

He looked into her eyes. "Wherever you're going."

She drew in a breath. "I don't want you to regret any of this. I think you've had a lot to drink. That's why you went skinny-dipping in the lake—"

"It's not why I went," he denied, shaking his head. "I'm not drunk on alcohol. I'm drunk on you." He paused, wondering if she was having second thoughts. "But if you've changed your mind…"

"No, I haven't," she said quickly. "Do you need to call Drew?"

"He's nineteen years old. He doesn't care where I am, but I'll text him that I'll see him tomorrow." He pulled out his phone, sent the text, and then looked back at Molly. Her hands were gripping the wheel. "You sure you're okay with this?"

"Yes. I just don't usually have this long to think about it."

"This long? It's like a five-minute drive."

"I know. It probably seems incredibly fast to you."

"It seems slower than slow," he said. "I've been wanting to be with you since the first second you knocked me over."

"I don't remember our first meeting that way. You were annoyed."

"I was shaken, but also taken," he said with a smile.

She smiled. "You seem very different tonight, Adam."

"The lake woke me up." It wasn't actually the lake; it was her, but there were some things he'd keep to himself.

She parked behind the store, then got out of the car, and he swiftly followed.

He only wished he didn't have a bum foot, or he could have moved faster. He could have carried her up the stairs and across the threshold and put her down on the bed. But he had to settle for hobbling up the stairs. When they entered the living room, she'd no sooner put her bags and keys on the side table, when he pushed her back against the wall, needing to kiss her like he needed to breathe.

She wrapped her arms around him, kissing him back with eager impatience that only ramped up his desire. He wanted more—fast. "I need you," he muttered.

"Then have me," she said, looking into his eyes. "Let loose, Adam."

"Be careful what you wish for, Molly."

"I'm not worried. I trust you. And I need you, too."

Her words brought forth a fierce wave of desire. They stripped off their damp, soggy clothes once more. The whirlwind that was Molly consumed him as they kissed their way into the bedroom with a passionate urgency that couldn't be denied.

They tumbled down onto the soft bed. He loved the way her body molded to his. He wanted to savor every inch of her, until she was gasping his name and writhing with pleasure. And she seemed to want the exact same thing, her hands riding up and down his back as he made his way down her body, touching, then tasting her breasts, drawing soft gasps of pleasure as he slid his fingers through the heat between her legs.

He only paused long enough to pull a condom out of his wallet because not even this wild version of himself could ignore being safe. He wanted to love her. He wanted to protect her. He wanted to be everything to her. He just didn't know if that would be enough.

But he wasn't going to worry about any of that tonight. He was going to live in this moment as long as he could.

Molly rolled onto her side as the morning sun drifted through the curtains. When her gaze moved over Adam's handsome features, she smiled to herself. His brown hair tumbled over his forehead. There was a dark morning shadow of beard across his strong jaw, which was finally relaxed. There were no serious lines running across his face. He looked happy.

Or maybe she was just putting her feelings on him because she felt almost giddy with satisfied pleasure. Last night had been more than she'd imagined, and she'd done some imagining over the past week. But she hadn't realized what an incredibly hot body Adam had been hiding beneath his clothes, or how wild and passionate he could be when he finally let go of his rigid control. She hadn't thought he could make her smile so much or that he could be so unbelievably generous. She also hadn't realized how much more she could like him.

That was scary. She immediately pushed that thought away. She didn't want to think past the next few minutes. She had this gorgeous, naked man in her bed, and she was pretty sure she could do anything she wanted.

She started by running her fingers down his bare arm, his bicep flexing beneath her touch, his skin deliciously warm. Then she snuggled closer and kissed the corner of his mouth—one side, and then the other.

Adam's eyes flickered open, and she gazed into the dark, deep blue that reminded her of the lake.

"Morning," he said huskily. "How did you sleep?"

"Great. Probably the best night of sleep I've had since I got here. I haven't quite made the place mine yet."

"Speaking of that, you need to get rid of that owl. I felt its eyes on me all last night." He tipped his head toward one of Phoebe's ceramic owls on the dresser.

"I thought you were only looking at me," she complained.

"Well, when you fell asleep, it was just me and the owl."

"I did fall asleep on you, didn't I? Sorry, but that was your fault. You were exhausting—in a good way." She gave him a kiss, then sighed. "Why do you have to look so good in the morning?"

"You look good, too."

"I feel like my hair is a tangled mess."

"I like it that way," he said, running his fingers through her hair. "I like everything about you, Molly."

"Spoken like a man who wants to have sex again," she teased.

He grinned. "That's the other thing. You make me laugh. You're fun, Molly."

"Well, thank you. I have to say you were more fun than I expected, and I'm including the skinny-dipping adventure. Do you think any of your friends would believe you stripped down and went in the lake with me?"

"I'm thinking we should keep that to ourselves, or I'll never hear the end of it."

"I guess it could be our secret."

"I appreciate that. You got me out of my comfort zone, Molly, and I'm glad you did."

"Sometimes we all need a push to try a different direction."

"Or a dare," he said with a grin.

"Or that." She paused. "Do you want some breakfast?"

"Maybe after…"

Her heart sped up at the promise in his eyes, and then she let out a little gasp as his hand covered her breast and his lips touched her neck. Then his hand moved down her body, leaving a tingle of nerves in its wake. "Yes," she agreed. "Let's eat later... much later."

It was almost nine when Molly got dressed and made her way into the kitchen, where Adam had already made coffee.

He held out a mug. "Perfect timing."

She reached for it, but he held it away. "Kiss first."

"Aren't you tired of kissing me?" she asked.

"That's like asking me if I'm tired of breathing."

She gave him a kiss and then took her coffee. As she sipped it, she realized he'd done more than make coffee. "What's all this?"

"Breakfast. Scrambled eggs and avocado toast."

"You might be the perfect man."

He laughed and shook his head. "Not even close. But I can make breakfast. And I figured you probably need to get down to the store pretty soon."

"I do. Drew will be here at ten as well."

"I'm not worried about Drew seeing us together. You don't need to be a secret, Molly."

"Okay, good," she said, happy to hear that. "I don't like hiding my feelings. But I'm kind of surprised you're willing to be so open."

"Well, I'm not planning to take out an ad anywhere, but I don't have a problem with people knowing I like you. It's not like our friends haven't guessed that already."

"That's true. Hannah was all over me about it yesterday."

"What did she say?"

"That I should go for it. She thinks you're hot."

"Hannah has always been one of my favorites." He handed

her a plate of food. "Eat."

She took her plate to the table and sat down. He joined her a moment later. "So, what time do you normally go to work?" she asked.

"Around nine."

"You're going to be late."

"I don't have any pressing cases, except yours."

She frowned at the reminder that she had a case. "I'm supposed to call Lance Baylor today."

"Don't bother. I already left him a message. If he shows up again, just say no. You have no obligation to let him in here."

"Okay." She took a bite of her eggs. "These are good by the way. I like the hint of pepper."

"Everything tastes better with seasoning."

"What are you going to do today besides talk to Baylor?"

"I still need to connect Ethan Mercer to someone in Caroline's family. I'm also going to check out some of Caroline's stepchildren. Maybe tonight we should empty the boxes together, zero in on what exactly you have."

"Do you really want to go through boxes or is that an excuse to see me?" she teased.

He smiled. "I want to do both. Let's multi-task."

"All right. Tonight, we attack the boxes. But today, I have to go through my inventory, reorder some items, refill the shelves and a lot of other stuff. The to-do list seems to be never-ending. I just hope all this work will pay off. I had a lot of business this past weekend, but it was the festival, and some people were curious about the store. I just hope they come back, and they keep buying. Otherwise, the money Phoebe had in reserve is going to go fast. I'm beginning to realize what a big risk it all is."

"No risk, no reward." He gave her an apologetic smile. "Sorry. That cliché is not helpful. I know, because my father used to say it to me all the time when I was playing sports."

"Are you close to your dad?"

"To both my parents."

"How often do you see them?"

"Probably six or seven times a year. They're in Denver. Sometimes they come up for a weekend, or I go there."

"And your brother? I know one is traveling—what about the other one?"

"Grayson has been sending some of his patients to the rehab center in Whisper Lake, so I've been seeing him more often."

"Are your parents retired?"

"My father retired from his accounting job a while ago. My mom works part-time for a literary agent, reading the slush pile."

"That sounds fun."

"She's apparently doing some writing now. She doesn't think it's too late to write her novel."

"It's never too late."

"Do you have anyone besides your mom in your life?" he asked. "What about grandparents?"

"My mom's parents died when I was about four. They were in a boating accident on their first big trip in more than two decades. My mom always lamented the fact that they'd waited so long to start having fun and then it was over. I think that's partly why she felt like she had to keep striving for more. She didn't want to leave anything for later."

"That makes sense."

"I never knew my dad or his parents. So, my family is just my mom and me. A few men have come and gone. Neil was the longest relationship she had, but that ended, too."

"Because she couldn't commit."

"No, she couldn't." That reminder made her feel a little unsettled. Was she going down the same path as her mother? She could fall for Adam; she knew that. *But what then?* She suddenly felt terrified. She didn't do serious. She was about fun, living in the moment. She didn't want to think about what might happen next. "I should probably get to work," she said, getting to her feet. She took her plate to the sink. "Thanks for breakfast. I hate to run out on you, but I have to do a few things before I open the store."

He got up, blocking her way out of the kitchen. "Molly, what's wrong?"

"Nothing. I had a great time."

"Your eyes just filled with shadows. What were you thinking about?"

"I don't know—just work, what I need to do today."

"That's not it. Talk to me."

"I can't do this right now, Adam. Everything is fine. We'll get together tonight."

She started to move past him, but he grabbed her arm, giving her a hard look. "Don't end this before it has even really started."

"End what? You don't want a relationship with me. You've been saying that since we met."

"Maybe I'm changing my mind."

"Well, maybe I just want to have fun," she said.

"Then let's keep having fun. There's no rush to do anything else."

His words eased some of her tension. "Okay. I like the sound of more fun."

"So do I." He gave her a kiss. "I'll see you tonight. Why don't I bring dinner?"

"If you want," she said, helpless to say no to this man, which was why she should probably stop having fun and end this—whatever *this* was. But she just couldn't do it. Not yet.

CHAPTER TWENTY-TWO

As the store slowed down late Monday afternoon, Molly grabbed the care package she'd put together earlier and walked down the street to Jackie's boutique. There was a stylishly dressed young woman organizing dresses on a rack.

She gave Molly a welcoming smile. "Hello. Are you looking for anything special?"

"No. I'm actually looking for Jackie."

"She had to step out. Do you want me to give her a message?"

"Actually, I'd like you to give her this." She handed the gift bag to the woman. "I'm Molly Trent. I run the shop next door, A Better You."

"I thought you looked familiar. I stopped by your sidewalk sale on Saturday, but you were helping someone else. I really like what you've done with the store. I'm Ariel Flint."

"Nice to meet you, Ariel." She was thrilled that Jackie's employee didn't seem to have a problem with her shop. "I'm glad you liked the shop. If you ever need anything, let me know."

"I'm actually interested in your yoga classes, but I noticed your schedule was pretty slim."

"I'm trying to get one of the former teachers back," she said, making a mental note to check with Elaine again. "I'll let you know when we add more classes."

"I'll make sure Jackie gets this."

"Thanks." As she left the boutique, she let out a breath. Step one in her plan to win Jackie over was done. Hopefully Jackie would look in the bag and not toss it out just knowing it was from her.

When she re-entered the store, she realized it was almost five, and there was no one around, so she went ahead and locked the front door, turning the sign to Closed. Adam had texted earlier that he'd be over around seven with dinner. And she was more than happy about that. Despite her morning panic, she wasn't ready to cut him off. She wanted to see him again. She wanted to spend more time with him. Just because something wasn't going to last forever didn't mean it couldn't last awhile longer.

Drew came out of the back room. "I just finished organizing that back wall," he said.

"I've been avoiding that."

"I noticed," he said with a gleam in his eyes. "But it's done."

"You really are a lifesaver, Drew." She paused. "You know, I've seen how excited you get when you're on the computer, when you're building something. Your mind is sharp. It wants to be busy. I know you're trying to figure out your next move in life. I hope you decide to lean into some of your talents. I'm sure you're a great partier, but you're other things, too."

"I guess," he muttered. "But it seems kind of boring to be a computer nerd."

"You don't have to be just one thing. Don't let people try to put you into some sort of box. And don't do that to yourself. Don't define yourself narrowly. You're a complex person. You have lots of talents. Embrace them all."

He shook his head in bemusement. "I have to say, I haven't met anyone like you, Molly. You're so comfortable in your own skin."

"I didn't grow up like everyone else. I had to be comfortable in my own skin, because everything else in my life was constantly changing: my homes, my friends, and the cities I lived in. You can roam around the world, but you're always with yourself, so I had to make peace with who I am."

"That makes sense, in a weird way."

She laughed. "I can be kind of weird, too." She paused as someone knocked on the front door. Looking through the glass window, she could see a man on the sidewalk.

"Do you want me to tell him we're closed?" Drew asked.

"No, I'll take care of it." She walked to the door and opened it. "I'm sorry. We're closing now."

"Ms. Trent?" he asked.

She looked at his unfamiliar face, at his nice suit, at the large canvas bag in his hands, and she suddenly realized who he was. "Oh, my God. You're George Marconi."

"Yes, Phoebe's lawyer. You were supposed to pick this up today."

"I'm sorry. I completely forgot." Her gaze moved to the open bag, where she could see a flash of gold. "Is that the urn?"

"Yes. I've also included the plastic bag that the hospital gave me with the clothes Phoebe was wearing when she was taken to the ER. I didn't know what else to do with them." His eyes filled with compassion. "I know this is difficult, but Phoebe wanted you to have her ashes until you knew what to do with them. I've included the note that I read you earlier."

"Okay." She swallowed hard. "I guess you should give her to me."

He handed over the canvas bag.

She held it in her arms, feeling the weight of the large gold urn. "Before you go, Mr. Marconi, I wanted to ask you about a missing diamond."

"A missing diamond?" he echoed. "Something that belonged to Phoebe?"

"No, it belonged to her friend Caroline. Apparently, it's missing, and a few people seem to think Phoebe has it. Did she ever mention it to you?"

"She did not. I would have made note of that in the items that you were inheriting. We went over jewelry and other valuable objects, and she had no individual piece of jewelry that was worth more than a hundred dollars, and most of it was considerably less." He paused. "Phoebe and I spoke a few days before she died, after Ms. Montgomery's death, but before she had gone through the items that Ms. Montgomery left her. If there's a diamond, it would be in the boxes that she had not yet opened."

"I'm still going through those. Caroline Montgomery's ex-husband is also asking me to let him look through the boxes. Actually, his attorney is asking me. Do I have to let him do that?"

"Absolutely not. Whatever Ms. Montgomery sent to Phoebe became Phoebe's property, which in turn became yours."

"That's good to know. I'm sure the attorney will keep pressing. Apparently, the diamond is worth over three million dollars."

"Would you like me to speak to the attorney?"

"No thanks. Not yet, anyway."

"Let me know if I can help." He took a breath. "My wife stopped by the store on Saturday. She said it looked amazing. She brought home a bag full of items, and she's been drinking tea, meditating, and sleeping better than she has in years. For some reason, she always thought Phoebe was full of hot air, but she said when she stepped in the store and spoke to you, she felt inspired."

"I had no idea I spoke to your wife, but it was crazy busy that day. I'm glad she's feeling good. That's what it's all about."

"Phoebe would be proud of you," he said with a nod. "She said there was only one person who could keep her legacy going."

"I'm still touched that she believed that. We hadn't seen each other in a long time."

"She felt close to you, as she indicated in her note."

"I was wondering about that note. It felt like she knew she was going to die. But she had a sudden heart attack. It was unexpected."

"Perhaps not completely unexpected. She was having problems with her heart several months ago. When her friend Caroline was ill, Phoebe started thinking a lot about her own plans. We sat down about a month ago, and she made her decisions."

"So it was very recent." She looked down at the urn. "I don't know where I should bury her, though. I don't understand why she didn't just tell me where to put her ashes."

"I don't know, either. But she seemed to believe the universe would deliver whatever answer was needed."

"Great. What about a memorial service? People have been asking me if there's going to be one, and I feel like there should be, but I don't know what she would have wanted."

"She didn't care about big ceremonies. But she did care about her friends. I don't suppose that helps, but she trusted you to make the decisions, so go with your gut."

"I will. Sorry again for making you come over here. I had it on my calendar, and then I didn't look at my phone. To be honest, I wasn't that excited to get this. It feels weird to know her ashes are inside."

He gave her a kind smile. "But her soul is flying. That's what she told me. She said when she was gone that she'd finally get to fly the way everyone thought she already could."

"No broom required," she said with a smile.

He grinned. "That's correct. Have a good night, Ms. Trent."

"Thanks." As he walked away, she stepped back into the store and relocked the front door. Then she took the bag over to the counter where Drew was waiting.

"You could have gone home," she told him.

"I just wanted to make sure you were all right."

"I appreciate that. I'm fine."

"So, what's in the urn, or do I not want to know?"

"Phoebe's ashes. I'm supposed to put them somewhere. Phoebe thinks I'll know the right place at some point."

"That's weird. She didn't just say where she wanted to be buried?"

"Nope. But she loved puzzles and challenging people. I guess we're playing one last game."

"What are you going to do with it? You're not going to leave it here in the store, are you?" he said with an uneasy look in his eyes.

"I'll take it upstairs."

"Good," he said with relief. "I'm going to take off then. See you tomorrow."

"See ya." She relocked the door after he left. Then she picked the bag up and moved into the back room. She checked the back door and then headed into the hallway and up the stairs to her apartment.

Once inside, she took the urn out of the bag and set it in the middle of the kitchen table. There was a folded note taped to the side of it. She opened it and read the short message that George Marconi had related to her over the phone.

But seeing Phoebe's handwriting made it all seem more real, and she had to blink the moisture out of her eyes before she could focus on the message: *I know you'll figure out the best place for me to be, Molly. I trust you to do what's best. I know you'll take care of me. I always felt connected to you, like you were the daughter I never had. Even though our time together was brief, I loved you very much, and I want the best for you. I believe that's in Whisper Lake.*

She wiped away a tear as she folded the note. She was touched and humbled that Phoebe had loved her so much and wanted the best for her. Now she had to do right by Phoebe. She looked at the urn and frowned. It felt wrong to put it on the table.

She tried a couple more spots, but they didn't feel right, either. Finally, she took it into the bedroom closet and put it on one of the shelves she'd recently cleared off. But that wouldn't work. She couldn't stick the colorful Phoebe in a closet.

"What am I going to do with you?" she muttered. "And I'm not talking just about right now, but about forever. Where do you want to be, Phoebe?"

There was no answer coming. She took the urn into the living room and put it on a table by the window.

"Now, at least you have a view." She felt a little silly to be talking to the urn. On the other hand, it made her feel closer to Phoebe. She sat down in the chair next to the table. "I was devastated when I heard you had died, Phoebe. It didn't seem possible. You were such a vibrant person. Even with all the time between us, I could still hear your laugh, smell your perfume, see your smile...and you were always in beautiful color. It's hard to believe you're not here anymore." She paused. "I do like the gold urn, though. You always loved gold."

She felt tears prick the back of her eyes once more. She hadn't had time to mourn Phoebe because she'd been so busy, or maybe she'd been busy so she wouldn't have time to grieve.

"I'm going to make you proud of me," she continued. "I've already got the store up and running. And we're making sales. There's an actual cash flow." She paused, gazing out at the street. "I do love Whisper Lake. I'm pretty sure you brought me back to stay. But I don't know if I can stay anywhere. I don't have relationships that last longer than a few months. I'm not sure I'd be any good at something longer. It's off with the old and on with the new. God, I sound like my mom now. Well, whatever happens, I'm going to keep the store going. Even if I leave, I'll put someone in charge. I'll never sell it. But it's too soon to make those kinds of decisions. I can almost see you shaking your head, telling me just to enjoy where I am."

She took a breath. "I don't know how well you knew Adam. But he's really something, Phoebe. He makes me feel things I've never felt before. It's scary. I don't do deep. I don't do love, you know. And it's funny because he doesn't think he wants to do love, either, but I think he does, and I think he should. Because he has a really big heart..."

"Anyway, that's enough for now. I'm kind of glad you're home. Is this what you were thinking? That I'd just bring you home?"

She thought about that for a long minute. "No, that seems too easy. You were a lot of things, Phoebe, but you were never easy. I hope I can figure out what you wanted. I'm definitely going to try."

With that, she stood up. She wasn't going to figure everything out tonight, and she wanted to take a shower before Adam arrived.

When Molly's doorbell rang just before seven, her heart leapt into her chest. She smiled to herself as she ran down the stairs to let Adam in. She couldn't believe how happy she was to see him again. The man had definitely gotten under her skin. She just had to make sure he didn't take over her heart, but that wouldn't be an easy task.

She threw open the front door, realizing her mistake a moment too late. The man standing in front of her was not Adam. He was at least ten years older, darker, and he had a tense look in his eyes.

"Molly Trent?" he asked.

"Yes," she said warily.

"I'm John Weatherly—Charles's son."

"Okay. If this is about the diamond, I don't have it. I can't help you."

"Are you sure?" He edged a little closer. "I know my stepmother packed a lot of shit before she died, and she wasn't all there mentally. The cancer treatments had taken their toll on her mind."

She held her ground, not letting him through the door. "I've looked through everything that Phoebe Haller received from Caroline Montgomery, and the diamond is not there." It wasn't the complete truth, but she didn't owe him that.

A grim look entered his eyes. "You better not be lying, Ms. Trent."

She swallowed hard. "Are you threatening me?"

"That diamond was given to my father."

"That's nothing to do with me." Relief ran through her as Adam's Jeep pulled up in front.

Adam got out of his vehicle and moved as quickly as he could in his walking boot. "Is there a problem?" he challenged.

"None of your business," John replied.

"I'm Detective Adam Cole," he said, pulling out his ID. "If I ask you if there is a problem, you answer. What's your name?"

"John Weatherly."

"He's Charles Weatherly's son. He's here about the diamond," she put in. "I told him I don't have it."

"She doesn't have it," Adam said, giving John a hard look. "I already told your father's lawyer that earlier today."

"She has to have it. It's nowhere else to be found. Caroline had to have given it to Phoebe. They were like sisters. Phoebe was the only one she wanted to see when she was dying." John ran a frustrated hand through his hair. "Look, the ring isn't just of monetary value. It represents the love between my father and Caroline, and he needs that back. He's been distraught since she died. And the diamond will make him feel like he hasn't lost everything."

Molly didn't know what to make of his suddenly sad story. Maybe if he'd told her that tale first, she would have been more receptive. "Look, I'm sorry for your dad, but I can't give you what I don't have."

"We just want to help you look," he said.

"No," she replied "You're going to have to trust me."

"It's worth over three million dollars."

"I thought it wasn't about the money," Adam interjected. "Do you know Ethan Mercer?"

"Who?"

"He broke into the store last week and a few days before that. I'm pretty sure he was looking for the diamond, too."

"I've never heard that name," John said. "Are you telling me someone might have already stolen the diamond?"

"Well, the guy hasn't come back, so who knows?" Adam said. "But what we do know is that Ms. Trent doesn't have it. You need to leave her out of this. Step back, Mr. Weatherly."

Adam's firm voice backed John away from her.

"Please keep looking," John implored. "It's very important."

She didn't know what to say, so she just moved inside. Adam followed, watching Weatherly walk to his car before he shut the door.

"Are you all right, Molly?"

"I'm fine. I shouldn't have opened the door without looking. I thought it was you."

"Did he say anything else before I arrived?"

"No. Do you really think Mercer stole the diamond when he was here last week?"

"It's possible. It wouldn't be big. He could have had it in his pocket."

"I almost hope he does have it, so I can move on."

"I know. How are you doing?"

"Better now that you're here." She leaned into his kiss, feeling like it had been forever since she'd had his mouth on hers.

"I missed you," he said, lifting his head, his eyes sparkling with desire.

Her stomach flipped over. "It hasn't been all that long."

"Today felt like a month."

She smiled. "I'm happy you're here, but you are empty-handed."

He started. "Right. I left the food in the car. When I saw that man staring you down, I was more concerned with what was going on with you."

"I appreciate that, but now I want food. I'm starving."

"So am I," he said with a laugh. "And not just for food. I'll be right back."

CHAPTER TWENTY-THREE

Molly stood in the doorway as Adam went to his car and retrieved a pizza box and a paper bag.

"I'm liking the look of dinner," she said, as he joined her. "It smells like onions."

"I got half veggie, half meat deluxe. Wasn't sure exactly what you like."

"I like everything," she said with a laugh, as they went upstairs to her apartment.

"I brought salad and chicken wings, too."

"And I got some nice wine from the liquor store down the street. Or would you rather have beer?"

"I'll take some wine."

She set the bottle on the table for him to open while she grabbed glasses, plates, and utensils. "What's Drew doing tonight?" she asked, as she sat down across from him. "Maybe we should have asked him to join us. I should have thought about that before he left."

"Cassie and her friends were playing volleyball at the beach and barbecuing hot dogs tonight. He had better options than you and me."

"They're spending a lot of time together."

"He's all in. I hope she feels the same. I'd hate to see him get dumped."

"I know. I want him to be happy for a while. He deserves some fun."

Adam gave her a dry smile. "When his father sent him here, he told me to make sure he didn't have too much fun. I'm not doing a very good job."

"He's nineteen, Adam. You can't stop him from doing whatever he wants to do. And you certainly can't stop him from falling in love."

"That's true." He gave her a thoughtful look as he poured her some wine. "Have you ever been in love, Molly? You know about my past. What about yours?"

She took a sip of her wine, contemplating her answer. "I've liked some men. I've dated a few for a couple of months. One went almost a year. But looking back, I can't say I've ever been in love. I'm not even sure exactly what that means. I had this one guy in college tell me that he wasn't in love with me, but he did love me. Then he said, 'Do you know what I mean?' I told him I knew exactly what he meant, because, you know, I was twenty, and I liked him. But I had no clue what the difference was."

"Maybe it wasn't really any kind of love, just caring."

"Isn't caring love?" she countered.

"I don't know. I'm not an expert. But it sounds like the guy was warning you that he wasn't that interested. He didn't want to get serious."

"Or even see me again. He basically ghosted me after that. So you were right; there was no love."

"Who was the guy who almost made it to a year?"

"Brandon. I was twenty-three and he was twenty-seven. I was in San Diego at the time. We were doing the SoCal beach scene—volleyball in the sand, body surfing, margaritas at night, rollerblading along the ocean. It was all very outdoorsy and almost felt like we were on vacation, which was probably why it lasted as long as it did. Neither one of us had a career job. I was waiting tables at a vegan restaurant. He was bartending." She shrugged. "I ended up moving to Austin, Texas for a year with my mom, so it ended."

"Did you like Texas?"

"Austin was cool. But we only stayed there about a year."

"What did you do for work in Austin?"

"I worked for a nutritionist for a while, who was part of a natural wellness practice. That gave me some insight into herbs, vitamins, and superfoods. We moved to San Francisco next, where I worked in skincare. I learned a lot about skin conditions, ointments and lotions. Oh, and I learned how much money people are willing to spend to look younger."

"And did they actually look younger?" he challenged.

"Sometimes they did, but I have to say I think it was always part of a bigger picture. Like they start focusing on their skin, but they also do other things. They drink more water. They get outside. They de-stress. The years fall away, and maybe the lotion gets the credit."

He smiled as he munched on a piece of vegetarian pizza. "I like that you can see the bigger picture."

"I like that you're trying to see the bigger picture, too. I felt like your mind was really closed when we first met. It feels more open now."

"My perspective had gotten too narrow," he admitted. "You helped me see that. I just had to get into a freezing cold lake for that to happen."

She laughed. "You wouldn't have gotten in that lake if you hadn't already opened up your mind."

"Are you kidding? The second you took off one item of clothing, I was going in that lake. And it was definitely worth it."

His words and the appreciation in his eyes sent a shiver down her spine. "It was worth it," she said softly. "I was surprised you could be so spontaneous."

"It surprised me, too."

"Because you'd forgotten that you used to be that way," she said. "Before Gina died."

"I was never that spontaneous, but I was certainly more before she died than after. Let's get back to you."

She groaned. "We already covered my romantic history."

"There has to be more."

"You know I moved around a lot, and I don't believe in long distance, so, no, there isn't more."

"What about friends? Who is your best friend?"

"Before I came back to Whisper Lake, I'd say it was Layla. I only met her when I moved to San Francisco, but we became close. Then she went and had twins, so our friendship took a back seat to diapers and bottles and all that, but she's a good person. Now, I'm feeling like Chloe and the rest of the gang could be friends, including your sisters, who are awesome, by the way."

"They're not bad. A little nosy, but otherwise okay."

"It's just their way of protecting you, like you protect them by being all big-brotherly and judgmental."

"Is that what they said?"

"Maybe not in those exact words. Who is your best friend, Adam? I know you have a lot of friends after seeing you at your birthday party yesterday, but who are you closest to?"

"Probably Brodie now. We work together and he's my brother-in-law. I like Justin, too, don't get me wrong, but Brodie and I probably have more in common."

"I can see that. What about childhood friends?"

"I've kept up with some over the years, but I don't live near most of them."

"Do you ever think about leaving?"

He shook his head. "No. I like it here."

"It doesn't feel too small to you?"

"It's growing every day. But even if it wasn't, I like feeling a part of the community I serve. I worked in Denver for a while, and a few other cities in Colorado before I came here. Whisper Lake has the right mix for me."

"That's good." She cleared her throat. "So how was the rest of your day?"

"It was fine. I didn't make much progress on your case and then I got sidetracked by another investigation."

"Is it something you can talk about?"

"Not at the moment, but nothing too serious. What about you? Was it another big sales day?"

"It was steady, not super busy, but enough that I felt good about things. Oh, I also had a brief chat with Phoebe's lawyer, George Marconi. I was supposed to pick up Phoebe's ashes, and I forgot, so he brought them by." She tipped her head toward the table.

Adam turned his head. "Well, that's a very bright and very large gold urn."

"Phoebe liked gold."

He faced her once more with a question in his eyes. "Is she going to stay there on the table?"

"I tried putting her in a dozen other places, and every single one felt weird. When I put her by the window, it felt right. She used to sit in that chair and look out the window. She liked to see the sun set over the mountains. She'd make herself a Manhattan and watch the sun go down."

"That seems like the right spot then."

"For now. I don't think it can be her permanent resting place, but I don't know where that should be, and she left it up to me. She gave me a note saying something like I would figure out where she should stay forever. I can't believe she didn't just tell me."

"She might not have known. It's a big decision to make, to even think about. She didn't want to do it, so she left it for you."

"But I haven't seen her in years and when we spoke, it was only on the phone. How would I know what to do over all her friends? They knew her better than me."

Adam gave her a sympathetic look. "Maybe she just thinks you two had a connection that will tell you what to do. At the end of the day, you're never going to know. She can't tell you."

She let out a sigh. "True. I just need to think about it, and also about a memorial service. But before I can get to all of that, I really need to make sure that I wasn't lying when I told Mr. Weatherly that the diamond wasn't here. Finish your pizza. Because I am going to need your help going through some boxes."

"So, rich people buy a lot of worthless shit," Adam declared after thirty minutes of looking through boxes filled with impractical and, at times, very unappealing objects. He was astonished by the amount of junk Caroline had apparently treasured enough to bequeath to Phoebe. He held up a ceramic snake. "How much do you think this is worth?"

"About a quarter at a yard sale," she said with a laugh. "But I could be wrong. Maybe it's a priceless ugly snake."

"I don't think so. I'm putting it in the giveaway pile."

"I won't stop you. I'm beginning to lose hope on finding the diamond. Unless..." She started taking apart a wooden doll.

"You think there's something inside that?" he asked in surprise.

"I know there is." She held out another doll that matched the larger one. "It will keep going, too."

He watched in fascination as she opened the doll to reveal a smaller one. In the end, there were five matching dolls, all with the same painted expression.

Molly held up the center of the doll, which was a tiny round box. "Last chance." She popped open the lid and then turned it upside down. "Nothing. I was thinking this was going to be it."

He smiled at her disgruntled expression. "It would have been a good place to hide a diamond. I certainly wouldn't have found it."

"One more box to go." She sliced open the tape on the last box. She lifted the lid and started to pull out something very furry, then stopped, her expression wrinkling with fear. "I don't know if I want to see this."

He stepped forward. "I'll check it out."

She put her hands over her eyes, as he pulled it out of the box and laid it on the floor. "Is it an animal?" she asked.

"At one time. It's a bear rug."

"Oh, God, there's not a head, is there?"

He laughed as he saw her bright-green gaze peeking through the hands covering her eyes. "No head. I'm not actually sure if it's real or faux fur."

She took her hands down. "Well, that's a relief." She looked at the rug. "I'm sure it's fake fur."

He wasn't that certain, but he wasn't going to tell her that.

She squatted down to touch the rug. "Oh, it's really soft." She sat down on the middle of it. "Very comfy. Maybe I should keep this."

"Really? Why?"

"Well…" She flushed. "Never mind."

"No way. Not with that expression on your face. Tell me what you're thinking."

"There's just something really sexy about a thick rug like this. It would probably be nicer with a fire going, some snow coming down outside, candles, a little music, maybe wine…"

His heart sped up and his body tightened at her words, at the image she'd created in his mind. Although in his head, she wasn't wearing anything but the rug. He knelt down, looking into her eyes. "I like the fantasy."

"Too bad we don't have all the extras."

"I don't think we need them." He put his hand under her chin, tilting her face upward. "Do we?"

Her eyes sparkled. "Really? Right here on the rug?"

He pushed her onto her back. "Right here, right now." He took her mouth with a passion that seemed to grow more intense each minute that they were together. He loved the way she kissed him back. He also liked the way she pushed him onto his back and then straddled him.

"My fantasy," she said with a wicked smile. "Do you mind if I have my way with you?"

"Are you kidding? Do whatever you want."

She slid her hands under his shirt, sending heat ripping through his body. Then she leaned over and kissed him, her long, silky hair covering his face. He greedily inhaled the scent of her, as she teased him with butterfly kisses that moved from his mouth across his jaw, her tongue swirling around the edge of his ear.

"You're going to torture me, aren't you?" he asked.

"Yes, a delicious, slow torture."

"You don't like to go slow."

"I do right now."

Despite her words, she tugged impatiently at his shirt, and he helped her pull it off.

Her eyes feasted on him. "I like looking at you, Adam."

"I like looking at you."

As her hand moved down his chest to the snap of his jeans, he sucked in a breath. "I like that even better."

"I know," she said confidently. "Don't worry. We'll do everything you want and everything I want."

"Then we won't be leaving here for days." *Or maybe years,* he silently added.

CHAPTER TWENTY-FOUR

"You look happy," Chloe told Molly as she stopped in the store Tuesday afternoon.

Molly started, having been completely lost in thought, a thought that included the night she'd just spent with Adam. "Sorry, I didn't see you."

"You were thinking about something else. Or should I say someone?"

"There might be someone," she admitted.

"A sexy detective? Lizzie told me that you and Adam stayed at the lake after his party."

"We did. He's really great."

"He is," Chloe agreed. "Is this going to be something serious?"

"I don't know. I'm not good at serious. But we're having fun."

"Is Adam on the same page?"

"I think so. We've been honest with each other."

"That's good. The man could use a little fun."

She gave Chloe a thoughtful look. "Is there something you want to tell me about Adam? You—you're not interested in him, are you?"

"No. I like him as a friend. That's it. Did someone tell you something different? I know there were rumors going around about Adam and me after Kevin and I split, but nothing happened. Adam was just helping me with Leo and being supportive. But we have never been romantically interested in each other. I just let myself lean on him for a while."

"He is a good person to lean on."

"Yes, he is. But he needs someone who wants more than protection, who challenges him, and I think that's you. He has smiled more this week than he has since I've known him."

"He is something else when he smiles," she said with a wistful sigh.

Chloe laughed. "You have it bad. So, when are you seeing him again?"

"We're going for a bike ride after work. Then he's going to barbecue for me and Drew and probably Cassie, who seems to be permanently attached to Drew."

"That sounds fun. So, I had another reason for coming by. Lizzie told me about some amazing pillow that guarantees a good night's sleep."

"It is an amazing pillow. No guarantee but I think you'll like it." She led Chloe over to the corner of the store where her sleep aids were displayed and handed her the pillow. "This is my last one. I just ordered more after the sidewalk sale. It's made of organic, non-allergenic materials, and it stays cool while you sleep."

"Perfect. I'll take it." As they walked back to the register, Chloe said, "How are things going with Jackie?"

"I'm not sure. I dropped off my first package yesterday, with no response. I stopped by at lunch, and she just gave me a tight-lipped look as I left a basket of goodies on the counter. There were customers in the boutique, so their presence might have prevented her from yelling at me or throwing the basket in my face."

"You're being very nice to her. If she can't see that, then she is beyond saving."

"I hope she can see that I'm trying. I do want to help her. I left a note today saying that Phoebe had left instructions on things that might make her sleep better. I wanted her to know that Phoebe is still looking out for her."

"Well, I can't wait to hear what happens. I have heard that you're impressing the hell out of everyone by knowing exactly what they need before they even ask. One of my waitresses said her mother, Joanne, came by this morning, and you knew exactly what vitamins she wanted before she even asked."

"I'm just following Phoebe's notebook, as well as adding to it," she said as she took Chloe's credit card. "Especially for the locals. That way, I'll know what items to keep in stock and what other new products they might benefit from." She handed Chloe the receipt. "Let me know how the pillow works out for you."

"I will. I better get home. My in-laws are in town, and they're babysitting Leo, but he gets very hyper around this time of day."

"Phoebe used to call this time of day the witching hour, and it doesn't apply just to kids."

"That's probably true. Have fun tonight, Molly. Say hi to Adam."

"I will."

After Chloe left, she rang up her other customer, who had found a couple of herb tinctures she wanted to try. When that woman departed, she turned the sign to Closed, locked the door, and ran up the stairs to change clothes.

As she moved through the living room, her gaze went to the bear rug that was still on the floor. Heat ran through her as she remembered the hours they'd spent on that rug before making their way into the bedroom. She flushed a little as her gaze also landed on the gold urn by the window. "I guess we put on a show for you, didn't we, Phoebe?" She paused, hearing Phoebe's laugh in her head. "I just wish you were here, and we could really talk to each other."

She walked over to the urn, kissed her fingers, and then touched them to the urn. "You were always about living life to the fullest, staying in the moment, but the more fun I have with

Adam, the more I care about him. The more I start to worry about what's going to happen if—when—our moment ends." She drew in a breath. "But it's not going to end tonight. I'll see you later, Phoebe. And by the way, if you have any idea where that damn diamond is, can you give me a sign, something…"

As the quiet surrounded her, she let out a sigh. "I'll have to figure it out for myself, won't I?"

Adam was on the phone when Molly arrived. He let her into his house and motioned it would be just a minute. While he was talking, she wandered around the spacious, one-story home with floor-to-ceiling windows of the lake. The décor was manly, comfortable, but also very clean and organized. Adam was a man who liked order. And she was a woman who had had very little order in her life and was almost scared when things were too neat.

They were very much opposites. But they also complemented each other. At least, she wanted to think so.

Besides being neat, Adam's house felt warm and inviting. There were a lot of family photos on a credenza. She walked over to check them out, seeing group pictures of a much younger Adam with his siblings and his parents. There were also bigger family pictures with what appeared to be cousins and kids, aunts and uncles.

As her gaze swept the table, she also noted the picture of Adam, Brodie, and three other guys holding a trophy on a basketball court. There was also a shot of Adam on a boat with a very large fish dangling from a hook.

"Sorry about that," he said.

"You're a fisherman?" she asked, pointing toward the photo.

"I don't catch a lot of fish, but I don't mind being out on the water in the early morning. I have a boat, and it's very relaxing. Have you ever been fishing?"

"No. It sounds like it would be a little boring."

He smiled. "But you're all about relaxation and de-stressing. That's what fishing is."

"I thought it was about catching fish."

"That's the icing on the cake. We'll have to go sometime."

"Maybe. I certainly wouldn't say no to a boat ride. Is it a speed boat?"

He laughed. "It is. We can go as fast as you want." He leaned over and kissed her. "How are you?"

"Good," she said, as an intimate smile passed between them. "What about you? Busy day? Was that call about my case?"

"No, it was about another investigation, but I'm still working on locating Ethan Mercer."

"That's fine. I'm hoping that he got the diamond, or he just gave up. Either way works for me. I don't want to think about it right now."

"Then let's go for our bike ride."

"I haven't actually been on a bike that moves in a while, just the one at the gym."

"It's fairly flat around here. You'll be fine. Come on, I have the perfect bike for you." He led her out to the garage.

She laughed at the bright-red girl's bike with the basket in front. "Seriously? You own this bike?"

"No. I borrowed it from my neighbor. She likes to bike into town and pick up fresh vegetables at the farmers' market. It looks like the right size for you."

"I just hope it's true that you never forget how to ride a bike. Not that I had a lot to forget. I don't think I rode more than two or three times as a kid. I didn't have my own bike, and we lived in a lot of big cities where you couldn't just hop on a bike and ride around town."

"Then you're really going to enjoy this." He handed her the helmet that was hanging from the handlebars. "Safety first."

She laughed. "Of course."

Like everything else, bike riding with Molly was an adventure. She'd started out wobbly and uncertain but after running off the driveway into his rosebushes twice, she'd managed to get herself out to the sidewalk with the dogged determination Adam was beginning to realize was a big part of her.

Molly was not a quitter. She rose to challenges. She didn't sink down and hide or look for someone to bail her out. She hadn't even wanted his advice on how to get the bike going. She'd been determined to do it on her own.

He knew at least some of her independence had been born in the fire of an unpredictable childhood. Molly had grown up knowing she had to adapt. She had to embrace change, or she'd spend her life unhappy.

What he didn't really understand now was why she seemed so ambivalent about staying in Whisper Lake. She should want the roots she'd never had. She should want to be part of a circle of friends, a supportive community. She should be ecstatic she had her own business. And they got along great, better than he'd ever imagined great. But he wasn't sure any of that was enough for her, and it didn't make sense.

She'd said something about having roots meant you couldn't fly, but she'd been flying her entire life. Maybe it was time to land, to make a home, a real home, one that wasn't going to change in a few years.

He tried to rein in his thoughts as they went into dangerous territory. He hadn't been looking for a relationship. He hadn't wanted a relationship, but he seemed to be in one, and he was having too good of a time to end it.

At first, he'd shied away from Molly, because her impulsive recklessness had reminded him not so much of Gina, but of the way he'd been when he was younger. He'd put that part of him away after her death. It had been the only way to get through the grief. He'd told himself that if he could survive the pain, he'd be done with pain. He wouldn't go down that road again. But he was already halfway down that road, and the irony was that he wasn't even sure that Molly wanted to be on the road.

He'd spent so much time pushing women away, afraid they'd want a commitment, it hadn't occurred to him that he might meet someone who also didn't want a commitment.

"Look at me," Molly suddenly called out. His gaze moved toward her as she lifted both her hands off the handlebars. "No hands."

He smiled at the pure joy and freedom on her face. "I told you that you could do it."

"It still feels good to actually do it." She put her hands back on the bike. "Should we head back?"

He nodded, even though he hated to end the ride. He had this worrisome feeling that every minute only brought him closer to a goodbye that he didn't want to hear. But he was thinking too far ahead. It had only been a couple of weeks. She wasn't going to leave anytime soon.

When they returned to the house, Drew and Cassie were there. Adam took steaks and chicken out of the fridge as well as some appetizer trays he'd picked up at the market, and then headed out to the barbecue. Drew, Cassie, and Molly followed, settling in at the patio table with sodas and appetizers.

As he got the grill ready, he listened to their conversation, amazed at how much Drew had to say. In a few weeks, the kid had really opened up. And Drew was sweet with Cassie, always making sure she had what she needed. He even got up to switch places with her so she wouldn't be looking into the sun. He was a good guy, and he was happy. That's all his dad had wanted, all Adam wanted.

He wasn't even half responsible for that happiness. Cassie and Molly had played a much bigger role, but he'd put Drew in a place where that could happen, and he was glad he'd done it.

Molly came over to the barbecue. "How's it going over here?"

"It's good. Everything is cooking."

"Your house, this view..." She swept her hand toward the lake. "It's beautiful, Adam. Do you still appreciate it? Or have you been here so long you don't notice it anymore?"

"I appreciate it every day. It never gets old. What's the longest you've lived anywhere?"

"Two years and eight months, and that was here in Whisper Lake. Only one other city made it past the two-year mark, but barely."

"I can't imagine moving so much as a child."

"I can't imagine what it was like to live in one house your entire childhood. Chelsea told me you never moved."

"No. My parents moved into the house I grew up in three months before I was born, and they're still there. I didn't leave Denver until after Gina died. I needed a change then. For the next six years, I moved around. But once Lizzie moved here and put out a tempting call to join her, I decided to make this town my home."

"Did you know right away that Whisper Lake was it for you, or did it take time?"

"I knew within a couple of weeks." He hoped she'd figure that out in even less time. "See, I can be impulsive," he teased.

"I don't think that's exactly impulsive but skinny-dipping in the lake and making love on a bear rug definitely added some cred to your ability to be spontaneous."

"I liked both. I only had one problem with the bear rug."

"What was that?"

"I kept seeing that urn in the window. I felt like Phoebe was watching us."

"We did give her something to see," Molly said with a laugh. "I know I need to put the urn somewhere permanent, but I haven't figured it out yet."

"You'll make the right decision," he said, as he flipped the steaks and checked on the chicken. "How do you like your steak?"

"Medium is fine. I'm not that picky."

He frowned. "Wait a second. Are we getting back to the low expectations? Because I want to cook you the perfect steak. Tell me exactly how you want it, and I will make it happen."

For some reason, his words seemed to bring moisture to her eyes.

"Molly? Did I say something wrong?"

"No, you said something really sweet. I'd like my steak medium rare, with a juicy pink center."

"You've got it. I won't let you down."

He wanted her to say she knew he wouldn't, but she just gave him a watery smile and moved back to the table.

He focused on the grill, because after his strong declaration, he better make sure he gave her exactly what she wanted. It was about time someone did that for her. And he wanted to be the one.

CHAPTER TWENTY-FIVE

MOLLY WAS STILL THINKING about her perfect steak the next day when she watched the clock tick slowly toward five on Wednesday afternoon. Adam had outdone himself with the meat, and she'd been touched that he'd wanted to give her exactly what she wanted. Maybe she did set too low of a bar for herself. Perhaps it was time to raise it.

She let out a sigh as she looked around the shop, which had been empty for the last hour. Her weekend rush had petered out. It had been so slow she'd sent Drew home early, and she was ready to call it a day herself. She'd gotten up early for her yoga class and while there hadn't been a lot of customers, she'd kept busy going through inventory and getting more familiar with the computer software that Drew had set up for her.

As the door opened, she was startled to see Jackie Hunt come in. Her face was drawn tight, as she stopped uncertainly in the middle of the shop.

"Hello, Jackie," she said, coming around the counter.

"I know what you're doing," Jackie said. "With all the little gifts. You think I can be bought."

"I don't think that at all. I just wanted you to know that I care about my neighbors and Phoebe's former customers."

"How did you know what she used to give me?"

"Phoebe kept notes on all her customers—what they liked, what they disliked, how she thought she could help them."

"That's how you knew all my favorite things," she muttered. "I thought you were a mind reader."

"I'm not a mind reader or a witch or a mystic or anything else along that line. I'm just someone who is trying to provide products that promote health and wellness, whether it be mental or physical. Phoebe mentioned in her notes that you suffered from insomnia."

"That was a private conversation we had. I don't like the idea of these notes. What else did she say?"

"Nothing personal. Just that she wanted to help you sleep." She paused. "You haven't been sleeping, have you?"

"No. It has been a difficult month for me, and Phoebe's death was shocking. That just made it worse." Jackie bit down on her lip. "When I heard the sirens, and I saw the ambulance pull up out front, I knew she was gone." She shook her head, her jaw tight. "I just wanted the store to disappear. It wouldn't be the same without Phoebe, and then you showed up. And I had other reasons I didn't care for you."

"Because you think my mother stole Neil away from you. He told me. I'm sorry about that, Jackie, but I'm not my mom. And I'm not Phoebe. I'm just me. And I hope we can make peace. I hope you'll let me help you."

"You already did," Jackie said, squeezing the words through her stiff lips. "I slept eight hours last night. It was the first time in a long time. Anyway, I brought you this. It just came in. I thought it might look nice on you."

She took the small satin bag out of Jackie's hand and was shocked to find a beautiful necklace inside. "This is gorgeous."

"It's made by a local artist. The colors felt like you, sunny and bright."

"Thank you, Jackie. It's beautiful."

Jackie's gaze swept the shop. "I see you've cleaned things up. That's good. I should get back to work."

She barely had a chance to mutter goodbye before Jackie was gone. She put the necklace on and looked in the mirror. The colors on the heart-shaped charm were beautiful, warm, and vibrant. They felt like love. Not that Jackie loved her. But she'd brought a peace offering, and Molly would take it.

The door opened again, and she turned around as Adam came in. The feeling of love washed over her once more. He gave a quick look around the store and then pulled her into his arms to kiss her. She was breathless when he let her go.

"What was that for?" she asked.

"I missed you last night."

"I missed you, too, but we both needed sleep."

He gave her a sexy smile. "Sleep is overrated."

"I know you think that. You told me that more than once this week."

His gaze moved toward the necklace, where her fingers were still touching the heart. "That's pretty. Fiery. Like you."

"That's what Jackie said."

"Jackie?" He raised a brow. "She was in here?"

"She gave me the necklace." Molly couldn't help but give him a smug smile. "I told you I could bring her around."

"She brought you a present?" he said in amazement. "That's unbelievable."

"It was a peace offering. She really appreciated the little gifts I've been giving her. She said that she hadn't been sleeping well, but last night she got eight hours. She was like a changed woman, Adam."

He gave her a look of admiration. "I'm impressed. You didn't kill her with kindness, you actually made her kind."

"I don't know if I'd go that far. But I think we have a chance to get along now, and I'm very happy about that. I didn't want to be in a fight with her."

"That's great, Molly. You're good at knowing what people need and then giving it to them."

"I got most of my insight into Jackie from Phoebe and also a little from Neil."

"But you still used it in the right way. That's a skill. Don't sell yourself short."

She liked that he respected her, that he kept pushing her to be proud of who she was, to state what she wanted, to not settle for less. "Thanks, Adam."

He gave her a quizzical look. "For what exactly?"

"Just…being you."

"I'll take that. What are you doing tonight?"

"I don't have any plans."

"How about we make some?"

"You and your plans," she said with a laugh. "We could just walk out the door and see what happens—which way we turn, where we walk. Who knows what we'll see, where we'll end up?"

"Sounds risky, but I like it."

"You're a cop. I can't imagine that sounded risky."

"With you, I'm never sure what's going to happen."

"Good. I like being unpredictable. I just have to lock up, and we can go." She turned toward the door, then stopped abruptly at the sight of the person peering through the window. "Oh, my God!"

Adam whirled around. "What's wrong?"

She pointed toward the window, to the woman looking right back at her.

"Who's that?" he asked.

"My mother."

"Your mother? I thought she was in New York."

"So did I," she replied as her mom walked through the door with a smile on her face.

"Surprise," her mother said with a gleeful smile. "Are you happy to see me?"

Molly was feeling a lot of things, but happy wasn't one of them.

Molly's mother, Diana Trent, swept in like a whirlwind, much like her daughter. She wore a flowy dress that seemed to catch the breeze even indoors. She was taller, thinner, and fairer than Molly, her hair a dark red, her eyes a light brown.

Adam didn't know why he was comparing them so carefully, but he was, and he liked that their eyes were different. He felt an odd need to separate the two in any way he could.

Despite Molly's startled reaction, the embrace between them was loving and warm.

When they broke apart, Diana's gaze immediately turned to him.

"Who's this?" she asked with a gleam in her eyes.

"Oh," Molly said, as if she'd just remembered he was there.

He didn't like that feeling at all.

"This is Adam Cole—Detective Cole," she added.

Diana's gaze turned to concern. "Is there a problem?"

"No," he said shortly, not sure why Molly had felt the need to throw in his title.

"Adam is here as a…friend," Molly said.

That wasn't how he would have described them, but he needed to put a pin in his growing annoyance. Molly had been taken by surprise, and if she didn't want to talk about their relationship with her mother, he needed to respect that.

"What are you doing here, Mom?" Molly asked. "What happened to New York?"

"Old news," Diana said with a wave of her hand. "I want to tell you all about it. I also have a fabulous opportunity to discuss with you. Why don't I take you and your friend out for a drink and some dinner? I know it's only five but I'm starving with all the time changes I've been through."

"Uh, I guess," Molly said, giving him a questioning look. "Do you want to have a drink and dinner with us?"

He would have preferred a more enthusiastic question, but there was no way he was leaving now. He wanted to get to know Diana. And maybe he wanted Diana to know that he was more than her daughter's friend. "That sounds good. We were just going to wander around town and do that anyway."

"Great. Just one second." Diana stepped back out the door, then dragged in two large suitcases and a tote bag. "I hope you don't mind if I stay with you, Molly. But if you do, if that gets in the way of your life…your friendships," she added with a sly smile, "I can go to a hotel."

Molly frowned. "How long are you staying?"

"Oh, goodness," Diana said with a laugh. "You know I hate to answer that question. Let's start with tonight. Can I put these somewhere?"

"I'm in the apartment upstairs."

"I'll just take these bags up."

"I can do that for you," he offered. He grabbed the largest suitcase and the tote bag while Molly took the smaller bag. Then they headed up the stairs. It wasn't lost on him that Diana made the trip with nothing but her small purse in hand. He had the feeling she was a woman who always had others carry her bags for her.

When they reached the apartment, Diana's gaze perused the crowded room. "Good grief, what's all this stuff? Was Phoebe a hoarder?"

"No. But she inherited a bunch of stuff from a friend right as she passed away, and I've been going through it," Molly said. "There's only one bedroom, but there's a pullout couch. You can take the bed tonight. I'll sleep out here."

"You're always so generous," Diana said. "I'm just going to freshen up, and then we'll go."

As Diana moved past him, he was hit with another heady

spray of her floral perfume. It was a bit much, but then she was a bit much.

"So, that's my mom," Molly said quietly as Diana disappeared into the bathroom. "You don't have to go out with us if you don't want to."

"I want to, unless you'd rather I didn't."

"She's going to ask you a lot of questions."

"I don't have anything to hide. Do you? Do you care if she knows we're together?" he challenged.

"No, of course not."

"Really? Because you seem a bit off."

"Well, that's generally what happens when my mother shows up." Molly squared her shoulders. "But it's fine. We'll have drinks and dinner together. If nothing else, you won't be bored, because my mother is very entertaining."

Molly was right. Her mother was entertaining. Diana had story after story to tell, and she knew just how to tell them, punctuating the high points with pauses of anticipation. And as they drank wine and ate pasta at the Lakeshore Bistro, those stories got even better, especially when she decided to tell him about Molly.

"Mom, Adam doesn't want to hear about my childhood," Molly protested.

"Not even the T-ball story?" Diana asked with a laugh. "Where you hit the ball and ran the wrong way all around the bases?"

"Ouch," he said. "That must have been embarrassing."

"I was six, so it wasn't that big of a deal. Besides, we moved three weeks after that, so it's not like I saw anyone again. And you told me it was great that I had changed the game, made my own rules," she reminded her mother.

"That does sound like me. It is better to change the game and make your own rules. Who wants to be ordinary when extraordinary could be just around the corner?"

He was beginning to see why Molly had gotten swept up in her mother's infectious, enthusiastic dreams. Diana Trent had a lot of charisma and was very persuasive.

"Now, what shall we get for dessert?" Diana asked.

"I'm good," he replied.

"Oh, don't be silly. Who can turn down a bite of something sweet? You'll share something, won't you?"

"Mom, leave him alone. Adam, you don't have to have dessert."

"It's fine. I'll have a bite of whatever you get."

"They have crème brûlée," Diana said, consulting the menu. "Or what about a flourless chocolate cake? You know what, let's get both." She waved her hand, and the server came over to take their order.

He added in a coffee, while both Molly and her mother ordered tea.

"So, there is something I want to talk to you about, Molly," her mother said.

"What's that?" Molly asked with trepidation.

"A fabulous opportunity." Her eyes lit up with excitement. "I've been offered a job in Paris. They want me to choreograph a Broadway show."

"That's amazing, Mom," Molly said.

"Very impressive," he added.

"It's been my dream for a very long time," Diana said. "The director is a fan of mine from years ago. I first met him when he was just a bit player in an off-Broadway show. Now he's moved to Paris, and as part of my contract, he's going to lease me a two-bedroom luxury apartment with a rooftop deck and a view of the Seine. I want you to come with me, Molly."

His gut clenched at her words. He immediately looked to Molly for a strong reaction, an immediate refusal.

"I just moved here, Mom," she said.

He frowned. That reaction was just a sidestep, and it worried him.

"Yes, but this is a rent-free luxury apartment in Paris, Molly," Diana continued. "How many times did we dream about going to Paris, walking along the Seine, going to the Louvre, drinking wine, and eating incredible food? It's only for a year. You can come back after that, if you want."

"I have a business. I can't just leave it."

"The store is up and running now. Hire a manager. I'm sure there's someone here in town who would want to run the shop. You can check in by phone. But this is Paris. This is our dream."

His tension increased with the uncertainty in Molly's eyes.

Would she really drop everything and just go to Paris because her mom wanted to do that?

He had a terrible feeling the answer might be yes.

"I don't know, Mom. I need to think, and I need to use the restroom," Molly said, getting to her feet. "I'll be back."

Diana gave him an optimistic smile when they were left alone at the table. "Molly always needs a minute when I throw things at her, but then she jumps right in. She's as adventurous as I am."

"She's mentioned that." He was disappointed that Molly even needed one minute to think about her mom's offer.

"You're unhappy that I'm asking her to leave Whisper Lake."

"It's her decision, her life. She should do what she wants to do."

"But you want her to stay."

He hesitated, then said, "Yes, I want her to stay."

Diana let out a little sigh. "You seem like a very nice man, and I can tell Molly likes you, Adam, but I don't want to see her get trapped in this small town. I want her to live up to her potential. I want her to see the world. I want her to have experiences she'll remember her entire life."

"Like I said, it's her call, but Whisper Lake has a lot to offer."

"It's not Paris."

"No, it's not. But it's a great town with wonderful people, and Molly has her own business, something she seems to love."

"And does she love you?"

He sucked in a breath at her direct question. "You'll have to ask her that."

"Love is a risk," Diana said. "It took me down a bad path a long time ago. I stayed away from it after that."

He'd stayed away from it for a long time, too. But he didn't want to do that anymore. He didn't want to be safe. He wanted to risk it all. *But was he going to risk it all on a woman who might wake up tomorrow and decide to go to Paris?*

Molly returned to the table at the same time as their desserts and she immediately changed the subject, asking about some of her mother's friends, which sent her mom into another humorous tale.

He could barely listen to the stories now. His stomach was churning. He'd known all along that Molly was impulsive and liked change, but he wouldn't have thought this kind of decision would be happening this soon. Maybe she wouldn't go. Maybe he should tell her not to go.

But how could he tell her that?

He was relieved when the meal ended. But as he drove Molly and her mom back to the apartment, he worried that the way her mother talked, Molly might be gone by the morning. Unfortunately, there was nothing he could say except goodnight.

He just wished Molly had something more to say, but she simply gave him a distracted smile and said she'd talk to him tomorrow. He hoped that conversation would go the way he wanted it to go, but he wasn't at all certain of that.

CHAPTER TWENTY-SIX

"So, what do you think?" her mother asked as they sat on the couch late Wednesday night.

"You're completely crazy."

Her mom laughed. "What else is new? You've always thought that. But we've had a lot of incredible experiences, haven't we?"

"Yes."

"Paris was always our dream."

She couldn't deny that. She'd always wanted to go to Paris, but she didn't know that she wanted to go now, or that she wanted to go for a year. "I have a lot going on here, Mom. I'm running the store, and I can't just turn it over to someone else before it really gets going."

"But it's Paris, Molly."

"Stop saying that. It's an incredible opportunity for you, but I wouldn't have a job there."

"You'd find something. You always do. You could teach yoga. I'll be making enough money for both of us, and we'll have a beautiful and free apartment to stay in."

"Why would he give you an apartment? Are you involved with this man, Mom?"

"We had a fling once, but we're not together now. He has

come into good fortune and wants to share it with me. It's as simple as that."

"Nothing is ever that simple. Maybe he wants to restart your relationship."

Her mother waved that idea away. "I don't think so, but even if he did, I'd say no."

"Even with the apartment on the line?"

"It's not a quid pro quo arrangement, Molly."

"It just seems too good to be true, Mom."

"You always say that, but you're not often right."

"Just some of the time." She let out a sigh. "Why are you really here, Mom?"

"You know why…I just told you. I want you to come with me."

"Because it's Paris, or because you want to get me out of Whisper Lake, and now you have an incredible offer to lure me away? I know you didn't want me to come here."

"The offer just came up. And I didn't want you to come here, because going back is never a good idea."

"Was it that? Or were you trying to keep me away from Neil? You didn't want me to find out that you broke up with him, did you?"

Her mother's eyes lost a little of their sparkle. "You spoke to him."

"Yes. He told me that he asked you to marry him, and that you said no, which seems odd, because that's the opposite of what you told me. You said you wanted to marry him, but he didn't want you. He told you that the two of you had no future and that he didn't want to be a stepfather."

"I don't need a recap, Molly."

She ignored that comment. "You were devastated. We had to leave immediately. You couldn't risk seeing him again. Your heart was broken."

"My heart *was* broken. I cared about Neil."

"You cared about him, but you didn't love him."

"I wanted to," her mother said quietly. "I really did. I thought I could be the woman he wanted. I even tried to be that woman, but I just couldn't be her. I couldn't settle down and live here forever. I didn't want to have more kids. I wanted to travel and see the world, and Neil didn't want any of that."

"Why didn't you just tell me that?"

"Because you were more in love with him than I was. You wanted him to be your stepfather."

"You hurt me when you told me that he'd turned his back on both of us."

A guilty expression flashed through her mother's eyes. "I didn't mean to say that. I was just desperate to convince you to go with me."

"Convince me? I was seventeen; I had no choice. But you should have told me the truth."

"I know. You're right."

"And you should have told me that you stole Neil away from Jackie Hunt."

"I did not do that," her mother said, coming to life once more with a new fight in her eyes. "Neil was not interested in Jackie. He wanted me. You can ask him that if you don't believe me."

"Neil said he knew it was over with Jackie, but he didn't break it off until after he met you. It would have been nice to have that information, because Jackie owns the shop next door and has been a bitch to me since I arrived."

"She was a bitch to me, too. Don't let her get to you. She's just a petty person."

"Actually, she's more than that. I've gotten to know her a little, and Phoebe left some notes about her background. Neil also told me she lost a child and then her husband left her. Did you know that?"

"I heard something about it. But I didn't break Jackie and Neil up." Her mom paused. "Did they get together after I left?"

"No. Or if they did, they're not together now."

"Then they weren't meant to be. Things happen for a reason, Molly."

She let out a sigh. "I need to go to bed."

"Really? I thought we could get in our PJs and watch some old movie together."

"I can't have a slumber party with you, Mom. I have to work in the morning."

Her mother gave her a disappointed look. "This is what I worry about, Molly—you getting stuck in a life that will hold you back. I know this is a cute town with lovely people, and it's fun for a while, but it's too small. There isn't enough here for you. Do you just want to run a little shop for the rest of your life? Do you want to see the same people day after day, the same mountains, the same lake?"

"Maybe I do. Staying somewhere would actually be the most different thing I could do."

"You'll get bored. It might not happen right away. But one day you'll wake up and wonder where your life has gone."

"How do you know that would happen? You never stayed anywhere. You never woke up one day and wondered where your life went."

"I have friends who married their high school boyfriends, others who moved to the suburbs or a small town like this one, thinking they were going to live some fairy-tale holiday movie. And maybe it's good for some people. But why would you want to settle when there is so much out there for you to experience? You're young. You're single. You're free." Her mother gave her a sharp look. "Or perhaps you're not as free as I think. Are you falling for Adam?"

She slowly nodded. "Yes."

Her mother sighed. "Well, he's handsome and hot, so I can't blame you. Does he want more than to be a small-town cop? Does he ever want to live in a bigger city?"

"I think he's happy to be here. I might be happy to be here, too." She wished she could be more definitive, but her mom had swirled up some of her doubts.

"You shouldn't stay because of a man."

"And I shouldn't leave because my mom wants me to be her wingman."

"I want you to be happy."

"What if being happy means I stay here?"

"I would hope for the best," her mom replied. "But I can't help reminding you that it's not Paris."

She groaned as her mother repeated the phrase she'd been saying all evening.

"Whisper Lake isn't going anywhere," her mom said. "Neither is Adam. But you could at least take a couple of months and have an experience you'll never forget. Just think about it, okay? Promise me you'll do that."

"Fine. I promise." She got to her feet. "And now, I'm going to bed. Do you need anything else?"

"I'm okay, but could we throw a towel or something over the urn?" her mom asked. "Phoebe never liked me that much, and I feel like she's staring at me with annoyance. She wouldn't be happy I'm trying to get you out of Whisper Lake."

"She probably wouldn't." She moved into the kitchen, grabbed a dish towel, and dropped it over the urn.

"Thank you," her mom said. "Sleep well, Molly."

"You, too, Mom."

"I love you, sweet girl."

"I love you, too."

It was the goodnight they'd shared for so many years but tonight it brought mixed feelings. She was happy to see her mom, but she'd known there was going to be trouble since her mother had first walked through the door, and she'd been right.

"I just made the biggest sale of the day," Diana told Molly on Thursday morning. "That woman I just waited on spent $422."

"That's impressive, Mom," she said, as she finished stocking one of the shelves with vitamins. Her mother seemed to have embraced her role as super saleswoman, much the way she attacked any part she had to play.

"I'm very good at moving merchandise."

"Yes. You are very talented at telling people what they want, even if they don't know they want it. Thanks for helping out today."

"It has actually been fun. Not that I'd want to do it forever." She lowered her voice. "And, honestly, honey, I can't imagine that you would, either. You're doing a good job, and clearly you've already made some friends here, but it's just a little store in a little town."

She let out a sigh. "Don't do that, Mom. Don't belittle the store or the town or the people."

"I didn't mean it that way. It's a beautiful town and you've made this store far nicer than I remember. It's very organized, too." She tipped her head toward Drew. "That young man is very sharp. He showed me the website he's building for you. And he mentioned that he set up the software system."

"Yes. Drew has been amazing."

"He might make a great manager."

"He's nineteen, and he's going back to college in a few months."

"Oh, well, maybe someone else then."

"I haven't decided anything."

"I know. I know. What are you doing for lunch?" her mom asked.

"I have to run some errands."

"I can do that with you."

"It will require a lot of boring standing in line at the post office. Why don't you go out, walk around? Chloe runs the Blue Sky Café. It has a great menu. It's on Silver Street."

"Are you sure you won't go with me?"

"I'm sure." She needed a little time away from her mom.

"All right. I'll see you later." Her mother grabbed her bag and headed out the door.

Molly took the empty box into the storeroom to be torn down and placed it in the recycle bin. Then she went back into the store and told Drew she'd be out for a while.

He gave her a nod. "No problem. Take as long as you need."

As she walked outside, a warm breeze lifted her hair, and she felt better than she had since she'd gotten up that morning. She hoped late summer would last for a while longer. She was really enjoying the weather.

Her enjoyment fled as she neared the park and saw the Jeep coming in the opposite direction. It was Adam. He parked, then got out and came toward her.

"I was just coming to your store," he said. "Where are you going?"

"Post office. I have a package to pick up."

"Where's your mom?"

"I sent her to Chloe's café."

"She's still in town?"

"Yes. I'm not sure how long she'll be here."

"Probably until she persuades you to go to Paris with her."

His dark-blue gaze settled on hers, and she could see a mix of emotions in his eyes. "I'm sure that's part of her strategy." She blew out a breath. "Are you angry, Adam?"

He gave her a long look. "Should I be?"

"I don't know. My mother dropped a bomb at dinner last night, and I'm sure you have an opinion."

"Do you want my opinion?"

She really wasn't sure. "I—yes. I would like your opinion."

He shook his head. "That wasn't at all convincing, Molly. Why don't you tell me what your opinion is? Your mother sold Paris hard."

"She does everything with full force."

"You're like her in that way. Whatever you're doing, you put all your energy into it." He paused. "You're just getting started, Molly. Your business is doing well, but it can grow a lot more. You already have good friends, but you have many more to meet. You could have a life here. I know you think roots can hold you back, but you've been flying your entire life. Maybe your new adventure is to stay somewhere, build something that will last."

"I'm not sure I can do it," she murmured.

"Maybe you won't know until you try."

"What if I try and I fail, and Paris is long gone?"

"You'll get there another way. There's always another way. Except for death, the chance of starting over is always there." His lips tightened. "But I can see why you have a hard time turning down your mother. She is very persuasive. I almost wanted to go to Paris with her."

She gave him a small smile. "She always makes the new adventure sound great, and most of the time it is. Even when it's not, like the time we moved to Florida, and the apartment we rented didn't exist. We ended up sleeping in a hostel, but then we met these two musicians. They were traveling to Nashville. We ended up going along and my mom got a job in their music video. It all worked out. She always makes things work out."

"How old were you then?"

"Ten or eleven. I can't remember."

"Do you think you missed out on anything because you traveled all the time?"

"Yes. I know my mom didn't do the best job raising me. I had no bedtime. I was around a lot of people who drank and smoked and did God knows what. But she loved me, and I loved her. We had fun. We were there for each other."

"Are you sure you weren't the one who was always there for her?"

She frowned. "You always ask the difficult questions."

"I just think she shortchanged you."

"I was there for her more than she was there for me," she admitted.

"And this trip to Paris. Is it really for you? Or does she just need you to be there for her? Or is there something else behind it?"

"I think she's afraid that I'll want to stay in Whisper Lake, and that I'll never take another trip with her. She doesn't want to lose me."

"You each need to have your own lives. And you like it here, don't you? I thought you said that having your own business was a dream of yours."

"Paris was a dream, too." She didn't know why she was arguing. She didn't disagree with him. But they were talking about more than Paris, about more than Whisper Lake. They were talking about their relationship; they were both too afraid to admit it. "I need to think about it all."

His expression filled with disappointment. "Well, if you need to think about it, you've probably already decided."

"That's not true, and I don't like the pressure of having to come up with a decision on your timetable."

"And I don't like having a relationship with someone who can't commit."

"We're not having a relationship. We're just having fun. Remember?"

"Well, it's not fun anymore," he said grimly. "Let me know what you decide. Or maybe I'll just find out one day when I walk by the store, and it's closed, or there's a new manager behind the counter. And what about Drew? He might need to know he's going to be out of a job. Do you want me to tell him?"

"No. Stop it, Adam. You're moving too fast."

"I'm not the one who moves too fast; that's you, Molly. You blew into my life like a whirlwind, and I've always known that you'd probably leave the same way. I have to go."

He was gone before she could say a word.

That conversation hadn't gone well. She wanted to blame it all on Adam, but she was at fault, too.

She hated that she even had a decision to make. She knew that whatever she decided, she'd hurt someone, maybe even herself.

CHAPTER TWENTY-SEVEN

THE REST of Thursday and most of Friday passed in a blur of anger and disappointment and a lot of other emotions Adam didn't want to deal with. He hadn't seen Molly because he didn't want to see her. He needed to get used to not seeing her, because she was probably leaving. But he couldn't completely put her out of his mind. Not just because of their relationship, whatever the hell that was, but because he was still working on finding a connection between Mercer and Caroline's family.

He finally got a break late Friday afternoon when he found a link between Ethan Mercer and Erica Kenny, Ray Kenny's wife. They'd worked together in a Denver bar five years ago, shortly before Erica and Ray had moved back to Whisper Lake. Ray Kenney was Caroline's stepbrother, who had seemed happy with his inheritance, but maybe that was a lie. Or maybe it was his wife who wasn't happy.

He spent the next hour digging into Erica, who had been completely off his radar until now, and another piece of the puzzle fell into place. Erica had a sister—Brenda Dunn, the cleaning woman, who had neglected to mention that she had any connection to anyone in Caroline's extended family.

The picture grew clearer in his head. Brenda had worked in

the house. She had found out about the diamond. Maybe Rebecca was in on it, too, and that's why she'd disappeared. He still hadn't been able to find Rebecca, but Brenda lived only a few miles away, and Ray and Erica were just on the other side of the lake.

Grabbing his keys, he headed to his car. He needed to find a way into the group, and he had a feeling Brenda was the weakest link. If he could convince her that the first person who talked would get off easier, he might be able to get her to open up.

Brenda lived in a small house not too far from downtown. He knocked on her door. It opened just a few inches, the chain still on. A middle-aged woman gave him a wary look.

"Brenda Dunn? I'm Detective Cole. We spoke on the phone last week."

"I don't have anything else to say."

"I do. Open the door," he ordered.

"I don't have to do that."

"Yes, you do, Brenda. You're in a lot of trouble. We need to talk." He put his hand on the gun at his hip as she took off the chain and opened the door. "Are you alone?" he asked.

She nodded. "Yes. What's this about?"

"Step outside."

She moved onto the porch. "Are you arresting me?"

"Should I?"

She gave him a terrified look. "It wasn't my idea. I didn't know that anyone was going to steal the diamond. I just told them about it."

"Told who?" he asked. "Your sister, Erica? Her husband, Ray?"

"How did you know?"

"Your sister worked with Ethan Mercer in Denver, and he broke into the wellness store three times, looking for Caroline's diamond. You knew about the diamond, because you were in the house." He let that sink in, then added, "Someone is going to talk first, Brenda. If I were you, I'd be the first one to speak, because that person always gets a lighter sentence."

"I didn't hire Ethan. I told Erica not to do it." Brenda twisted her fingers together. "I never should have said anything about the diamond."

"How did you know about it?"

"I heard Caroline talking to Phoebe. I peeked into the room when I wasn't supposed to, and she had the biggest diamond ring I'd ever seen in her hand. She said she was going to give it to Phoebe. That there was no way Charles was going to have it. She'd made sure of that. Phoebe asked her how. And she said Rebecca had put a fake diamond in the safe for her."

Another piece of the puzzle fell into place. "Did Caroline hand the ring over to Phoebe?"

"I don't know. Rebecca was coming down the hall, and I didn't want her to see me, so I ran into the next room."

"Then you told Erica about the diamond?"

"Not until after Caroline died. She was talking about Ray's inheritance and how she thought he should have gotten more because Caroline was a rich bitch, and I agreed. I said I heard she was giving this huge diamond to Phoebe."

"And that started the plan in motion," he said. "Your sister hired Mercer, didn't she?"

"Yes," Brenda admitted. "After Caroline died and the boxes all got sent to Phoebe, she told him to find the diamond."

"Was Phoebe alive when he got to the store?"

Brenda nodded. "He didn't expect her to be there. He pulled his gun on her, and he said she gasped and put a hand to her chest and then she just passed out. He saw some people walking down the street, and he was afraid they were going to think he killed her, so he left."

"And he almost killed a little girl as he sped away," he said grimly.

"I don't know about that. He tried again to get into the store, but the alarm went off."

"He went back two more times, but he kept running into the new owner."

"Yes. He said he was done a couple of days ago, but Erica kept pushing him to try one last time. She told him she'd give him a bigger cut."

His pulse leapt. "He's going to try again?"

"I think so. I told Erica to make him stop. I don't want anyone else to get hurt."

He didn't know if he believed her concerned attitude for even one second, but he had more pressing concerns. He called for backup, then cuffed Brenda.

"I thought you weren't going to arrest me," she said, tearing up. "I'm just a cleaning lady. I don't have much. My only mistake was to tell my sister about the diamond."

"You can tell that to your lawyer," he said harshly. "When is Mercer going to try again?"

"Soon. They know you're asking a lot of questions, and they're getting desperate."

"How much does Ray know?"

"He doesn't know anything. Erica and Mercer have been having an affair for years. She wants the diamond ring so they can start a new life."

"And what's your cut?"

"Ten percent of whatever they sell it for. She said it would probably be close to fifty thousand dollars. I've never had that much money in my life."

"You took ten percent and gave your sister ninety percent?"

"She and Ethan have to split it. She said they're taking more of a risk than I am."

"And yet you're the one in cuffs," he said, as Brodie arrived in his squad car. He explained the situation to Brodie and asked him to take her down to the station. Then he got into his car and headed to Molly's. If Ethan Mercer was going to try again, he needed to get her out of there.

Molly paced around her apartment Friday evening, feeling restless and unsettled. Work had kept her mind off Adam, her mother, and big decisions. But now she wasn't at work, and she didn't know what to do with herself. As her gaze moved to the urn, she said, "Well, Phoebe? Got any ideas for me?"

As soon as she'd asked the question, she realized what she needed to do. She needed to think about Phoebe, about where her final resting place should be. Her gaze moved to the three photo albums that Caroline had put together for her best friend. She'd only ever looked through the first one. Maybe there was a clue in one of the albums. Caroline had known Phoebe better than anyone.

She grabbed all three books and took them to the coffee table. She sat down on the couch, looking at the titles scrawled across the first page of each book: *This Was Us* on the first book. *This Is Us* on the second book. And *This Could Have Been Us* on the third book.

The first album had taken Phoebe and Caroline to age sixteen. The second album began when the women were in their twenties. They were getting out of a limo at what appeared to be a movie premiere. Caroline was on the red carpet talking to interviewers while Phoebe waited in the background. There were also photos of Caroline alone or with one of her husbands. She was pictured all over the world: in front of the Taj Mahal, riding an elephant in Africa, drinking champagne in front of the Eiffel Tower.

Then the album turned to Phoebe: There was a ribbon cutting in front of her store, and this time it was Caroline in the background. Other shots caught Phoebe singing at Micky's Bar and Grill during karaoke night, dressing up like a witch on Halloween, reading a book at the lake, and then surrounded by a troop of Girl Scouts at a jamboree. Phoebe and Caroline had gone in different directions in their lives, that was clear.

The third album intrigued her with the title. What had Caroline meant when she said *this could have been us?*

As she turned the pages, her pulse began to race. There were only four photos, one on each page with a caption written beneath.

The first photo was a strip of pictures taken at a photo booth. They were in their forties, but they were making faces like kids. The caption said: *Life was funnier when we were together.*

The second photo was taken at the wedding of Caroline and Charles Weatherly. Phoebe was standing right behind Caroline. She appeared to be her maid of honor. The caption said: *I was always running away. I wish you would have stopped me.*

Her heart pounded against her chest, as a thought crept into her head.

The third photo showed Phoebe and Caroline standing on the edge of a bluff overlooking the lake and the mountains, their arms thrown wide as if they could fly off that mountaintop. They were probably in their late teens. In fact, it might have been just before Caroline had moved away. The picture was captioned: *You told me to be brave that day. I said I would be, but I wasn't. I didn't tell you how I felt. I couldn't admit it then or for a lifetime. I often wish I could go back to our mountain of dreams and have the courage to speak.*

She suddenly knew where this was going, and the fourth photo confirmed it.

The two women were at a baptism, and this caption was even longer: *We both could have had children. I was too afraid of what people would think. I was too afraid of what I thought. But like I told you when you came to see me yesterday, you were always in my heart, even if we weren't together. It's too late now, but I want you to have something special. Please don't send it back, Phoebe. I gave every other part of me away. But the diamond, the symbol of love, should be with you. I bought it with my money, and while I thought about giving it to Charles, because I was still pretending I loved him, I couldn't do it. He wasn't the one. The diamond was always meant for you. With all my love, Caroline.*

Emotion put tears in Molly's eyes as the truth rang through her. Caroline had been in love with Phoebe. And it sounded like Phoebe had been in love with Caroline. But they'd lived their lives apart.

And the diamond… Caroline had given Phoebe the diamond.

Someone must have read the note that Caroline left in the album. Or they just knew that's where the diamond had gone.

But where the hell was it?

It definitely wasn't in the boxes. But Caroline had said she was sending it to Phoebe. It might have come separately before Phoebe died.

She desperately hoped that was the case because Phoebe had probably never seen this album. She'd never read these words. She took some small comfort in the fact that Caroline had said she'd talked to Phoebe and told her some of it, at least.

Getting up, she paced around the room, wondering where the diamond could be. And then her gaze lit on the plastic bag that had come along with the urn. She moved across the room to take another look in it.

The dress and shoes Phoebe had been wearing when she died were in the bag as well as a bra and underwear, Phoebe's watch, and a necklace with a small gold heart. She pulled out the items, her heart breaking as she smelled Phoebe's perfume. As she laid the dress over the back of the chair, something fell out of a pocket. Her jaw dropped in shock at the stunning square-cut diamond ring.

Phoebe had not only seen the ring, she'd gotten it. She'd known that Caroline loved her.

It was sad to think they were now both dead.

Her door suddenly burst open, and she whirled around in surprise.

Her mother was pushed into the room by a man standing behind her, a man with a gun—Ethan Mercer.

"I'm sorry," her mother babbled. "He said he was your friend."

The man shoved her mother toward the wall, as he pointed the gun at Molly. "I knew you had it. Hand it over."

She swallowed hard. *How could she give the ring away? It was meant for Phoebe.*

But Phoebe was dead, and if she didn't do what he asked, she might end up in the same condition.

"Diamond or her," the man said, pointing his gun toward her mother. "Don't believe me?"

"No. I believe you," she said quickly. "Don't hurt her. You can have the diamond, but first, tell me who you're working for. Is it Charles Weatherly?"

"What do you care?"

She licked her lips. "I want to know who's getting this ring."

"Someone who deserves it." He put out his hand. "Give it to me."

As he spoke, she thought she saw a shadow behind him. Impulsively and probably stupidly, she tossed the ring in the air. As Ethan reached up to grab it, Adam barreled through the door and slammed into him, knocking him to the floor. Her mom let out a scream as the gun skidded across the floor.

As Adam fought with Mercer, she scrambled to get the gun. But once she had it in her hands, she didn't know what to do with it. She couldn't shoot and risk hurting Adam, so she just kept it at the ready.

There was no trace of Adam's injury as he fought to subdue Mercer, and his anger was palpable as he swung his fist into Mercer's face. Mercer hit back but as Adam sidestepped, Mercer lost his balance. Adam took advantage of that to tackle him once more, finally knocking the wind out of him. Then he rolled Mercer onto his stomach and cuffed his hands behind his back.

She blew out a breath of relief, as Adam got to his feet. "Your face," she said. "He hurt you."

"I'm fine. What about you, Molly?" he asked with deep concern. "Did he touch you?"

"No. How did you know he was here?"

"I didn't know. I was just coming to warn you that he might try again. But when I saw the open door and heard his voice, I knew I was a little late."

"You were just in time."

He walked over to her and held out his hand. "Give me the gun, Molly."

She hadn't even realized she was still holding it. She handed it to him and then looked toward her mother. "Did he hurt you, Mom?"

"No," her mother said, her face pale, her eyes still terrified. "He said he was your friend, Molly. I didn't know until I let him in that he had a gun." Her mother picked up the diamond ring that had fallen onto the floor. "Where did you get this?"

"It was given to Phoebe by her friend Caroline." She looked at Adam. "I finally went through the albums. Caroline was in love with Phoebe. She just couldn't acknowledge it. I think Phoebe loved her, too."

"Caroline and Phoebe?" he murmured in surprise. "But Caroline was married three times."

"I guess she couldn't find happiness when she was living a lie."

"Where did you find the ring?"

"In the pocket of Phoebe's dress that she was wearing when she went to the hospital. The hospital gave the bag of clothes to the lawyer, who gave it to me last Monday with the urn. I never looked in the bag until tonight." She paused, her gaze moving to Mercer, who lay stunned on the floor. "Who is he working for? Do you know?"

"It was Erica, Ray Kenney's wife."

Her eyes widened in surprise. "They're the ones behind this? I thought you were going to say Charles Weatherly."

"No. Erica and Mercer are having an affair. It started when

they worked together in Denver. They heard about the diamond from Brenda Dunn, who is Erica's sister. Brenda cleaned Caroline's house once a week and found out about the diamond. She knew Caroline had given it to Phoebe."

"But Ray got twenty-five thousand dollars."

"In Erica's mind, that wasn't enough.

"That's crazy," she muttered.

"I'll tell you all the details later, but I need to take care of him." Adam called dispatch to request a squad car.

While Adam was on the phone, her mother came over to her and gave her a hug.

"I was scared for you, Molly," her mom said, fear still lingering in her eyes. "Why did you even hesitate for one second to give him that ring?"

"It seemed wrong. I knew how much Caroline wanted Phoebe to have it. But I also knew I had no choice. I was just afraid he was going to shoot us after I gave him the ring."

"You threw it really high in the air. Now I know why they didn't play you in softball."

She laughed. "I did that on purpose, Mom."

"You saw me outside, didn't you?" Adam asked, as he rejoined them.

"I saw a shadow, but I didn't see your face. I was just trying to knock him off-balance in some way."

Adam met her gaze. "You are very good at knocking people off-balance."

She gave him a weak smile. "And you are very good at rescuing people."

"Why don't you take your mom in the bedroom while I deal with him?"

"Okay."

She led her mom into the other room as the police and EMTs arrived. They sat down on her bed. "That was a little too close," she murmured.

"It wouldn't have been close if I hadn't let him in," her mom said with regret.

"You didn't know, Mom. And it's fine. It all worked out."

Her mom gave her a tired and somewhat sad smile. "You used to hate it when I said that."

"I know. You always tried to make bad things good, and sometimes it annoyed me. But I guess I take after you."

"I wanted you to take after me. In some ways, I felt like you were my little sister. I was so young when you were born, and I was so scared, trying to be a mother. I didn't know what the heck I was doing. But as you got older, and we became best friends, as well as sisters, and mother and daughter, I thought we were two peas in a pod. I guess I've had a hard time letting you go the last couple of years. I know you're an adult now. You have your own life to live. I just want to be there for it."

"You can be, Mom."

Her mother gave her a long look. "But not in Paris."

She shook her head. "No. Not in Paris. Not now. But I wouldn't mind coming to visit for a few weeks."

"Of course. I would love to see you." She paused. "And maybe you'll bring Adam."

"I don't know what's going to happen with Adam. We had a fight the other day."

"I caused that."

"Yes," she said honestly. "The thing is, Mom, when you show up and pitch me some great idea, I have a difficult time saying no. You always make things seem so great, and I hate the idea of missing out. For a minute there, I actually thought about going to Paris. It was a dream we both had, but I had another dream, one you didn't share."

"To stay here. I know I ripped this town away from you, once. I had no right to do it again. I guess I've always been a little afraid of Whisper Lake. When you wanted to stay here before, I panicked. I was scared our adventures would be over. And when

Phoebe called you back from the grave and gave you her whole life, I was terrified that this time it would be the end."

"It's not the end, Mom. It's just a new chapter. You should go to Paris and have that dream. But I'm going to stay here and build my business and make friendships that will last more than two years."

"And you want to see where it will go with Adam."

"I'm not sure if it will go anywhere. He doesn't trust that I won't suddenly leave. He lost someone he loved when he was much younger. She died very suddenly, tragically, and even though this is completely different, I don't think he can handle the uncertainty of losing someone he might love, even if it's just to another job or another city."

"Well, you need to convince him that he's wrong."

"I don't think that will be easy."

Her mother gave her a knowing smile. "I suspect it won't be as difficult as you think. The man is in love with you. You just need to be persuasive."

"I'm not as good at that as you are."

"Then it's time to step up and do better. If I can't have you in Paris, then I want you to be happy here. I know I didn't always do right by you when you were young."

"You did fine. We had some great adventures, and we'll have more in the future. I want you to be happy, too. Be sure to send me a lot of pictures from Paris."

"Every day." Her mother paused as Adam came into the room. "Is it all clear?" she asked.

"Yes. Mercer is on his way to the medical center and then to jail," Adam said. "Brenda is already at the station. Erica and Ray Kenney will be taken into custody as well. It's over."

"Did Ethan confront Phoebe?" she asked. "The day she died?"

"Brenda told me that Ethan said he was surprised Phoebe was there. He pulled out a gun and she gasped and clutched her chest and that was it. I think she died instantly. There were people coming down the sidewalk in front of the store. He was afraid someone would look in and see him standing over her, so he ran."

"And he almost killed you and that little girl."

"He was the one driving the car, yes. Brenda told me that Mercer got frustrated when he couldn't find the diamond and kept running into you, but Erica forced him to try one last time. When I heard that I came straight here."

Her mother stood up. "I'm going to make tea and then start packing. I'll let you two talk."

As her mother left, she got to her feet. Adam came closer, but not as close as she wanted him, leaving a few feet between them, which seemed like miles of uncertainty.

Her mom was right. She needed to fight for what she wanted, but she had to start with a thank-you.

"You saved my life, my mom's life, too," she said. "I'm very grateful, Adam."

"I don't want your gratitude, Molly. I want more than that. I don't like the way things ended between us." He paused. "But maybe I'm too late. Your mom wants to start packing."

"Yes, she does."

"Well, you need to know something, Molly. And late or not, I'm going to say it."

A knot grew in her throat at the look in his eyes. "What do I need to know?"

"I'm in love with you." His words came out in a rush. "But that's not all. I love you, too. I don't want there to be any confusion."

Tears filled her eyes as she remembered her silly comment about not knowing the difference between falling in love and loving someone.

"I know it's fast," he added. "But you like fast."

She smiled at the hopeful gleam in his eyes. "I do like fast. And I'm not falling in love with you, Adam; I'm already there. I'm also not going to Paris. My mother is packing for herself. I want to stay in Whisper Lake."

"Are you sure?"

"Yes. I want to see what might happen with us, if you're willing to take a chance on me. Are you?" With his history, she could understand his fear of losing someone he loved.

"I am. I don't know what the hell I was fighting so hard against, Molly. I know life and love don't come with guarantees. I didn't have the right to pressure you into trying to give me one, especially since we've only known each other a few weeks. I panicked when I thought you might go. I wasn't ready. I wanted more time with you. It was killing me to think I might not have it."

"I'm sorry that I didn't say no to my mom right away, that I didn't reassure you. Honestly, saying yes to my mother is an old and bad habit."

"She made it sound amazing."

"She did, but I didn't want to go with her."

"Not even to Paris?"

She smiled as he mimicked the way her mom kept saying Paris. "Nope. Although, I wouldn't mind going on vacation there, but not to live. I want to make a home. I don't know why I've been fighting so hard against that, either. I have always wanted a real home with roots and ties to a community, to friends. I told myself not to want any of that, because I didn't think I could ever really have it. I didn't want to be disappointed. The only way I got through the ups and downs of my childhood was not to want anything to last so that it wouldn't hurt so much when it didn't. I'm going to have to work hard not to think that way."

"I completely understand. Here's something else you should know. You said I saved you tonight. That might be true, but what is also true is that you saved me long before tonight."

"From what?" she asked in surprise.

"From a life that was too controlled, predictable, narrow, and short-sighted. You brought back a side of myself I buried along with Gina. I want that side back, Molly. I want to go skinny-dipping. I want to make love wherever we are. I want to try new things." He paused. "I love this town, and I'm happy to work here forever, but it's not as important as you are. I don't want to hold you back, Molly. I want you to still be able to fly. I just want you to take me along if you do. I can work anywhere. I can live anywhere. I want you in my life, whatever that takes. And I also want adventure. I want a full, rich, complicated, messy life."

Her heart squeezed tight at his words. "Be careful what you wish for, Adam."

He shook his head, a smile in his eyes. "No more being careful. I've spent too long playing it safe. I'm just sorry I didn't tell you this before tonight."

"You needed time to figure it out. I needed time, too. Tonight, I went through the photo albums that Caroline had made for Phoebe. I saw their lives play out in front of me, how they were together and then apart, and yet always in the background of each other's lives. They wasted so much time not telling each other how they really felt."

"They grew up in a time where it was harder to be honest."

"I don't even think it was just that. They couldn't be honest with themselves…at least, Caroline couldn't. I'm not as sure about Phoebe. She never married anyone. When she'd travel, she'd sometimes come back and mention something about a lover, but when I think about it, she never said man or woman." She paused. "I just hope they really had a chance to talk to each other before they died. As soon as I closed that album, I knew I had to tell you how I felt about you, no matter what your response might be. I had to try. I don't want to have regrets at the end of my life."

"I'm glad you told me."

"I'm glad you did, too."

He gave her a slow, burning smile. "So, we see where this thing goes?"

"Absolutely. We can start as soon as my mother leaves."

"Then I think we should help her pack."

She laughed and moved into his embrace. Their kisses now felt deeper, richer, and filled with emotion. It was exhilarating and terrifying all at the same time. She'd put her heart on the line, but Adam had done the same, and his willingness to do that touched her deeply. Love had always been a risk for them, but together, they were willing to take it.

As they broke apart, she gazed into his eyes and said, "Phoebe told me in her note that Whisper Lake was where I belonged. She was right. Maybe she really could read the tea leaves."

He smiled as he gazed into her eyes. "Maybe she could."

EPILOGUE

One month later

"Fall is definitely here," Molly said as she stepped out of Adam's Jeep. A cool breeze washed across her face as the fall leaves drifted to the ground from the nearby trees. Even the lake looked colder, a strong current churning up the waves lapping against the shore.

"Are you ready?" Adam asked as he came around the car.

"For fall or..."

"Everything," he said, as he gave her a compassionate smile. "Today won't be easy."

"I'm okay. It only took me six weeks to figure out where Phoebe's ashes should go. It was so obvious."

"Only because you looked past all the noise and the secrets to see the truth."

"The truth that Caroline and Phoebe loved each other, even if they never lived that way or publicly acknowledged it."

She'd learned a lot about the two women in the past month. She'd talked to all of Caroline's relatives, even the ones who had tried to steal the diamond, as well as Phoebe's friends in town. She'd also discovered that Caroline's attorney still had Caroline's ashes. Caroline had asked that her ashes be joined with

Phoebe's whenever that day might come. She wanted their ashes to fly together from a beautiful mountaintop in Whisper Lake called Dreamspinner. It was where one of their pictures had been taken when they were teenagers, when they were running free on the mountain, the lake in the background, love on their faces.

Ava Washington, Caroline's attorney, had also told Molly that Caroline had placed a caveat on her wishes and only said that Phoebe needed to agree. But since Phoebe had died only three days after Caroline, there had been no time to talk to her, and Ava had been waiting to see what Phoebe's wishes for her own ashes were. That, of course, had been left to Molly.

As she looked at the flat, wide bluff with the magnificent view, she knew she was making the right decision. She turned back to Adam, thinking she'd made another right decision when she'd decided to stay in Whisper Lake.

"Thank you for being here," she told him.

"Where else would I be?" He slipped his arms around her waist as he gazed into her eyes. "I love you, Molly."

"I love you, too, Adam. This past month has been amazing. I feel so blessed, grateful, lucky, happy…"

"And scared?" he asked, with a knowing smile.

"You're beginning to know me too well."

"We are not too good to be true, Molly."

"It feels that way," she murmured. "Old habits are hard to break, but I'm getting better at setting my expectations higher and not waiting for the other shoe to drop."

A smile spread across his handsome face. "And I'm getting better at not trying to control everything."

"Well…"

He laughed. "Okay, but I'm trying."

She grinned. "I know you are, Adam. You're naturally protective, and I love that about you. Also, some of your plans have turned out to be really good."

"Speaking of plans. The reason I wanted to come up here

before everyone else was because I wanted to ask you something."

Her heart sped up, as he stepped away from her. He pulled out the urn and set it on the ground between them. "I want Phoebe to have a front-row seat to this."

"What is this?" she asked, her heart beating fast against her chest.

Adam dropped to his knees in front of her and pulled out a small velvet box. As he flicked open the lid, her breath caught in her chest at the diamond ring nestled inside.

"Oh, Adam," she breathed, tears gathering in her eyes. "It's beautiful." An intricate silver thread worked its way between two diamonds. "It's us."

"It is. I never imagined I could love someone so much. You're my best friend, my lover, my shooting star. I know forever scares you, Molly. And maybe this is too fast and you're not ready. If that's the case, I'll wait. I just wanted you to know that I'm fully committed to you, and to wherever life might take us. I don't need guarantees anymore. I don't need roots or predictable schedules or anything else; I just need you. Wherever you go, I go. Even if that means we spend a lot of time with your mother."

She laughed. "You're too much, Adam."

"I hope I'm not."

"You don't have to give up your life for me."

"My life is you," he said forcefully. "You know how stubborn I am, so don't try to argue."

She got down on her knees in front of him. "I'm stubborn, too. And I'm willing to give as much as you are. You're right, Adam. Nothing else matters but love. I don't want to go anywhere else or do anything else. I found my life here with you, just like Phoebe thought I would. My answer is yes. I will marry you. Can I have that ring now?"

He slipped the ring on her finger and then they met in the happiest, most loving, most committed kiss of her life.

She looked over at the urn. "Thanks for bringing me home,

Phoebe, so I could find my love and my life." Turning back to Adam, she said, "I'm a little surprised you decide to propose in front of an urn at a memorial service."

He laughed again. "It felt right. Phoebe needed to be with us."

"She's always going to be with us." She drew in a happy breath. "But I love that you thought about including her. You really are a man who thinks of everything."

"I wasn't sure if you wanted your mom here, too." He paused. "I don't want her to think I'm taking you away from her. I know how much she loves you."

"You are the sweetest man." She cupped his face and kissed him again. "But this was our moment."

At the sound of cars, they got to their feet. A small procession of vehicles soon lined up along the road. They'd kept this part of the memorial small. Because Caroline and Phoebe had been private about their feelings for each other, she wanted to respect that. But after this, they'd be celebrating Phoebe's life with a big lunchtime bash at Micky's Bar and Grill with half the town.

Ava Washington, Caroline's attorney, was the first one to get out of the car. She was a tall, beautiful Black woman. She was accompanied by Kim Collins and Ray Kenney, Caroline's step-siblings. It had been clearly determined that Ray had had no knowledge of the scheme his wife had cooked up with her sister and her lover, Ethan Mercer.

Because Phoebe had had no relatives, Molly had invited her attorney, George Marconi, as well as her group of friends for the send-off. Justin and Zach were both out of town. But Chloe, Hannah, Gianna, Lizzie, Chelsea, Jake, and Brodie came out of the next two cars. She knew they were there to support her as much as they were there for Phoebe, and she appreciated it. She hadn't just found love with Adam in Whisper Lake. She'd found a circle of forever friends.

When the group was assembled, they made their way to the edge of the bluff. Ava and Adam held the two urns as the three of them faced the small group.

"The most important thing to Phoebe was love," Molly said. "Loving yourself and loving each other. She was a lot of things—crazy, quirky, loud—but most of all she was kind, and she lived with her whole heart. Caroline and Phoebe wanted to be together, and now they will be." She nodded to Adam and Ava.

They opened the urns as a sudden breeze came up. In unison, they tossed the ashes into the wind blowing out to the lake, to the mountains, to eternity.

She didn't even realize she was crying until Adam wiped the tears from under her eyes and gave her a hug. In his arms, she took a moment to pull herself together, and then they joined the rest of the group, where each of her friends embraced her so tightly she could feel their love, too.

Then she turned to Ava, Kim, and Ray.

"This was perfect," Kim said. "Caroline told me the last time I saw her that she had so many regrets in her life, and they all had to do with her being too afraid to be honest with herself and with others. I think this is exactly what she would have wanted."

"I hope so," she said. "I'm glad you came. I hope I can get to know you both better."

"I don't know why you'd want to," Ray said, his voice heavy, his expression wary. "After what my wife and sister-in-law did to terrorize you. Mercer could have hurt you."

"He didn't, and you weren't part of it."

"I should have known what they were up to."

"As we've seen from Caroline, even people we love can keep secrets from us."

"That's true. Thanks for having us here."

She nodded as the three of them returned to their car, along with George Marconi, leaving her and Adam alone with their friends.

"Can I ask what you're going to do with the diamond?" Hannah enquired.

"Well, with Ava's help and with Charles's reluctant cooperation, we've been able to prevent the diamond from going to

Charles," she replied. "After much conversation with me and others, he finally was able to acknowledge that Caroline's great love was never for him, but for Phoebe."

"So, you'll keep the diamond?" Gianna asked.

"No. I'm going to sell it, and I'm giving the money to the charities that both Caroline and Phoebe supported. Sharing their love with others less fortunate is really what they would have wanted."

"That makes sense," Hannah said. "But you could have kept it. It was yours."

"I have a new diamond now." She took her hand out of her pocket. She'd been subconsciously keeping the ring tucked away so that she wouldn't distract anyone from Phoebe's memorial.

She laughed as her friends squealed with delight, and Brodie and Jake slapped Adam on the shoulder. And then everyone was hugging her again. Chelsea was the last, and tears were in her eyes.

"I'm so happy for you and Adam," she said. "You both deserve all the happiness. And now Lizzie and I finally have a sister-in-law."

"It's about time," Lizzie said with a laugh. "It took you long enough, Adam."

He laughed. "I just had to wait for the right woman to show up in town. Thanks to Phoebe and maybe a little help from the universe," he added dryly, "she finally came."

"I'm so glad you believe in magic again," she murmured, as she moved into his arms.

He smiled. "I believe in you, Molly. That's the magic."

"Kiss her already," Hannah said.

They laughed, then kissed, then laughed again as they joined their friends and started moving into the future together.

WHAT TO READ NEXT...

Don’t miss the next Whisper Lake Novel

NEXT TIME I FALL

Are you up to date on the Whisper Lake Novels?

Whisper Lake Series

Always With Me (#1)

My Wildest Dream (#2)

Can't Fight The Moonlight (#3)

Just One Kiss (#4)

If We Never Met (#5)

Tangled Up In You (#6)

Next Time I Fall (#7)

ABOUT THE AUTHOR

Barbara Freethy is a #1 New York Times Bestselling Author of 70 novels ranging from contemporary romance to romantic suspense and women's fiction. With over 13 million copies sold, twenty-five of Barbara's books have appeared on the New York Times and USA Today Bestseller Lists, including SUMMER SECRETS which hit #1 on the New York Times!

Known for her emotional and compelling stories of love, family, mystery and romance, Barbara enjoys writing about ordinary people caught up in extraordinary adventures. Library Journal says, "Freethy has a gift for creating unforgettable characters."

For additional information, please visit Barbara's website at www.barbarafreethy.com.

Made in United States
North Haven, CT
28 March 2022

17612072R30181